ENGRAVED
on
MY HEART

BETTY LOWREY

To order additional copies of this book, contact:
Bookwhip
1-855-339-3589
https://www.bookwhip.com

Monday's child is fair of face	Sophia/Kathryn Preston/Kane Alberson
Tuesday's child is full of grace	Susan, mother of Caroline, Sophia, Barkley
Wednesday's child is full of woe	Caroline, daughter of Susan & Hugh
Thursday's child has far to go	Oliver Devoe, fiancée of Caroline
Friday's child is loving and giving	Barkley, son of Susan & Hugh
Saturday's child works hard for a living	Susan's father, Anson, her Mother, Star Caplan
The child born on Sunday is fair and wise	Hugh Preston, husband to Susan

Folk lore from the 1500's

Chapter 1

They were young and in love.

"This can't have a happy ending," his parent's said. "Who is she? We have to send him away awhile."

"I like that boy," her parents said, "But we have to lay down the law to her, impetuous as she is anything could happen and with his parents being the staunch leaders of the community they think they are...well, our daughter could end up with a bucket full of troubles."

Twenty years later

"Does it ever strike you funny, my mother ask one day as we were talking, that that family with all their finery are toilers of the soil just as we are?" Susan turned to watch Hugh's reaction to her question.

"Nothing funny about farming," Hugh replied. "But, you are going to have to keep your eye on our daughter. Susan, she is too impulsive. I know life will settle her, but for now she throws herself into anything she does. I'm telling you, if anything happened that boy's family would be down our throat."

Susan laughed, reaching over to curl her hand around Hugh's neck and pull him close. Placing a kiss on his cheek, she said, "You are afraid they are too much like us."

His eyes met hers. She could make him melt with that lilt in her voice, smile on her lips and come hither look in her eyes. "We barely made it to the altar. If your daddy hadn't recognized problems and headed us off...." Hugh's eyes were warm with love. "You have a very wise daddy and a loving mother."

"They love you. That's for certain." All pouty lips, she added, "Probably more than me. It seems so."

"God was kind to me," Hugh replied. "I get to marry the girl next door, didn't have to search far and wide and then her daddy sets me up in farming. You can't beat that."

"I can only wonder what that was about," she replied. "Daddy was frugal with money. Had to be in this business but I heard Gram say he could make the Eagle squawk. Still, he saw something in you to take you on."

"What he saw was a hard working dud of a boy trying to become a man without a penny in his pocket. What did you see?"

"I saw this fellow, lived just down the road, handsome; wore white T shirts that smelled fresh washed and maybe dried hanging on the line in God's sunshine, broad shoulders, curly black hair...ummm. He made me...."

Hugh braked to a halt, pulled to the side of the road and put the truck in park. "Who was he?" He leaned across the console, pulled Susan into his arms and demanded, "I want to know who you were fooling around with?"

Susan fell into his arms, a spasm of giggles taking control of her body. "I've never loved anyone but you, you, big fellow." She knew his arms would tighten as he pulled her closer and the kiss would be worth every hurt the console between them made digging into her body. "You know the neighbors will talk if any one of them comes by and sees this."

He silenced her words, his lips claiming hers. "Suz, Suz. I love you." The kiss ended, Hugh slid back into his seat, Suz hers and they went on down the road. "So you loved that guy, huh?"

"Still do," she said straightening her clothes. "He's the best, can't imagine life without him. He is engraved on my heart."

"We could have starved to death that first winter when my crop failed in spite of your Daddy's advice."

"Nah, Dad wouldn't let us starve and even if he meant to for a lesson, Mom would've sneaked us food."

"Through sickness and health, starvation and prosperity, right?"

Sitting tall in the seat, all dignified and wise, Hugh Preston appeared to the world a man with his act together. Only she knew the waves of emotions that traveled his veins. He held no grudge toward any man and he'd been slighted time after time in the business they called farming. Undermined and kicked down, some might say but Hugh said it was all in the way a man perceived it; if you want to grow and get ahead don't worry about another man's motive, just keep yourself straight, don't let your nose get out of joint and let God judge those who would misuse you.

He did have one flaw; however, Suz was his sounding board. When times got really rough he'd come to the house, throw his hat on the nearest peg, slump into the kitchen chair as he placed his arms on the table in a resolute way and sit staring at her as she worked around him doing the necessary tasks until finally she sat opposite him and said, "tell me."

She listened. Maybe it was the ditch board decided in August to clean out the ditch; yeah, that one, the ditch that ran alongside his leased land and guess where they would be dumping the dirt? On top of his beautiful near ready beans, just a month from harvest. Or, perhaps the neighbor decided to clear out a patch of saplings and the excavator came across Hugh's land and wiped out the standing crop. Then there was the time the landlord accused him of not caring for his unirrigated land when Hugh was using his own wells, pumping the water a half a mile to water said landlord's land when the man was too stingy to provide his own irrigation equipment and he had the gall to say that when his crop was thriving at Hugh's expense? No, sometimes it was too much and Hugh had to speak it out of his system and when he finished he retrieved his hat and walked out of the house a man on a mission, cool calm and collected to show the world you could live among your neighbors without righteous indignation, when they did you wrong. All the while Suz steamed with new found anger and resentment that the neighbors were so uncaring. "I'll die of an ulcer," she would mutter, "while that man smiles at the world."

So it went, Suz and Hugh birthed three children, two girls and a boy. The birth of the second daughter was long and hard, that one kept turning and the doctor was concerned breech birth too much for Suz with her small frame. "She's wearing down, Doc," Hugh said, his eyes troubled. "Please, do something." And the doctor did, which meant Suz had a week or two longer recovery than usual and Hugh saw that she had help. About that

3

time the flu season was rampant and Hugh fell to it, trying by day to plant crop, by night wearing a bandana tied around his mouth and nose, lifting baby Sophia Raine from the bassinet and the three year old Caroline Dawn at his heels ready to hold the bottle, hand daddy the powder and always knowing where the items were he might need.

"You need to go back to bed, little girl," he would say as she scooted into the chair as snug as a bug by his side. "Sophia is just hungry and has to be fed. Daddy can do it."

"Is Momma going to be all right?" The days were filled with Suz trying to keep up by day and by night sleeping through many of Sophia's feedings, always apologizing the next morning.

"Oh, my darlings," she would say. With troubled eyes she studied this man she loved. "You need your rest and I can't even keep my eyes open."

"It's all right," he would say. "Soon you will be up and around; yourself again."

Already Suz felt the concern. She and Hugh wanted to try one more time for a boy but this had its effect on her. "Give it time, Babe," Hugh comforted. "A few years when you've forgotten the pain and the loss of blood...you may feel different about having another baby. We don't know it would be a boy, anyway." But Suz knew he would never lose the desire to have a boy to follow in his footsteps. Hugh seemed the picture of health, as had she, but now; this bout of recovery seemed a caution for what lay ahead in their future.

Life progressed, the girls grew and as they walked through the community seeing fathers and sons, Suz often saw the wistfulness of Hugh's desire to have a boy. Suz had not forgotten the pain. Sophia was seven years old and she was approaching thirty. "I guess we need to think about your boy," she told Hugh. His eyes sparkled as he lifted her up into his arms and nuzzled her cheek. He was happy already.

Within a month, Suz was pregnant and the pregnancy was without problem. Hugh Barkley Preston was born on a January morning. "You sure you want to name him that?" Mrs. Preston asked. "It sounds like a law firm."

"Oh, Mother," Hugh chided. "What's the difference in what you named me? Hugh Don Preston? That was a bit unusual in that day, wasn't it? Just so happens little Hughie was conceived when we went over to Barkley Dam on a little weekend jaunt." He began to laugh, seeing his mother's discomfort.

"That's a bit more information that I requested," his mother replied.

Suz lay on the hospital bed listening to their discourse. Mrs. Preston, rigid and unbending had set the perimeter of their relationship from day one, she was Mrs. Preston and Suz must prove worthy to retain the title when she was gone. Until that day there was only one worthy of the name and she was it. As Hugh's mother, he belonged to her. When they were out, Suz was to walk behind them, Hugh holding to his mother's arm, tucking her into the car, seeing her order was processed first all those little things that would drive most young wives crazy. It helped Suz that Mr. Preston liked her. "For heaven's sake." she would remind Hugh, "we work together, why does that disturb your Mother?"

"Mother disturbs easily," he would reply. Yes, she does, Suz agreed silently.

They took their baby home on the third day and life settled down with two sweet quiet girls becoming as rowdy as the next door neighbors boys, watching little Barkley grow from infant to toddler, knowing Momma went through a time of healing and not understanding at all when they overheard her explaining to her own mother, "they cut me in the same place and delivered before hours went by."

Hugh's mother cautioned the girls should not roll in the floor and play so wildly with their brother. Suz's parents could sit hours watching their antics and not utter a word of advice.

Suz thought it hilarious while Hugh was torn and a bit indecisive his part in the triangle of him, his mother and herself. "You don't have to agree with everything mother says, just try to respect her."

"Lord help me, Hugh. She has such high standards but I'll admit any woman who can leave her house every day of the week looking as though she just stepped out of the most fashionable saloon has my vote, chasing these kids fair wears me out, that's why I wear my hair shoulder length and no fuss, make up is a minimum and my wardrobe is mostly denim." She did a little dance around his chair.

He pulled her down on his lap and kissed her. "You are beautiful and you know it."

"You think so?" She preened and fell onto his chest. "You like this baby burp stain on my blouse?"

"We can afford a new blouse for you. Once we couldn't, but now we can." He was unbuttoning her blouse. "The kids are at school. Your Mother has Barkley and it's a rainy day. Let's go buy you a new blouse."

On another day, Hugh came to the house, "Bert's wife is sick. He has to take her to the doctor, seems she's too sick to drive. Do you think you could keep the seed truck up for me? Everyone else has a job and if we are to get these beans planted before the rain, it surely would help."

"Let me get supplies together and we will be there. Down on the forty?"

He nodded on his way out. "I'm good for I'd say maybe an hour, then I'll need the truck. How's that?"

So it went, Suz had no schedule when it came to Hugh, whatever he needed she was available, but when the girls became active in school, Hugh saw she was overextended and hired help. "How you doing today, Missus Chauffeur?" He'd ask, tousling her hair and going on to each girl. The girls protested, "Oh, Daddy you messed up my do."

He'd grin. "Your do?" Glancing around he'd say, "Where's my boy? Hey Barkley, Dad's gotta go to town, you wantta ride with me?" He'd tweak the girl's noses; give Suz a kiss that always went into longer time than the girls wanted to watch. "Turn your heads," he'd say when he heard their ugghs. "You'll grow up someday, around thirty years old and want an ole boy to kiss you."

"Thirty, huh?" Suz would ask, eyebrows raised. "Let's see Caroline Dawn is thirteen and Sophia Raine three years behind. Hmmm. That's a lot of chaperoning Big Guy." With a slap on her behind Hugh left with his son tagging along.. "There goes a happy man," Suz would mutter. "Lord, let it last, please."

The year they celebrated Caroline Dawn's sixteenth birthday, they purchased a fairly good but used Volvo from the neighbor, Mrs. Rhodes, whose husband had died three years prior and the vehicle had been sitting in the shed all that time, undriven, as Mrs. Rhodes had a newer model car.

"Four thousand dollars for fifty thousand miles, I guess if we do the math, what is that about eight cents a mile?" Hugh scratched his head, thoughtful, "What matters is the safety of the vehicle, putting the girls out there for every other goose-neck on the road."

"Isn't that red-neck, Daddy?" Barkley asked.

"I was trying to be nice, Son."He grinned. "Only you and I share the difference between a red neck and a goose neck." He tousled Barkley's hair. "You ready to go out and drive that tractor?" Barkley's eyes lit up.

"Be careful with my baby," Suz cautioned. "We waited a while for this one." Barkley grinned.

"I'm going to disc that whole eighty, Momma."

"You just be sure you don't get sleepy and fall off that seat. You hear me?" She stooped to plant a kiss on his cheek. "If you get sleepy, you stop and tell your Daddy. There's no shame in that; the shame would be we lost a fine boy like you. You understand?"

"Yes, ma'am." Father and son left, the one striding across the lawn toward the shop, the other trying hard to keep up.

"Sometimes I don't know about this farming," Suz muttered. "Men strive to own a piece of land but truth is, the land owns them and she is a demanding mistress."

"You talking to someone on the phone, Momma?" Caroline Dawn came into the kitchen. "I have piano in an hour, Mom. Do I get to drive by myself today?"

"Well, yes, if you're not counting your sister. She has lessons too. And there's no need me having to go."

"Tell her she can't drive, Mom. She waits til we get down the road and starts in on me, and she doesn't have license, yet. She has to wait, just like I did. What's wrong with her, she thinks she can skip."

"It was true; Sophia thought she could skip a few steps in many things. She played the piano with a passion, fast and furious not reading the music many times but playing by ear while Caroline played for the school's orchestra and followed the printed sheet, completely accomplished and with grace. Sophia was her own person, striding along behind her father; her interest lay in mechanical things. Forget there were household chores. Caroline chose the indoors, she could do those. Sophia reined outside.

Before they could realize the years had passed Caroline Dawn was graduating high school and planning college. Sophia Raine had become the darling of all things extra curriculum. In order to do that she had to keep the grade level up which meant in spite of herself studying, learning the most important subjects that would carry her through life and to Hugh's surprise she not only had a bent for mechanical things but she was very good in the mathematics of life.

"Sophia, must you do everything? You leave very little time for us."

"Oh, Daddy, I'm with you all every Sunday. I'm good at what I do, that's why they choose me."

He glanced across to Suz sitting at the sewing machine, bringing to life yet another strapless dress in bright blue taffeta. Sophie had been chosen as candidate for the basketball team's queen. "I thought you just made her a dress, that wispy pink thing that I thought dipped to low and you stitched it up an inch or so?"

"You are right, handsome," She stood up and ruffled his hair as he pulled her into his arms and kissed the tip of her nose. "She was last month's Miss Cordiality. It seems they like her, those teachers and her class mates. At least if I sew the dresses it doesn't cut into our budget so much. Just yards of material and…" She couldn't help but rub that area of her back that ached from sitting too long.

"And your time," he said nuzzling her ear, working his way around to kiss her soundly on the lips. "Don't think I don't appreciate what you do, but it takes your time, too." He grinned, "Truth is, I wanted you to run down south with me, we've had an offer to rent some ground. We could use it."

"It's Saturday. I need a break and I can finish this Monday if you don't have plans for me, then."

"Barkley, stay with your sisters. Sophia, Caroline, no fighting. I'm going with Dad."

They left to a chorus of okay, mom. Hugh held her hand to climb up into the cab of the truck and then hurried around to the driver's side. "Hey," he said, climbing in, "Our kids wouldn't fight."

"Oh, no. You need to stick around, Mister. Those girls are something else these days. They used to be so docile and compatible. Is that the word? Whatever the word it doesn't fit now." She shuddered.

He shook his head, "what is it? Hormones?" He whistled. "That kid that keeps coming to sit with us every other night. Doesn't he have a home?"

"Sophia says his parents are divorced. You know them. His dad is a farmer, though I hear tell a turn row farmer." She thought about his description. Hormones. Maybe she was experiencing hormones.

"Doesn't want to get dirty, huh?" Hugh scratched his chin where the day's stubble of beard was already visible. "He doesn't look like anyone I know. What's his last name?"

"Kirkland, from the neighboring community, but Dalton attends our school because his Mom's a substitute teacher." Susie found herself fidgeting in the seat, for some reason she wasn't comfortable.

"Dolly?" Hugh glanced her way. "I forgot her last name. Let's see, she married the Harpo guy from St. Louis, first, then, yeah…it's coming to me. She wasn't a teacher, or didn't even have college until after that first divorce when her parent's told her she just as well get educated and get a job."

"And you suddenly know all this, because?" Her usual patience seemed to have flown out the window.

He grinned. "She and I were classmates. She had the hots for me." He watched as she bristled and moved closer to the passenger side door. "You don't need to fall out on the road, Suz, I didn't have an eye for her…she was old man William's daughter and he had set his eye on me to farm his land. We do still farm it, you know…how did this little tidbit of information escape your little ole eagle eye?"

"So…truthfully, you've let that little bit of info stagnate in your teeny weeny little brain all these year." She seethed. "You always insist I tell you…everything…like I'm your possession and that escaped you?"

"Guess I was busy trying to pay for diapers for the toddlers, and planning on the day you said we could have our boy, which by the way, thank you very much." She was settling down. "You never rile, what's happening with you. Something I don't know about?" Worry crept into his voice. "This is not you."

"It just so happens," she retorted, "Our toddlers are teenagers, our boy is eight going on fifteen and I did have a conversation with Mr. Williams, once, when he told me he had handpicked you for his son-in-law but my dad beat him to the draw." Her eyes had turned violet blue. "How was I to know his daughter wanted you, too? Honestly, Hugh. A woman needs to know these things to protect her territory."

"Have I ever strayed?" He loved seeing her flare over her need for him to be hers alone. Those eyes were beautiful. "Could you be feeling a little jealous, Suz Q?"

"Don't call me that. You're being sarcastic and no, not jealous, protective. You wouldn't know a woman making a pass at you; if they lay down stark naked in front of you…you… you are so vulnerable."

"Uh, uh, uh." He wagged a finger between them. "That's double talk, one wipes out the other." On second thought he didn't tell her Molly had a name in those days for being a little too easy with the boys. Time would have changed that with Molly realizing ladies were a bit more subdued.

She felt like a shrew but she couldn't help spewing a bit. She had gained five pounds and couldn't figure out why and now this info…a bit overdue to her way of thinking, because her husband was a good looking man. In fact, Hugh Preston was downright handsome even if he was her husband. He seemed to get better with age, on the other hand the five pounds she had gained this month were making her miserable…it would be five now, five later and five more down the road, she just knew it.

"Hey, Babe?" He waited for her to look his way. "Aren't we in deep water over nothing?"

She sighed, feeling weary and defeated. "Yes, I guess we are. As you often say, those days are water under the bridge."

"Hmm. Do I say that?" He grinned. "Must be true then." He turned off the main highway onto a field road. "This is the ground we are thinking about."

"Who are we?"

"You and me, who else?" He was out of the truck and around to her side in no time flat, opening the door and pulling her into his arms. "Okay, Suz Q, what's up?" She started to resist but he held her firm.

"I honestly don't know. Just a feeing something's going to happen, I guess."

"Yeah, it is." He released her but held on to her hand. "Come on, let's walk this ground and see what we think of the soil."

"Isn't this the old Ellington homestead? You know the grandma went to our church until about two years ago."

"It is and her grandson lives in Chicago. He's a doctor, Oncologist I think. It seems Mrs. Ellington was in assisted living but she fell and broke a hip, contracted pneumonia and died. The son had died before his mother and the grandson has no interest in farming but he remembered his grandmother saying we were nice folks."

"That's an interesting recommendation for farming someone's ground." She replied, peering down at the soil Hugh had kicked loose. "It's sandy loam, right? Good soil for about any crop."

"Except for that corner over on the Northwest, there's a strip of gumbo. Otherwise, pretty good, huh? Looks like it, not ice cream but near." He laughed. "All our lives we've heard the ground along the Interstate is the best soil in Missouri, ice cream, they say. Well, this may not be at the top but it's pretty good. So what do you think? Take it on?"

"The question is, do we have enough equipment to farm it?"

Hugh removed his cap and thought a minute. "We will be stretching it, but right now I can't see adding to ourselves financially when we've already got a full load. Let's try it and if we see we have to we will lease the equipment we need until we can purchase."

She nodded. She knew what was coming next. It always did and for that she was thankful. Hugh kept the cap in his left hand and reached for hers with his right. They bowed their heads. "Father in Heaven, we come to you now with grateful hearts we are given this opportunity to farm more land, help us to be pleasing to thee, to our new land owner and always to each other. We thank you for all blessings, Lord, for our family that we know you watch over, we just ask that you are always with us in our decisions. Amen."

Suz thought back on all the times they'd made decisions, and most of the times it was as if the devil was taking note. They had to take everything into consideration in their younger years and earlier days of farming and to this day not much had changed. If they purchased anything it seemed a big rain followed that kept them out of the fields. Farming was a timely business, striving to plant the crop at the right time and hopefully be able to keep up with its needs until it was ready for harvest and then that was a whole new game. If you were hampered by weather every one suffered.

Some years were a struggle. They'd worked through a few and come out with enough to break even, except the one they lost first to flood; the irony was that same year they then had drought. That year took out a lot of farmers and they had hung on as Hugh said by the skin of their teeth.

They rode home in silence, Hugh holding her hand, no longer feeling the resistance. It was when they arrived and Suz slid down from the truck seat Hugh felt a horrifying concern. "Babe?" He reached for Suz as she seemed to wilt down to the ground. Her face had paled and she seemed lifeless. "Girls," he hollered. "Sophia. Caroline Dawn." He was trying to pick her up but she was dead weight. "Something's wrong," he told his daughters as they came running, Barkley close behind. "Help me get Mom inside. Open the door there, Barkley."

"Dad?" Caroline's voice was strained and she was near tears. "Dad, did you see where Mom had been sitting?" Caroline had rushed ahead and laid towels on the sofa where he was placing Suz. "Dad?"

His expression was grim. "Yeah, I saw. Let me call the doctor and see what we are to do. I think ER but I'm not certain."

Sophie was whimpering and for once she had her arms around Barkley in a death grip. "Dad?" She was the first to see Suz coming around and dropped down beside her. "Mother. What happened?"

"I honestly don't know." Suz voice was weak. "I had this one great pain but I thought it was like a muscle spasm but worse and as soon as I could stand it would go away…but that's all I remember."

"Mom," Caroline was bending down, trying to speak softly but the other two kept pressing in. "Mom, you are bleeding and its bright red. I think Dad's going to take you to ER. He's talking to doctor Mays, but Mom…I've never seen so much blood. Do you hurt?"

"Sweetheart," Suz reached up to touch Caroline's face. "I don't feel anything. I think I'm in shock."

"But Mom, you weren't around anything to shock you, were you?" Barkley sounded mystified.

Sophia shook her brother, lightly. "Not that kind of shock, Barkley. Shock, like, I can't believe this."

Tears dripped off Barkley's chin. "I don't know what you're talking about. Let me hug Momma."

Suz opened her arms. "I'll be all right, Son." Barkley's thin little body was quaking against her own.

"You're not going to die are you, Mom?"

"We have to go, Babe." Hugh still had the phone in his hand and laid it on the end table. "Girls you have to take care of your brother, we have to go now. Doctor Mays said Mom might be hemoragghing."

"No, we're going," Caroline's chin was set as her eyes flashed a stern meaning to her dad. "She's not just yours. She's our mother and we're going."

"Then there won't be any bickering," Hugh said, his own eyes pinpoints as he bent down beside Suz.

"I need a bath, before I go anywhere," Suz said. "I feel sticky. You'll have to help me."

"No bath, Babe, the doctor said come now, to ER, he'll meet us there."

"Why?" Suz was disoriented and couldn't grasp the meaning behind his words. "Now?"

Hugh was ready to lift her into his arms but she protested. "I can walk." She tried, her knees buckling and she would have fallen except for his hold on her. She was on the edge of fainting again. "I can't...."

"See that everything is turned off, Sophia. Caroline we'll need more towels. Barkley get in the back seat between your sisters and everyone put their seat belts on, no fussing, just do it. We don't have time for more problems." They were out the door, Sophia turning the lock and pulling it shut behind them. Caroline was running ahead to open the truck door and laying the towels on the seat, but her heart nearly stopped when she saw the blood dripping from her mother's pant leg. She slid onto the console instead of getting in the back, "I'll hold her, Dad. Either that or we put her in the back seat but maybe we shouldn't move Mom again." Hugh nodded and closed the truck door.

Dr. Mays came from the building as they pulled beneath the veranda. A second later a wheel chair appeared. "Good Lord," Dr. Mays exclaimed. "No time here, but we should've brought a gurney." He was pushing the wheel chair himself, Suz doubled over and the attendant running alongside one arm ready to catch her if she toppled. "Hugh, you'll have to wait out here with the kids. I'll take good care of her and call you when I'm sure she's out of danger." To the attendant he said, "Call my office and tell them I want Susan Preston's records faxed over immediately."

"Why Daddy?" Barkley was scared and the look on his father's face told him his Dad wasn't much better. "Why did he need a gurney and why is he having her records sent over?"

"Mom's lost a lot of blood son." He couldn't rid himself of the picture of those sodden towels on the truck seat a congealing mass of red trying to thicken, which meant a lot of blood had passed through. *Lord, God, he was praying silently within himself, take care of her. Don't let her die.*

It was an hour that seemed two before the doctor returned. "Hugh, could I speak with you alone, please?"

"Is my Momma dead?" Barkley was up standing his ground when his dad would have quieted him, except his own thoughts were mirrored in his son's eyes.

"No, Son, your Momma is alive," the doctor said gently. "I just need to talk business with your dad."

Hugh stepped over to Barkley, "Sit down Son, and let ole Dad talk with the doctor and I promise I'll explain to you later, if I can, what's going on. Now, let's let mom get the attention she needs. Okay?" He kissed Barkley on top of the head and walked over to where Dr. Mays was standing.

"Hugh, did Susie know she was pregnant?"

Hugh's world reeled for a minute. "No, Ben, she didn't. That's one thing she would have told me."

"Well, it's serious business. You know the trouble she had having Sophia, then Barkley was a big decision and she waited a number of years to have him." He sighed, heavily. "Of course, you know all that first hand, but I'm reviewing it all in order to say this. Suz was on the pill, right?"

Hugh nodded. "I seriously doubt Suz ever missed one pill. She loves her kids but she did have problems bearing them."

"Yes." Dr. Ben thought how to say the next words. "You may have saved her life getting her to ER when you did. I know Susie and she probably would have said I'll be all right just give me time, but in this case she could have bled to death."

"What is it, Ben? You're scaring me to *death* and you see how it's affected the kids, all that blood..."

"She could have bled to death, Hugh. We've given her blood. Don't worry it was her type. I checked the records carefully. What happened was a pregnancy developed outside the tubes. They were probably scarred in the past pregnancies, I don't know, but this happened in the tubes and the embryo had no place to go because of the blockage. Strange things happen, Hugh. Susie made it farther than any ectopic pregnancy I've witnessed before."

"Susie was pregnant?" Hugh's voice rose but dropped sharply. "A baby was growing outside the womb?"

"It happens. Except this one progressed to the stage it had no room to continue growing and that started the bleeding due to…" The doctor hoped he wouldn't have to finish the sentence.

Hugh felt the need for support and reached out to touch the wall, finding himself fairly leaning away from the doctor and into the space, his head down, trying to come to grips…"It's death threatening?"

"It could have been, but you got her here in time." Dr. Mays touched Hugh's arm. "Given time she will be all right."

"What do you mean, given time?" Hugh's voice rose again, until he heard the shuffle of his kid's feet behind him. He must listen to Ben. He trust him. They'd gone to school together. Now, he locked his eyes on Ben's long white coat, a pocket on one side with his name above and an inch down a larger pocket that held a small note pad. Why would he need a note pad? He tried to focus on Ben's words.

"There's recovery, Hugh. Some women feel guilt in not realizing what was happening thinking they could have saved the baby, but in this type pregnancy she couldn't, you can't transplant an embryo at this stage…I don't know what the experts say…that's not my line of doctoring…but evidently Suz didn't know. She knew her body was different and possibly thought she was going through the change. She's been in no shape for us to talk about this. That's where you come in, you're going to have to be prepared for what comes next and only God knows what that will be. Women are different. What affects one may not the next…but they all grieve the loss of a life…and you best know your wife."

"Ben, give me a few minutes. I've got to get myself together, outside just me and the Lord. Talk to my kids, assure them their Momma's going to be all right. She is, isn't she?" Hugh's eyes were pinpoints focused on Doctor Mays like a cat on a mouse. "You tell them something that's hopeful. You hear?" Hugh stomped off, one hand behind him directed toward his kids. "Stay there," he ordered. "Stay."

The hospital parking lot was a string of cars of nondescript color, a blur on his vision as he stomped the distance from the visitor's entrance to the highway, it's lanes of admittance and exit ablaze with red markers and a steady stream of people in vehicles coming and going. He had one fleeting thought, how many had lost a child that day and had they known they were going to lose that child?

His stomach tightened as he felt the urge to vomit, Suz could have bled to death. She wouldn't give in to not feeling well. No, Suz had to sew up a formal dress, wipe the kid's noses and feed them and he wanted her with him at every turn. She never said no, she might say later, but no wasn't in her vocabulary and maybe one day it would kill her if she didn't learn she couldn't keep the pace, not with the kids and not with him. He had to help her change their world. So much of it was his fault. He wanted her with him. He would die without her…but if he didn't learn to let go, Suz might die.

When he thought he had the situation under his belt he returned to the waiting room. Caroline eyed him strangely, Sophia was engrossed with a teenage boy she seemed to know and Barkley was doodling on a note pad. It looked familiar, perhaps the one Ben Mays had in the pocket of his long white coat.

"What'd he say, Dad? Do we get to go in and see Momma?" Barkley had waited for him to return. "I wanted to come walk with you, Dad. But you needed your time, didn't you?"

"That's very wise, Son." Hugh tousled Barkley's hair and pulled him under his arm. "Yeah, I did."

"But now you can tell us, Momma's not going to die?" Barkley's eyes had turned the color of blue Hugh saw in Suz, while Sophia and Caroline's eyes were brown as his own, Caroline's nearly black.

"I don't think God's ready for Mom, Barkley. She lost a lot of blood, but they've tried to replace it."

"Where'd that blood come from, Dad?" Barkley's mind could not fathom a body could bleed that much.

"I don't know, Son. What's important is the doctor said we must take good care of Mom."

"We will." Barkley grasp the information. He was relieved now there was something to work with.

Hugh had sunk into the waiting room's sofa that seemed to be occupied by his children and he had pulled Barkley with him, needing to feel that warm body that reminded him so much of Suz. Now he felt Caroline's eyes on him and Sophia had joined them, leaving the boy sitting over by the window.

His eyes met Caroline Dawn's. "You kids need to go find something to eat and then Caroline, you can take these two on home and see that Barkley goes to bed. You can pick me up sometime tomorrow. I'll call you."

"So it's that bad? Mom's staying the night?" Caroline had feared as much and she wanted mom to stay.

"Mother is never sick," Sophia began, cut off by Caroline's pursed mouth and warning glance. "Well, she's not. If we say, don't you feel well, Mother. She says she's fine."

"Well, this time she's not," Hugh replied softly, "and it's up to each of us to help her through this."

"What is *this?*" Sophie's question was almost petulant. "I mean, aren't we old enough to know?"

"It's my fault," Barkley spoke up. "Dad wants to tell you later. He thinks I'm too young. Right, Dad?"

Hug leaned forward his head in his hands massaging his temples. "Son, I don't understand, yet. So you all go." He stood, digging in his pocket and then taking out his wallet. "Here, go eat and then do as I said. Caroline will take care of you and I'll see you tomorrow, maybe then we'll know something."

Hugh felt their kisses on his cheek and the hugs were comforting but Barkley's was fierce. He watched them walk to the truck and drive out onto the highway. Caroline Dawn was a settling influence. The other two had now become her wards and they'd have a hard time if they didn't follow instructions. A sudden thought of Sophia's unfinished dress crossed his mind, he knew already his second daughter had thought of it and kept that piece of information to herself, but already she was planning its completion.

He settled back onto the sofa, laying his head back to rest his eyes but all he could see was the blood. "Sir? Mr. Preston? Would you like to see your wife? We have her in the room all bathed and clean." He rose to his feet, wondering that Suz had suffered and he was worn from it all. He was as tired as if he'd done a hard day's work.

The nurse led him down the hall, their shoes making soft squishing sounds on the tiled floor. She opened the door, quietly, and there lay Susie asleep on the white pillows, a small tube running up from the underside of her wrist to the small clear bottle on the stand by the bed. Her dark hair fanned out around her face making her appear even paler, the dark lashes a fringe on her cheeks. "We've given her a sedative, Dr. May's instructions. I'll leave you alone now, just use the light if you need us." She pointed to the line with the small black button and was gone.

Hugh pulled a chair next to the bed and laid his head on the mattress by Suz. Already his mind was locked in a prayer of thanksgiving. There, as he communed with his Lord, the picture of bright red blood was replaced by Suz framed on the white sheets her even breathing a solace to his worried mind. The room was dark, he realized he'd heard the nurses come at intervals to check on Suz but he hadn't roused. Now he felt a hand rippling softly through his hair. "Suz?" His hand sought hers. Tears welled up in his eyes as he raised to kiss her cheek. There were no words necessary, they would come later. Her arms went around his neck as he lift her up slightly, his hands cradling her there on the pillow as their tears ran together. "Suz. I couldn't lose you. I've been scared to death. Suz?' He had such a need to say her name over and over, for his own good he had to feel her wrapped in his arms, her heart beating next to his and the softness of her. God help him now he knew, he thought he was dying for lack of her.

Another nurse came to the bed, checking the bag atop of the stand and then as quietly as she had appeared, no words, no admonition to lay the patient back on the bed, a moment of a door to the closet opening, a soft thump of something added to the bed and then silence. She was gone. Suz slept; her hand curled in his and he though wound up in strangeness pushed his long legs beneath the bed and laid his head on the second pillow that had mysteriously appeared from the closet by the nurses hand.

Chapter 2

The kids showed up the next morning before the nurse bathed Suz. "Momma?" Barkley stood by the bed, squeezing her hand. She was weak and had closed her eyes after they changed the sheet beneath her. Suz requested the change, knowing her children would be there any moment. Now Barkley was peering at her, his eyes deep in worry, mirrored by his dad's and his sisters. "Mom? Are you asleep." With his heart quaking, "Dad?" He demanded Hugh look his way. "Is Mom all right. She can go home?"

"I doubt she can go today, Son. In a few days. You and your sisters need to clean the house and give her a proper welcome home."

"I did, Dad. Last night. I know Mom wants me to keep my room better and I'm going to. I even threw away the ginger bread house we made at Christmas. I thought if I sprayed it it would keep but Sophia said it stunk."

"It did." Sophia crossed her arms in front of her body. "Make no mistake, it had rotted. You had to throw it out."

"Well, I did," Barkley huffed, his attention on his mother again. "Momma, wake up. Please, Momma."

"You are such a worry wart," Sophia complained. "Let Mother sleep. You can talk to her when she comes home."

"Are you spending the night here, Dad?" Barkley turned loose his mother's hand and fixed himself beneath Hugh's arm, his own arms around his dad's waist. "I missed you, Dad. You and Momma need to come home."

The nurse had entered and heard Barkley's words. It seemed the whole staff attended the church where the Preston's went. She had heard the story, and this was her first shift for the day and Susie Preston was her patient, too. "Well, sweetheart, looks like your Momma won't be going home today." She stooped to look Barkley in the eye. "I know you want her to stay until her body is ready to go home, don't you?" Barkley nodded. "Then why don't you take your dad out to eat something while we give her a bath."

Hugh nodded agreement and led the way from the room. "That meant vamoose, scat, get out of there," he grinned at Barkley. "Mom woke up during the night, Son. She's going to be all right."

They would keep Suz a few hours longer. "She lost so much blood, Hugh, she needs to stay but Susan has set her head to go home." Doctor Ben explained. "She has to take it easy for a week, maybe two, and then with all your help she can cook a light meal, maybe once a day but not cleaning," he glanced to where the children hovered waiting for their dad to relay the message. "Looks like you all can manage. Just remember, Suz could have died. She didn't..." He let the words sink in, "but recovery will take a week or two on the physical side."

The doctor had privately told Hugh, "this will be an emotional scar for Susan, I don't know how long that will affect her." Now, Hugh's next question stood between them. "I know Suz, Ben. I think you have an idea what I'm going to ask, but she'll be after the answer."

The doctor rubbed his chin. "We did the best we could to know, Hugh, and that possibility doesn't often present its self, but because Suz lasted longer than most... we are pretty sure."

"You have been able to discern this," Hugh searched for words. "I mean, you said it would be pretty far out...babies cannot survive outside the womb...but you've been able to tell..."

"It was a little boy." Ben saw Barkley's eyes take on a minute of joy, and then sadness closed in.

Hugh's reaction was as Ben expected. "If only," There Hugh's words muffled, "If I'd got her here quicker..." Ben saw Hugh's pain. "Is it my fault? We were looking at a field, I knew something was wrong but this… she'll be so disappointed."

Doctor Ben picked up Hugh's words, "I've only known of one miraculous birth due to the baby forming outside the womb…and she was born prematurely but the girl is college age now and that's what she's doing, going to college. She's our miracle baby, but other than Angela, don't you think that name is appropriate?" Ben smiled a bit, thinking of the young girl. "She is every bit as precious as her name. I think God intervened and she lives as a testimony to the fact, He gives and takes according to his will."

"But our baby couldn't make it?" Hugh felt his insides caving in. He wanted to crawl up on the bed and let Suz hold him, so acute was his pain in their loss, but Caroline and Sophia were waiting to hear and Barkley had moved back. Who knew what the kid was thinking, Hugh mused. His own thoughts were crashing around in his brain. Suz said last night; they must not let the medical world rob their child. "Our baby will need a name and a memorial; private just our children and us and maybe the grandparents." The medication was taking hold, she slept and they did not discuss it further.

It was now or never, "I have to ask, Ben. Was there enough of our child to have a memorial? That's what Suz wants."

"I know Susan." A moment of sadness crossed Ben's face. He was a doctor, trained and encouraged not to get involved, but this was his high school friend. "In most cases depending on how far into the pregnancy; the hospital takes care of the remains. We have legal obligations and we do have sensitive disposal, but in this case for Susan I think the closure will help in her healing in the days ahead for you both to make the decision of how you want this handled." Hugh was motioning the children away as he moved toward the nearest wall. They understood and returned to the sofa, to huddle together.

Ben watched Hugh seek the support he needed to stand. "Your private arrangements will be respected. The hospital will record the baby as miscarried, proper documentation will be given you to take the remains for a private memorial and I will tell you we have had a small number of families do this."

"You must not open the sealed canister. It will fit into something of your choosing; We may have something you would like or a small wooden or ceramic box found in one of the local craft stores; preferably one with a seal. I know this can be done by information I've gleaned at the hands of those who have experienced it. Burial would be at your discretion since the baby was not over twenty week's gestation and there are no legal requirements at this time."

"I don't know how we missed this," Hugh replied. "Susan had her monthly period."

"It happens," Ben replied. "No two pregnancies are alike and a woman's body is God's own miracle." He sighed. "I have appointments to meet, Hugh." He clasped his friend's hand. "I'm truly sorry for your loss. I will release Susan around three this afternoon. We will have the baby's remains ready and hopefully if she's up to it, and I know Susan…then your family can find closure to begin the healing."

They watched Susan's doctor walk down the hall. Hugh would take the children home after one stop. They would wait for their mother's release and then if she wished they would bury their brother. "Daddy," Barkley stared up at his dad. "If we have a baby brother to bury, doesn't he need a name?"

"I guess he does, Son," Hugh replied softly. "What do you have in mind?"

"Joshua." Barkley whispered, but the girls were listening. They didn't scold, as he'd expected. "Joshua," he heard them test the name on their lips but daddy was saying, "Let's see what Mom wants."

Hugh helped her into the gray jogging set she'd requested to wear home. Light weight and soft it seemed to fall off her body, had she lost weight in the process or had there been swelling he hadn't noticed? His guilt was eating away, how had he missed the signs and caused her such agony? "Ready?" The nurse was waiting outside the door with the wheel chair, a hospital requirement for departing patients. Beverley, from their church, in her nurse scrubs leaned down to place a kiss on Susan's cheek. "I'm sorry," she whispered and both women's eyes filled with tears. Hugh followed them to the truck.

A single sob escaped, as she asked, "How are the kids taking this?" They were leaving the hospital's property; she glanced at the signs wondering if they were leaving something behind. As if knowing her thoughts, Hugh reached for her hand.

"We have the baby, Suz. I know you are wondering. You can say, Babe." She seemed to slump down into the gray clothes. "We don't know what to do, without you telling us. What are we to do, now?" She was waiting, the question hanging in the air. "The kids are all right. Barkley says we must name the baby brother."

"You wanted a boy so badly, then we got Barkley and you seem happy, but now, I've lost this one."

"It's not your fault." He squeezed her hand. "There's a reason, we just don't know what it is, yet."

"I feel so...lost...I don't know what I did wrong."

"I feel so guilty, Suz, that I didn't take better care of you; I didn't know...is my worst excuse. It wasn't lack of loving you, Babe, it was...me, I didn't know..." He glanced her way, "and as for having a son, I am happy but if we'd had ten girls I'd still love every one of them."

"Doctor says no more babies', Hugh."

"We never planned for another but if we'd been given this one to keep, we'd been happy there, too."

"If Barkley thinks we need a name," she gave a half-sob-laugh, "then Barkley had one in mind."

"Joshua."

"Joshua," she repeated. "Joshua. Jesus other name, we studied that; I don't know if Barkley's class did or not, but it means church or salvation....I recall...we can check it out...Joshua. Salvation." She was silent until they turned into the home drive she said, "If you and the girls agree, we will bury our Joshua...I think at the foot of my grandmother's grave. It will be such a small little box, no one would ever know and when we visit her we can visit him."

Suz parents were there, standing on the front porch, waiting with her children, their faces as sad as her own. Her mother's arms welcomed Susan and her Father waited for his moment when he placed his weather beaten arms around them both. "It will be all right, in time, daughter," he said, "but you'll never forget."

Hugh's mother reached for his hand. "You holding up?" He nodded. "This is a bit much," she said.

"It's a small box, Mother," Caroline Dawn explained, her hands caressing the beautiful grain of the small wooden box, that held the remains of her brother; cherry finished, the lid sealed, a small cross where an opener should have been. "It is normally used by people who cremate and keep the ashes." She was hesitant to go on but her mother was waiting. "I found this larger container it will fit into, the man who had the box said no rain or offering of the elements can penetrate, but it's up to you if you feel it ruins the beauty of the box."

"No, Caroline, you have done well. Its protection and you have thought it through." She motioned for Caroline to come near.

"I didn't want to hurt you, Mother," Caroline went down on her knees before Susan. "Were we supposed to bring the baby into our house? We didn't know what else to do until we bury him."

"It's a big job," Susan whispered, "thank you." Now she opened her arms toward Sophia and Barkley. Their hearts in their eyes, tears streaming down their cheeks they came, as the three were closed in by their mother's arms. "Of course it was all right to bring him into our home. Had things been different he would live here, as it is he will live in our hearts. Now," she allowed them to move back where she could look into their faces, "are we in agreement of our baby's name?"

"Joshua," they said in soft unison as she and Hugh nodded.

Chapter 3

Sophia Raine was on a roll, her nose in a snitch and her attitude hard to bear.

"You cannot expect Mother to finish that dress," Caroline hissed. "She is not strong yet, and you have this selfish idea she can sit at that machine and finish something just because you need it. Forget it."

"I can't forget it. Two nights away and I don't have a dress for the event. What am I supposed to wear? My pajamas?"

"You can wear the dress I had for last years Prom."

"I will not, everyone will remember it. That's not fair, and you know it. What if I'm crowned Queen? Then there're more pictures and people, especially the kids will be comparing it to when you wore it."

"I truly doubt anyone cares that much. Once the crowning is over, it's forgotten except by those who lost."

"You are so hateful."

"And you are selfish." Caroline finished putting away the dishes and closed the dishwasher. "You need to get the dust mop and take care of the floors before mother decides to do it herself. It's a simple thing and it makes her feel better if anyone drops in to visit."

"I'll be glad when you go back to college."

Caroline gave her own significant little laugh; reminisce of Hugh's when he was being sarcastic, "Why? So you will have all this to do by yourself? If your room is anything to compare to, we'd live in a hovel. Clean it up, Sophie, and grow up."

"You're so grown up?" Sophie sneered. "All you are is a simpleminded prig. Quit bossing me and telling me what to do. I just want my dress finished. I can't help mother had a baby. She and Dad shouldn't have been fooling around, anyway. It's embarrassing; you in College, me a junior in High School and our mother gets pregnant. What is that about?"

Caroline threw the dish cloth on the sink and grabbed Sophia's wrist, pushing her against the wall. "I've had enough of your high school drama, life isn't all about you Sophia. I'll tell you what it's about; Mother and Dad love each other. That's the real reason to have a baby, not some back seat fiasco with a pimply faced boy in a car or someone that doesn't give a rip about you. Do you get my meaning?"

Sophie pushed her away. "I don't know what you are implying."

"Then don't let it happen. I know exactly what and who you are playing around with. You want me on your side? Then settle it down. Right now is not the time to worry mother and daddy. You think you're so grown? Then figure out a way to get that dress finished. Ask one of the Grandmother's."

"I can't ask Gramma Caplan, she just had a cataract removed and Grandmother Kathryn," Sophie shuddered, "She's so stiff, she'd think I was imposing."

"They're both excellent seamstress, but you're limited, either shut up or ask Grandmother." She sighed; "Maybe you ought to clear this with Mother, first. Grandmother has a way of taking the upper hand."

Hugh and Barkley had just left. Susan was sitting at the breakfast table having coffee when there was a knock at the door. "Come in," she hollered. Hugh's mother came into the room. "Kathryn, what a nice surprise. Would you like a cup of coffee?" She glanced quickly to the clock on the wall, not yet seven.

"No. Where's Sophia? I told her I'd be here early."

"Is something wrong?" Susan started to rise. "The girls are still asleep. Barkley's with his dad."

"No, nothing's wrong, except Sophia said she had a dress needed finishing for the queen candidate thing for the Basketball team."

"She did?" Susan's disappointment was evident. "I was working on it when…"

"I heard the door bell, didn't I, or was it a knock?" Sophia came straggling into the kitchen. "Oh, Grandmother, I overslept," and to her mother, "I forgot to tell you Grandmother's going to finish my dress." Making a quick exit, she hollered back, "I'll get it, grandmother, the machine, too. We can sit it there on the table where there's plenty of light."

"I'm so sorry to inconvenience you, Kathryn, I had no idea she called you." Susan picked up her cup to move away from the table. "It's three forth finished but the straps need adjusting and if you get the length I think I can sit and hem it. There's a lot of yardage in the skirt."

"Why aren't you up and around, yet?" Kathryn studied her daughter in law. "Women used to have babies and be back taking care of the family the next day; shouldn't be different with a miscarriage."

Susan paled. "It's the loss of blood. According to Doctor Ben I'll have to rebuild and for a while he says my body will tell me rest and sleep are necessary. I admit I fight it but I seem to want to sleep a lot…"

"Maybe that's depression that it happened at all." Sophie returned with the machine and Kathryn stepped aside as she sit it on the table and plugged it in. "I'll need scissors. Now where's the dress." She cast her eyes on Susan as Sophie disappeared to bring back the dress. "You and Hugh aren't kids anymore; maybe It's time you take more seriously what creates a baby. You have three kids and if you don't know what caused them, then get a book."

Caroline was coming down the hall and heard her grandmother's word. Stopping suddenly out of Kathryn's sight, her mother knew she was there, but Caroline realized someone had entered the house and was standing just inside with a hand on the knob of the kitchen door, seemingly stalled in his steps whether it was Barkley or her Dad, she didn't know. They listened as Susan defused those caustic words.

"What happens between a husband and wife in their own bedroom is private, Kathryn. I thought you would understand that."

"You two have always been out of control, his hands all over you, you smiling…"

"If Hugh loves me, Kathryn and wants to touch my body and if I smile because I'm happy he loves me, why are you against that?"

"It's time you grow up. Both of you," Kathryn snapped. "People are interested in Hugh."

"Could be you're jealous," Caroline said, coming into the room. "I'm happy my parents love each other." She never raised her voice, smiling now at her mother, first, and then Kathryn as she leaned to bestow a kiss on Susan's cheek. "Didn't Grandad Preston show you attention like Dad does Mother?"

"That's none of your business," Kathryn snapped, suddenly aware her son had stepped into the room.

"He tried," Hugh replied. "I remember." He cast troubled eyes on his mother. "Good morning, Mother. Are you over stepping your bounds?" Now his glance went to Susan who was shaking her head wanting no further trouble. "You know, Mother, through the years you've shown such disregard for Susan and all I ask of her was to be respectful to you, but while she's not on her feet health wise at this time, I do think this is inappropriate."

"She's always come between us, you know that." Kathryn approached him as if no one else was in the room. "Right now, out in the community all I hear is poor Susan had a miscarriage. It's embarrassing."

"Is it?" He studied her. "I'm trying to figure that out. Why is it embarrassing? Life happens."

"Privacy is a good thing. The two of you need to consider it an asset. Don't bandy your lives publicly."

"I think, Mother, this was bad timing. I'm glad I had to return for the check book to hear what goes on when I'm not around. I can't tell you the times I've come home to find Susan distraught after you've either called or made your visit to give her your opinion and do you know what she says?" Kathryn only raised an eyebrow listening. "She says, your mother really loves you, Hugh Don Preston."

"Yes, I do," Kathryn replied. "You married beneath yourself; you could have had someone with standing and taken our name further. Are you aware the community wants you on the School Board"

Hugh sat down at the table with a weary thump scooting the chair on the floor. "There was no marrying beneath, Mother. You dress like a million and I don't know your bank account. I think you reference the simplicity of Anson and Star Caplan. Susan's parent's may not wear designer clothes, but they're probably worth a million financially…I don't have that information, either, but tell me, do you recognize their stability, the calming effect they have on people, their genuine happiness?"

"Pshh, it's probably put on." Kathryn met his stare head on. "Don't try shaming me, Son."

Hugh spread his arms wide. "What about here, Mother. Do you see happiness? Would you rather I married the rich girl down the road and lived a life of misery?" He got to his feet. "Wonders never cease, that you would choose this time, years down that road." His voice rose and frustration creased his brow. "Twenty years down the road to spew this nonsense. I suggest you fold your tent and go home and come back when Susan's up to countering your opinion….and your words from this time on need to be couched. Do you understand?"

"Daddy," Sophia came from the hall where she'd stood with the unfinished dress hanging across her arm. "Daddy, Grandmother came to finish my dress." Tears sprang to Sophia's eyes. "Please."

"All right." His voice was harsh. "It would serve you well, young lady, to think the next time, before you create such a mess. Susan, you're dressed. Get your medicine, whatever you need. You're going with me. Riding won't hurt you and I'll see it's cool and you can rest. Caroline, bring us a pillow."

End of day, Kathryn watched as Sophia removed the machine from the table. The dress was a dream on her granddaughter. They'd even shared a few laughs. This one was more like her. Caroline, was her father's daughter, perhaps mother's too, all fact and to the point honest. She didn't bend. This one did.

"I never meant to cause a problem," Sophia confessed as Kathryn was leaving. "I didn't want anyone to say you couldn't come." She caught Kathryn's expression. "Not Mother. Daddy, he'd of said, not yet."

In the truck at the far end of the field, Susan saw Kathryn's car on the Highway that led home. She had mused all day over Kathryn showing up unexpected, Sophia's wide eyes as if caught in a trap and Caroline coming to her defense over something that should never have been discussed in the first place. Only Barkley was spared the family conversation. Sweet innocent Barkley, eight years old and happy was driving the tractor for the guys picking up poly pipe from end rows. Cotton was ready to be laid by, now the heat index would tell the story of harvests yield.

Hugh had admonished her to lay back and rest, but the activity of the farm interested her. She'd had opportunity to catch up on the lives of the employees, listened in as Hugh spoke with representatives from the chemical and seed companies, out to make contact and glean information from Hugh on the products they supplied. She lay back to think of the day's adventure.

There was a knock on the truck window. "Hey, Susan, you asleep or just restin' your eyes?"

She raised the seat to sitting position. "Frank Jolly." Susan smiled, "Open the door and get in. It's cooler in here." He climbed in and offered his hand. "Good to see you, Frank."

"I heard you'd been under the weather, and big daddy, there," Frank pointed to Hugh standing by the Spray machine talking to the employee running it. "He said he brought you with him today to keep you out of trouble. How you doin?"

"In time, I'll be fine, Frank. How's your family?"

He grinned. "Well, they're puttin' up with me. You know we got the Rodeo comin up?"

"Rodeo?"

"Yeah, we call it that. That's why I wanted to see you. I sent the invitation home by Hugh but no one replied. We need you there, Susan. Hugh's going to get an award."

"For what?"

"Stayin with our company this many years when the competition out there has been fierce and he could've gone elsewhere." Frank rubbed the back of his neck. "Heck, there were probably times he could've, and probably saved a dollar or two."

Susan smiled. "I know what you're talking about, that overseas conglomerate that contacted him. They'd supply his chemicals at a better rate to get their foot in the door, except that was it, supply and no rep to come around to see everything was applied according to instructions and whether those applying understood the instructions. Some off-brand chemical that Hugh wasn't sure would be what it read on the label."

"That was one of them," Frank agreed. "Don't know if you've met Guy Chris over in Sand County? Well, he bought in on that deal…had a fine beginning of crop, cotton blooming in the top, got a heavy rain and couldn't get in the field, so he had his flying service fly on the product. That was last year, mind you, he's lucky if he's making crop this year. Whatever it was went into the ground, but on top it turned his crop brown and it didn't come out of it. Prospects of three bale cotton produced nothing."

"I'm surprised with all the rules and regulations that chemical got into the country."

"Quite frankly, Susan, if that happens and too many of our farmers take advantage…"

"It will affect your company?" She leaned forward interested. "Is that what you're saying?"

"Not exactly." He coughed. "It might…but what it does to the land, and if it mists over to other farmers fields we could have a real problem on our hands, it's enough to take a few farmers out of business."

"If the information's out there, Frank, why would a farmer even consider it?"

"Some don't want the info, other's reject it thinking they can make it work but the bottom line is everything needed in producing a crop cost more, some are straining at the bit, lack of funding and hanging on by a straw if they can't afford price on products that work they second guess by purchasing an inferior one, they're not thinkin, they're just tryin to make it one more season; all the while knowin they're on their way out."

"I hate to hear that." They noticed Hugh had finished with the sprayer and was headed their way.

"Well, Susan," Frank was opening the door. "It was nice talkin' with you. Now don't forget. I'll send you the info and Susan, It's going to be a formal affair. Wear that dress that's hangin in the closet, if you're like my wife, you wonder why you bought it?" He grinned. "She said she had a dream."

Frank left after a few minutes with Hugh. Hugh climbed into the cab. "Did y'all have a nice visit?"

"I guess," she replied. "He was telling me about a dress his wife had hanging in the closet."

Hugh gave her a peculiar look. "That sounds strange. Have I kept you out a bit too long?"

"I think so. I'm going to be dead on my feet."

Hugh closed up the shop, pulled the chain across the farm drive and secured it on the pole extensions welded specifically for placement since there had been a group of teenagers terrorizing the community the last year. Susan was asleep. Her head had been on his shoulder and he'd placed the pillow there momentarily. She looked peaceful and he hated waking her.

But she felt the truck stop on the back drive to the house. The thing was, her knees buckled when she tried to step out onto the ground. Hugh leaned down, lifted her up into his arms and said, "let's see if we still got it in us to make it up those steps." Susan giggled and tightened her hold around his neck.

Caroline only grinned but Sophia's eyes seemed to squint angrily their direction.

"Something bothering you, Sophia," her father asked. "You seem a bit tense."

"I don't want to have to worry every time I see you and mother together that we're going to have another baby. I agree with Grandmother, it's embarrassing."

Hugh laid Susan on the sofa, straightened and stood there, his lips pressed together, his mind in a whirl. "Grandmother said that, did she? And you agree." His voice was steel cold. "Sit down, Sophia." Protesting, she started to back away. "Young lady, I said sit. If you were younger, I would spank your butt, but seeing as to how Mother has put her two cents in and you are a lot like her, I'm going to skip that part and go right to the heart of this matter."

"Now, I realize it's not a thing often talked about in today's families, I guess everyone's supposed to know everything from the television and this is certainly not a dad to daughter item." He'd started this thing and he intended to see it through. "Sophia, why do you think a man and woman marry?"

"I don't know." She practically molded into the upholstery of the chair. "They love each other."

"Yes." His eyes bore into hers. "I won't have my mother or my daughter telling me what they think I should or should not do. Now, there's a wonderful physical thing happens between some people, not all, just so happens it does with your mother and I. We love each other. We like each other and I'm just about fit to be tied this has come up. It's embarrassing only in the fact we're discussing it, you and I."

"Hugh, please." Susan was sitting upright on the sofa. "I implore." Caroline went to her mother.

He cut her off. "Hells-bells, Suz. It's ridiculous, my mother...our daughter, discussing whether we should make love or not." He snatched the cap off his head and threw it across the floor. Striding across the room, he pulled a large ottoman in front of Sophia, "Give me your hands," he said, his lips as tight as ever.

"Daddy, don't hit me." Sophia's shoulders were shaking as tears slid down her cheeks.

There were tears in Hugh's eyes. "Sophia, I would never hit you. It was a figure of speech a while ago. Now," with one finger he lift her chin. "Look me in the eye. I'm going to tell you something. The love between a husband and a wife is something to cherish. We lean on each other. We share hurt and we share all the joy and happiness we're allowed. I want that for you. What I don't want is my mother souring you on that part of life." He gave a deep sigh, pulling one hand free to brush away the dampness to his face, then taking back her hand.

"My daddy was a bear of a man and he loved life. He was more outgoing than me, meeting people with a gladness, where as I do, but I'm a bit more quiet, I think, not reserved but my point here he was very demonstrative with Mother and Mother, was more caught up in what people would think if he leaned over to kiss her cheek out in public, I don't know where that comes from but she was stiff and unbending." He blew out a breath of air. "The best I can hope for you is you save yourself, Sophia, find a love that puts you above all those little side roads situations that can cause you sorrow, embarrassment and pain. Now that's where embarrassment comes in, if you forget who you are and let some old boy talk you into climbing in the back seat of a car with him and from there you lose control…sweetheart, that's embarrassment."

Sophia sat up, indignant, a scathing look going to Caroline. Caroline shrugged. "I haven't said a thing."

"No, she hasn't," Hugh agreed. "I see that old boy that's coming here every night, Sophia, and I'm telling you right now we're going to head this thing off. Nip it in the bud. Embarrassment is when you do wrong and it ends up hurting the whole family. Love is something I want you to understand is special." He drew up to stand pulling her out of the chair. "I love you, Sophia, don't be harsh about your mother and me. Don't let your grandmother lead you down the wrong path. Be who you really are. You are my daughter and I want the best for you but get this straight, the kind of love I have for your mother is nothing to embarrass anyone; it's what I want for you someday, just give yourself time." He kissed the top of her head, just as Barkley came through the door. "And Sophia, I want you to call the boy," Hugh said, "and tell him your daddy insists tonight is family night and he need not come tonight."

"Hey guys, what's going on?" There was so much dirt on Barkleoy's face a white ring was around his eyes from wearing the sunglasses his mother insist he wear knowing he would be disking with a tractor that had no cab and the wind would whip the dirt back on him. Hugh began to laugh. Barkley put both hands up as if to protest. "Is there something funny and I missed it?"

"Come on, everyone," Caroline was saying. "Barkley, wash up. Sophia, set the table and I'll put the food on. It's ready in the oven. Somehow I just knew we'd be delayed and I wanted to keep it warm."

Later, leaving the girls to tidy up the kitchen, Hugh entered the shower with Susan, toweled her off and slipped the gown over her head and put her to bed. "That was completely unexpected," he murmured. "I don't know why in the world I chose to go through that with Sophia. At first I was angry, then…" He shook his head as if to clear the cob webs, "Then, it was if Sophia wasn't seeing the picture clearly and I felt I needed to explain it to her." He wiped water from the floor from his own feet.

"Unexpected like your mother this morning," Susan whispered. "Hugh, I'd spared you that, if I could."

"So that's what you've meant the many times, that she comes in thinking she can say what she wants?"

"I didn't say it like that." Hugh was removing the towel around his waist, slipping into a pair of boxers and climbing in the bed beside her. "I try really hard with your mother, Hugh. It's like if she won't let anyone break through that shell and love her."

"I know. I lived it." He pulled Susan into the hollow of his body. "Are you okay, being out all day?"

"Just extremely tired," she said, yawning. "I love you, Hugh." Her eyes were closing. "G'nite."

"I can't let it go, Suz. Should I feel shame explaining what I did? It has plumb wore me out."

He could feel her smile as she said, "Turn loose, Big Daddy that one needed to hear it. Someday it will be one of the wisest words of wisdom she'll remember and it came from you."

Chapter 4

Caroline returned to college; Sophia and Barkley started school. Suz was physically better but often quiet and she and Barkley seemed to have an understanding. He'd find her after supper and sit as close to her side as possible. It seemed to bring both comfort. Hugh was coming in late hours. The corn was harvested, in the bin for now. The early soybeans were ready but not yielding as much as expected. "That's a concern," Hugh said. "I'm thinking next year we'll reduce down to maybe two crops. The corn was beautiful to watch growing but with price down, we can't do this another year."

"What are you thinking? Cotton?" Suz lay the invoices received in the day's mail on the back of the counter. "What if everyone and his brother decides the same?"

"Got a better idea?" She saw the worry in his eyes as he turned to her. "You ran the spread sheets. What do you think?"

"Right now, it looks like cotton would be the better choice, but then there's the Farm Bill to deal with and whether there are tariffs. If we have a glut on the cotton market and the tariff's prevent the product going out…" She sighed. "Then we're stuck."

"I hate to bring up another problem." Hugh come around the desk, slumped down into the chair opposite Susan. "Did either of our young workers tell you our neighbor down the road told them they'd beat our wages if they'd come over to their farm?"

"Grant and Tab?" She closed down the program she was working on. "When did this happen?"

"This week. They gave their two week resignation this morning and I told them to come talk to you."

"Well, they didn't." Huffing a disgusted breath of air, she said, "Your Dad always said it looked like you trained them, then someone else stepped in and took them away. I thought we were paying decent wages."

"We are, but the Alberson's have worked their men too hard, that's my understanding and lost three, this year. So they came after Grant and Tab. Of course they could see which piece of equipment they drove. Exactly what they need right now and they know they're skilled for the one's they'll need later. If it's true, Tab says this fall they doubled their pay, then next year they'll go back to same as paid here."

"How can they afford to double their pay? Even if only for this year's fall harvest?"

"How can they not? They want crop out of the field and if their men left, they don't see it any other way. So they go after their neighbors help and that leaves us two men short."

"Let me absorb this." Susan had just talked with the two late yesterday evening. "They hated to tell me, didn't they?" She thought of all the times she'd taken them snacks. Young men were always hungry. But right now, time was still moving forward. Maybe the event was not number one on their chart but for Sophia it was. "Do you plan on us going to see Sophia march as one of the queen candidates?"

"What's going on, that crowning is usually after Christmas."

"They didn't get it done last year and they've set everything earlier this school year."

He nodded. "I'll do my best to get in here early enough to get a shower. Just fix me a sandwich for on the go. You can feed Barkley anytime and tell him I don't have a job for him this evening."

"Mom," Barkley came through the door like a puff of wind. "Mom, Tab's nephew, Andy Jobe's, in my class. He tried to make me mad, Mom. He said Tab and Grant are going over to the Alberson's. They won't be here anymore, 'cause they're working there. I told him he's crazy. I saw them here this morning."

"They told your Dad this morning that they'll be leaving." She saw tears well up in Barkley's eyes and his hands went into a clench.

"They can't leave, Mom. Dad needs them and Tab, Tab lets me ride with him and he's always careful like you want. He says, "Barkley, never get between a tractor and an implement. Someone might run over you.""

"That's true, Sweetheart." Susan set down, pulling him o her side. "They've been offered a lot more money to work there."

"But Daddy trained them. They owe him something."

"They don't see it that way, Son. Maybe you wouldn't either."

"I won't be like that." Barkley's chin jut forward, his eyes squenched. "They're just rats, that's all."

It was time for the march. Half time on the court with scores nearly tied. They could hear the band tuning up. Arriving after first quarter, they were sitting on the end of the bench, the steps to the top immediate to their right. As usual the school's security team stood in front of the glassed paned doors that led from the gymnasium into the hall of the high school. The Security always interested Barkley; he liked to know they were there if needed. Making his usual late appearance Kane Alberson and his new girlfriend were coming up the steps. Kane saw Hugh turn his head as if interested in something Susan was holding. It was a ruse to ignore his presence, handsome and commanding as he was.

"Hey, there, Hugh." Kane stopped by Hugh, glancing down the row at Susan and Barkley. "How you doin', fellow. I heard you lost two of your best men this week, anything to that piece of gossip?" Barkley heard the conversation and he didn't like it. He moved up toward the top, finding a place on the outer edge by the steps. Three more rows to the top and that's where Alberson would head to rest his back against the wall. He saw his daddy stand to full height, at least four inches taller than Kane Alberson.

"I believe you'd know all about that, Kane, seeing as how they gave your farm address where they could be reached. Yeah, they said you were going to pay double. Sounds like your desperate, but the men, well they're well trained. Trained by me...all that patience and time, invested, just wasted on the likes of you. There'll be paper work for Grant...but not for Tab," Hugh replied sitting back down.

"Better man always wins, Preston." Kane followed his girlfriend on up the stairs. Barkley was watching.

Three more steps toward the top, Alberson lay a hand on Barkley's head just as Barkley's leg went out. Later, his friend would say he heard a cracking sound as Alberson reached out for support but none nor no one was there. The one knee hit the step in middle of the board that went across, the other gave a squishing sound as Alberson tried to gain purchase; doing an unexpected split, there was a thump unrecognizable, and Barkley's eyes were on that mouth, that kept talking and the hand, searching for what, he didn't know. Alberson wore a look of surprise as his knee smashed on the solid oak step. "You little monster," he swore at Barkley. "You little rat, I could crush you. Your Daddy's gonna be sorry." He was leaning in on Barkley, his eyes blazing whether with pain or anger.

Barkley stood up hollering. "Help me, help me, the man he's going to hurt me…get him away….away…away." The security team left the door; they were coming up the steps in a run. "Who's the rat?" Barkley whispered in Kane Alberson's ear. "Leave my daddy alone."

On the way home, Susan asked, "What have we come to, our family can't have a decent outing, there's always someone ready to mess it up." It was a sobering thought. "If we are doing it ourselves, it's got to stop. Now." In the back seat, Barkley was nearly asleep. He couldn't really say how it happened but it had and if he could muster the courage, need be, he'd do it again. Kane Alberson had no right to talk down to his Daddy. Turning a deaf ear wasn't always the right thing to do and maybe not a wandering foot, either, but tonight it happened. Maybe Kane Alberson would think about things, too.

Hugh reached for Susan's hand and squeezed it. "I saw Sophia in line with her escort. Her expression was anything but happy. I'm sure she was relieved the disturbance was by her brother and not me."

Susan reviewed it all in her mind. It was an evening of deep sighs. "I know. But it almost was. I'm grateful that whoever was in charge of the crowing of Basketball Queen had the foresight to have the band start playing and as soon as Alberson and his date were ushered out, the crowning continued." Tiredness claimed her, she couldn't seem to pull out of her own personal ordeal. "Sophia looked beautiful," she said, yawning, "Your mother did a good job, finishing the dress. I guess you noticed it wasn't the kid that usually sits on our sofa, her escort?"

"He looked older than the others. Is he still in school?"

"No, he was the previous year escort to the reigning queen, in college now. Caroline knows him."

I don't understand any of this, they've started out the new school year with unfinished business, last year's crowning because of the late fall tornado that took the roof off the gymnasium, and now they've brought in one of the older ball players. Why?"

"They scheduled this game to kick off the season and that young man, who was our daughter's escort was something, maybe a past captain of the team; seems they all need a bit of encouragement after the months of struggling without a gym to practice in and a shorter year." Her mind went on to a different subject. "What was that little huddle and discussion between you and several other farmers, in front of the glass doors where security stands?"

Hugh laughed. "You won't believe this, they ask if I'd run for school board, next community vote will be in the spring."

"And would you be interested?" She smothered another yawn behind her hand.

"That's a good question; I'd be running against Kane Alberson. That could get vicious"

"Who's the girlfriend? I didn't recognize her."

"You should've, that's Sherry Newell, she's was affiliated with the National Cotton Council, but I understand she has since been offered a job involved in promoting the product. She gathers the info the government puts out and applies the part that's beneficial to us rednecks; Maybe she works with the Council too, presenting information needed to make people want to buy items made from cotton. I've seen her at the meetings among local farmers and even the farm service. But she did seem to get stalled speaking to Kane's daddy when he brought a relief ride in for Alberson."

"I didn't make the connection, she's daughter to whoever's farm Kane is taking over. Right?"

"Yeah, I should've been on my toes and contacted her daddy as soon as I heard he was retiring, maybe Kane wouldn't have scored that one. Mr. Newell might have rented us a chunk of his land; most farmers don't put all their eggs in one basket. But if the story going around is right, he did lease it all to the Alberson's, and namely Kane will be in charge of it. Yeah, Kane scored that one."

"So that's what it is now, scoring on each other." She pushed her feet against the floor board of the truck. "It was almost too much for my first night out…I'm dying here to fall into our bed."

Hugh glanced back to their sleeping son. "I think the disruption got to everyone. It was unnecessary."

"Well, she's a pretty woman. I don't know her though." Susan's words slipped away, as she closed her eyes. "I guess the candidates were going to the Burger Shack to celebrate who won and who lost."

"Sophia has something to thank you and her grandmother for doesn't she if the dress helped her win?"

"Hugh, considering you'd have inquired about part of the Newell operation, do we need more land?"

"It's come to that, Babe. If we are going to pay for all these expensive products, the seed and chemicals not to mention the price of the equipment, yeah, we are going to have to find more land to farm."

"And us losing two hands which means two short if we don't find replacements before harvest." Her voice was weary with tiredness. "I guess you want me to start the search for skilled drivers."

"Yeah, you go on-line and I'll keep my ear tuned to what's going on local. It'll be all right," he replied. "I can tell you are worn through, let me get the door and then I'll wake Barkley and get him in." The truck tires crunched on the home drive. "Nothing like the green green grass of home, is there, Babe?"

Susan headed for the bedroom. "Seems to me, this energy replacement thing is taking its time. I'm sorry, Hugh, but I've got to go to bed. It's almost been too much day for me."

"That's to be expected. Ben said you lost a lot of blood." He wanted to help her, but how? " I'll get Barkley in."

Barkley was climbing out of the truck, grinning sheepishly. "Dad? I'm hungry. Can we have something to eat before we go to bed?" Hugh glanced at his watch. "It's not that late, Dad, I already looked."

"It may be cereal."

"Nah, there's ice cream, Mom always keeps ice cream." Barkley led the way to the kitchen.

"Son?" Hugh paused, a spoon full of ice cream in mid-air. "Did you have anything to do with Alberson tripping on the steps at the ball game?"

"I honestly don't know, Dad." Barkley wore a troubled expression. "I wanted to, and I was sitting on the edge, but I think it happened when he slapped his hand on my head, I wasn't expecting him to do that."

"You moved away from us, Son. Why?"

"He was talking bad to you, Dad. I didn't like it and you always say I'm not to talk back to older people."

Hugh kind of whistled beneath his breath, "No, and you sure don't trip them." He pushed the empty bowl to the center of the table and leaned his elbows on the table. "For some reason, Alberson likes to bait people and seeing as he enticed Grant and Tab to come over to his headquarters, I was handy tonight." His expression matched his son's. "We need to stay out of Alberson's path, Barkley. It's not that I fear him but that I have to take our crop in there and I don't need any problems."

"Does that mean, Sophia, can't be around Thorn, then?"

Barkley saw his dad's head raise as he stared into the distance. He didn't know Thorn ."You know, Dad, Sam Lansky's son, your friend Miss Emily's boy?" Barkley saw his dad trying to make the connection. "I hear things Dad. They say Thorn is really Kane Alberson's kid. And he looks just like him."

"What does this Thorn person have to do with Sophia?"

"Thorn Lansky was Sophia's escort tonight, Dad. They brought him back in. The whole thing was different. Thorn was past captain of the basketball team, the one from last year moved off and you know the other one died so they brought him back to do the crowning."

"How old are you?" Hugh was rising from the table. "Honestly, Barkley, where do you get this information?"

"Well, Tab and Grant talk a lot and I listen but the kids at school know everything."

"But that's not Thorn as you call him that comes to sit with us every night…although I've not been around for television much lately."

"Nah, that's just one of Sophia's friends. "His last name's Kirkland. I think he just likes the family since his Mom and Dad divorced."

"You are a walking encyclopedia," Hugh exclaimed. "At your young age."

"Yeah, but now my source has left," Barkley placed his bowl in the sink. "I sure will miss Tab and Grant. They were teaching me how to drive the spray rigs. Now, they won't be here through harvest and I won't learn nothing."

"Anything." Hugh corrected.

"Yes. Dad, I heard some people talking. They said Mom was asked to sit in on the County Council. Is she going to? What is that Dad?"

"Yes, Mom was asked but she told me she's thinking it over. I think the council needs help in meeting the needs of the county so they have a group from different areas, you'll have to ask Mom." Hugh's thoughts returned to the previous subject. He hadn't realized Sophia's escort was Emily's son.

Barkley went to his room and Hugh found the day's newspaper and settled into the recliner. Maybe he'd scan the paper to see if anyone was looking for a job, but how could he put an unskilled person on that expensive machine? His mind returned to the fact Barkley had so many facts and knew more than he did about Sophia's date. He couldn't caution Tab and Grant, not to talk such matters, now they were gone. Yeah, he'd known about Emily's son with Alberson, it had been rumored. She hadn't really admitted Kane was the boy's father but if it was true what Barkley said and the two looked alike, well, others would come to the same conclusion. But he believed Sophia too young to date an older boy, not until she finished high school. It appeared the Kirkland boy was a decoy. Hugh shook his head, a rue smile playing about his lips. Seemed the gossip mill was a factor in their lives anymore. He shook his head to clear the cob webs, what he'd heard that day about a former classmate, was too much. Dolly Kirkland, the boy's mother was practically running a brothel. No wonder the kid showed up at Sophia's home every night. For Barkley's sake he and Susan must instill good in their boy by their own actions.

Susan stirred, to see the clock on twelve thirty. She let her hand run the sheets on the other side of the bed. Hugh wasn't there. She checked and found him in the big recliner, the day's paper on his lap and Hugh in deep sleep.

"Hugh?" She pat his arm. "Hugh, wake up, you need to come to bed, honey. You'll sleep better."

He was rubbing his neck. "I was doing pretty good right here, wasn't I?" He gave her a lazy grin, "But I think someone made a gooseneck out of mine."

Chapter 5

*I*n the sleepy little town of Alberson, the founder's grandson left the Suburban by way of the Passenger seat. "Four hours to get a leg in a cast," he swore, "I know that kid intended to trip me." He gave an acidic laugh that only reached the midnight air. "Ole Preston's got quite a kid, all wrapped up in a lithe little body, probably don't weigh sixty pounds and he had the gall to trip me?"

"Come on, Babe," Sherry Newell, Missouri's own Miss Cotton Cheer leader encouraged him to take the crutch and put it under his arm as she waited for him to make the first step toward the back door to his house, already the garaged door was descending. "Please Kane, I'm tired, I know you are." She yawned, "I agreed to spend the night for you to get used to the cast and crutch. They are troublesome things."

"Tell me again, if the knee's not splintered as we feared and the leg not broken, why the cast?"

"The doctor said wear it a week and between it and the crutch taking the weight off, if that is a fracture you'll be better in the long run. You've got enough people to take care of you a week, Kane."

"If you only knew," he muttered, struggling with the first step up, then the second and the third to open the door. "Thanks for staying." He knew to treat Sherry right or forfeit the lease on the new ground. He needed the ground next year with a cotton gin to feed. He'd run through this year's draw. But now that the old man had turned the operation over to him, he had to watch every penny. Run right, the gin was the goose that laid the golden egg, every area of it needed inspection and preventative care before the season began. Down time was loss. He wondered if the old man had his own man spying on whether he was doing the job he had promised. Sherry's daddy wasn't just a shareholder in the gin, he was their main supplier. Retiring he needed someone to take over the reins, so to speak, guide the farm in its production and Kane was the man. If he buckled down to the task, Kane was a good farmer. What he didn't understand his cohorts did. Looking to them for advice tied them together, they thought in friendship, but Kane laughed to himself knowing before friendship even entered they were useable assets. Praise them enough they'd give him their wives.

He'd had a few men's wives. It wasn't what it was cracked up to be. He wasn't one to be cautious, they were. Especially if there were children involved, but more likely if there was an old money pre-nupt signed. Fifteen years the wife gained little if there was a divorce, last twenty or twenty five she could get by the rest of her life, educate the kids and enjoy a yearly vacation.

His father kept an eye on him, but the grandfather's eye was downright evil. "I tell you what, Kane," if it's true the first generation makes it, the second abuses it and the third loses it, meaning the family fortune, you just as well know I'll not stand by and watch that happen. You mind your business, earn my respect and we won't have any problems." The old man had crawled him many times, always leaving Kane to wonder who fed him information.

"No one worked harder than your grandfather," Tom T, his own dad reminded, "but he's serious. He didn't break his body making a living in this Bootheel dirt for you to take advantage. I didn't and you shouldn't." James Terrill Alberson, his grandfather, known as J.T. had earned a name of respectability. Kane was known for more frivolous ways but the playboy third generation set that were his friends could care less. They were high flyers, in their minds entitled to the niceties inheritance brought to their lives. Tom T. was old school like his father, J.T. They worked different areas, but Kane was the one supposed to bring additional acreage under their flagship.

"You got a flair for meeting the public," J.T. said. "Your daddy prefers watching after the farm and its employees; see what you can do for the gin. We've invested the money, now we have to feed it." That was seven years past Kane's bout with college, a career in marketing and the end of one marriage and beginning of another when he'd moved home and come on board the family enterprise. The second marriage last through the first ginning season. Kane being the handsome fellow he was, eye candy to the female employees found the evening shift enticing. He stayed away from those under twenty one, but the others were handy; Gina, the second wife, sultry and possessive, closed in on him Christmas day. She had photos, places, evidence. "We are looking at annulment. I'll be keeping my position in the office. You, stay out of my way. If we have business, we handle it as such, other than that, you are nothing to me. I told you, it was high stakes." He started to protest, "You have no business staying on." She gave him a cold eye. "Don't fool with me, Kane. Your Grandfather's on my side. I think you get the picture?"

Then there was the boy. That's how he thought of him; a child born to Emily Matthews. He knew the kid was his but she said, "no and there will be no testing, as if you really care, anyway." Times like tonight when the Preston kid stood up to him, with a grain of salt he thought of the son he knew was his and wondered what it would be like to have the boy following his footsteps. But Emily married Sam Lansky and Sam was raising his boy. He couldn't fault Emily. Sam was a good man. He didn't run in the inner circle Kane frequented, and he didn't seem to suffer any illusion he would benefit from it. He had to think how old the boy was now; Nineteen, maybe twenty he guessed, second or third year of college.

Unsettled that tonight he'd suffered the fall before God and the whole community, he struggled trying to sleep. Then, there was Sherry in the next room. She'd made it clear they were friends, nothing more. "Don't try anything with me, Kane. I've got a plan for my future and it's not with you." He had laughed. She was a straight shootin' gal and they had a lot of fun together and right now he was so loaded down with the old man's expectations, he didn't need the entanglement a woman brought, and then there was the debt, debt neither his father nor the old man were privy to. He had to take care of that himself. If he could stall until first of year, the bonus he'd receive would take care of it…if they'd wait.

He was shocked when his father showed up at the ballgame, not to view the game, nor the crowning but to see what happened to him. "They told me you broke a leg." Tom eyed him like a cat after a mouse, "Mainly,

I came to see if you were drunk. I catch you that way in public with us this close to ginning time when we got that church group interested in bringing us their cotton, you won't be running the office on a daily basis, you'll have the night shift. There's no alternative, especially if J.T. finds out."

"Don't you think I'm a little old for you to be lining me out, here, when there's definitely something wrong with my leg, maybe a broken bone or a splintered knee cap?"

J.T. barked he came in the car in case they needed to change vehicles and Kane had replied, "Not on your life. I don't need your help."

Sherry standing within hearing distance, he didn't care to flaunt his dirty laundry. "You're sounding like J.T." He couldn't stop his mind, thoughts kept pouring into his head. The Church group had come into the community three years previously and shown their expertise in recognizing the type of soil they'd bought and found the best crop to grow on it. Cotton. At first they'd used a gin affiliated with their faith, but when the gin mysteriously burned to the ground, the church decided not to rebuild. Tom nor J.T. hadn't trust him to do the ground work. No, J.T. at the ripe old age of ninety had done the footwork, driving into their complex in his old but shiny as new nineteen ninety one Lincoln, wearing his gray trousers and black sports coat, because J.T. shared the same housekeeper as the manager of the Church farm and she told J.T. that fellow worked in a suit and liked those he did business with to do the same.

The clock on the living room fireplace mantel struck two times, and still he couldn't sleep. It made him wonder, Tom frequenting some hyped up school function they'd delayed nearly a year due to the death of the school's star player, wasn't Tom's regular routine. The family did support the school events, but tonight? He almost had his mind set on the reason being one he'd denied himself. The paper had given the names of the Queen candidates and their escorts. Thorn Lansky was to escort Sophia Preston. The years he was away, he'd not given the boy much thought, but now, knowing there could come a day he'd meet him face to face, the fact was ever with him. He wondered how the boy shaped up.

He heard Sherry patter down the hall towards the kitchen and then the light cast a beam on the door facings. The refrigerator door opened and shut and in a few minutes she padded back to where she slept. "Sherry?"

She stuck her head inside the room. "I'm sorry, I didn't mean to waken you."

"I can't sleep."

"Pain?"

"Not physical, just too many thoughts going through my head."

"Like what?" She flipped a switch and a light came on in the room where she had slept.

"Dad showin up at the game. Thinking about that church group saying they'll bring their cotton to the gin." She came into the room, a glass of orange juice in her hand. "I don't know, everything's under control, but my minds too busy to sleep." She offered him the juice. He took a sip and hand it back. She finished it, set the glass on the bedside table and crawled in the bed beside him.

"Don't get any ideas. I know how it is when you got things on your mind and no one to run them past." Turning on her side, she settled into the sheets. "What does your housekeeper use on the bed linen? They smell nice."

"Like I'd know." He grinned. "You sure you don't want to play house?"

"I'm sure." She pat his arm. "We're way beyond that anyway. A person needs at least one friend they can count on and we have lasted a long time, so let's don't ruin it."

"How come you don't go home to your daddy's house when you're in this area?"

"It's awkward." She sighed, "Mother dying, Dad remarrying and her having grown children. Some women can tie two families together, unfortunately, that's not one of Adele's attributes." Her fingers threaded the sheet material, "I guess its seeing the things Mother loved dearly in her care now and her children are comfortable coming home to her, but I'm not."

"You like living in Memphis?"

"I do, and that's where my work is."

"You are going to be an old maid."

"I'm anything but an old maid." She laughed. "The night life is invigorating if you want to participate but I can't hold up my end of the bargain for the Cotton Industry and wine and dine its list of important people."

"They expect that of you?"

"I don't think I can truthfully say they do, but some of the board members imply things and I do get invited to a lot of parties. If I didn't like my job so much, I'd get out of Memphis."

"Where would you go?"

"To Texas."

Kane began to laugh. "I can't believe you said that."

"What's so funny about Texas?"

"You'd go to the state that produces the most cotton in the U.S and you're trained in the product. What do you think you'd do differently, become a chambermaid at its fancy hotels? No, you'd stay in the industry and all you'd have is a somewhat different change of scenery, and the same expectations."

"Shut up and go to sleep," she snapped, placing a pillow over his head. "And you owe me, in the morning I want to run a few statistics by you I'm using for the Cotton Producer's Wives tea coming up this weekend."

"We're awake, just give me a run down right now. Maybe if you talk, I'll drift off."

"A lot of help that will be." She sighed. "I'm not sleepy either. Was that O.J. spiked?" He snorted. "All right, I intend to challenge them first, that's after the warm fuzzy welcome. Then I'll say, We are looking for a log, and that's where you, the wives and mothers of a generation of cotton wearing individuals come in. As you know, Cotton Incorporated has a catchy saying, The Fabric of Our Lives. You can't beat that, but we hope to match it. What we need is a symbol that identifies our product no matter what state or country we live in." She glanced at him for encouragement. "I plan to continue with a few facts they may or may not know, but their minds will be on that logo, don't you think?"

"Give me the facts, and I'll let you know where my mind is when you finish."

She punched him. "Our enterprise has stemmed from the National Cotton Council being established to address the environmental issues always before us."

"Such as?"

"Well, possibly the biggest accomplishment was when legislation was introduced in nineteen fifty eight to eliminate the boll weevil."

"You sure it wasn't Eli Whitney's cotton gin in seventeen ninety four." His laugh was a bit more husky and it was apparent sleep was on its way. "Just don't tell them the cotton industry is the most toxic crop in the world and it uses twenty five percent of all insecticides in the world. They'll burn their white shirts."

Sherry, would remember the next morning, she shook her head thinking he wasn't listening at all. She had no idea where her speech would go, but the cotton farmer's wives were a high toned group of interesting women and she was excited to meet with them.

He woke her the next morning. "Hey, you any good at scrambli' eggs?" She scrambled out of his bed.

"Well, I certainly didn't mean to sleep here."

"I know, your eyes closed before mine but if it's any consolation, you're being here helped." He was studying her. "Honest to goodness, Sherry. If that's what you wear to bed every night, you'll never get a man."

She glanced down at the baggy cotton bottoms she loved and the oversized T-shirt she salvaged through the years that rolled up tight and fit in a corner of her suitcase. "I save these for when I'm around you," she said, sweetly. "And I don't have time to scramble eggs, Mr. Macho. See what you can do."

She was dressed to a T when she stopped in the kitchen. He was leaning on the crutch, seeming to know what he was doing as he stirred a pan full of eggs on top the stove. The coffee smelled great and the bacon even better.

"I've been thinking, Kane. Since we are friends, you need to work on your attitude toward that Preston fellow. He didn't seem such a bad lot and I liked his kid."

"Yeah, well, he rubs me the wrong way. Ever where I go I hear he does things right. He is a man of integrity. A man of principle. I hear his name mentioned repeatedly in town."

"Now why would the community be talking about a man like that?"

"They want him to run for school board."

"I guess that means you intend to?" She raised one beautifully arched brow. "Come on, Kane, you don't even have a kid in school."

"IS that a requirement?"

"You don't have time."

"Neither does he," Kane retorted. "Now sit down and eat this wonderful breakfast I prepared for you." He slid into the first chair, pointing her into the opposite. "I must say, you look dashingly beautiful today, Sherry. I was worried when I woke up and saw you in my bed in those awful clothes."

"No telling what your nemesis wife wears to bed. I hear matrimony makes you wear silk and such," she grinned. "Just kiddin. I got a few of those, myself, but comfort is all when you work a day job."

It was a two and a half hours drive back to Memphis and thirty minutes through the maze of workers on the bridge. She could never distinguish what they were doing from what was never done but the barrels were in place, the sign that said punishable by law if you ran over a worker, etcetera, and etcetera. After that delay she was relieved when she finally drove past the Pyramid. The Pyramid seemed finally to have found its purpose, when purchased by Bass Pro Shops, it now held everything imaginable, sane items to ridiculous. To each his own she muttered, her thoughts turned to Kane and his opinion of her sleepwear. That was her first laugh since leaving the Bootheel Ridge area. Kane was mecurial. He could be sweet or mean hearted and you didn't know how quickly it could happen. It just happened.

Applying lipstick, fluffing her hair and gathering her briefcase, Sherry was ready to face the Wives of Memphis for the cotton farmer's wives tea. "Good morning, good morning," her voice breathless and full of wonder, Sherry greeted them and within five minutes she had them in the palm of her hand.

Chapter 6

$\mathcal{T}$he morning after the Basketball team crowned Miss Sophia Raine Preston as the Queen, Queen Sophia was having a difficult time rising to go to school. Barkley waited patiently at the kitchen table. Susan felt tension in the air. She was relieved Hugh had left. Since her miscarriage Hugh had not known what to do with her. This, she knew by the way she often glanced up to find his eyes on her as though he studied her. "If I lost you," his words continued to repeat in her mind. "But you didn't," she replied.

"Sophia," she called down the hall. "Get a move on. You have five minutes left." Susan buttered a piece of toast, spread strawberry jam on top and placed it on a napkin by Sophia's car keys. Barkley hugged his mother, pulled on his back pack. "You leaving me," she asked, kissing his forehead. "My patient boy."

"Love you Mom," he said, "I'll be sitting in the car. See you this evening."

Sophia came running down the hall, pecked a kiss on her mother's cheek, picked up the toast and was on the way out. Susan glanced to the driveway where a silver late model car was making entrance. She wiped her hands on the apron she wore, just in case, but Hugh didn't bring the visitor to the house. She sat down at the desk to pay bills. An hour later he came to find her.

"Did you see we had visitors?" She nodded. "I couldn't believe why they were here." She tilt her head a bit, that look on her face, waiting. "It was a realtor. No, he didn't want to buy our place." Susan was trying to figure this one out. "It was a two-fold visit, school board and land…for sale."

"Would you really consider the school board? And the other, well that's something."

"First I heard about it was Mother's comment and I tried not to read anything in to it." Leaning across he picked up a sheet of paper from her desk, tore it in half and said, "Write whether you think we should enter this service to our community by running in the election for school board member. That's number one, yes or no. Then, on the other half write yes or no we will look into purchasing land. Yes or no."

"Ready?" His eyes held amusement. "This just jump kicks us to what we have to discuss, or not." He turned, his back to her. "Ready." He marked his paper and turned around to face her. "Let's lay them face up and see what we think."

They laughed together as he pulled her out of the chair into his arms. "I bet the president's council doesn't find it that easy." His eyes warm as liquid on Susan, his voice became husky, "Have I told you how often I thank God He gave you to me to travel this road?"

"No, not lately," she whispered, "But that's probably because my dad gave me to you free of charge."

"I've tried not to bother you." He gave a mixed laugh-tinged with self -pity, he thought. "But I'm dyin.'

"I know," she said, pushing back the cap, smoothing his hair. His hold tightened on her. They were each other's life line. Those beautiful brown eyes which were the window to Hugh Preston's soul at this moment held a question. She took his hand to lead him to the bed room. Gently Hugh picked her up and carried her.

September was upon them, the field roads were dusty throwing a fog behind the truck wheels that flew through the air, dusting the first rows of crop along each side. "It feels good," Hugh sang the words and pound the steering wheel. "How do you feel, Mrs. Preston?"

She laughed at his enthusiasm. "I believe Barkley calls it pumped. I feel like, the Calvary's arrived."

"Crops look great, our four remaining men have the machines ready to roll, we have a promise of two others joining us and it feels good to know we are ready to get this crop out of the field. We had our last watering, the poly pipes being picked up as we speak and I can't tell you…" He burst into complete laughter, "Like if you don't know all this…we've been through it, rained out, replant, spent more on chemicals and labor…thought it would break us a few times and we just kept going." He squeezed her hand. "How do you explain that, Suz?"

"Faith in God and tenacity."

"Yeah, holding on." He pulled onto the cross roads of the field, braked to a stop and waited for the dust to settle. "Shall we?"

She climbed down from the truck to join him. He reached for her hand and they bowed their heads. "Lord, God, our heavenly Father, we are filled to the top with your goodness that we are so near harvest and it makes us think of the goodness and mercy you have given us, those times we had doubt and worried over what to do. Now another task lies before us to bring it in out of the fields and you know Lord, we are short-handed and we rely on you to supply our needs. Thank you for all you've allowed us, now our hearts cry out to you, help us to finish this huge task we've worked toward. We ask safety for our crew, help us to take time in what we do and not rush that someone would get hurt. We rely on you, Father. We ask your blessing on our family help us to stay in your will. Lord, we love you. Our hearts are full as we thank you for bringing us this far and asking you to stay with us til this crop is finished. Amen."

"You didn't mention the land," she said quietly as they returned to the truck. "Nor the school board issue." He opened the door for her to get in.

"I just felt the need to wrap in prayer what we're beginning to undertake." He stood there, his face an expression of hope where it sometimes seemed hopeless. "Two men short, Suz. What are we going to do? We have two pieces of equipment we need to get the cotton out of the field that has no driver."

"I'll drive one," she said. "Sophia is geared to this kind of thing; maybe after school she could help us."

"Babe, you've had your own upset this year and I can't, I mean we can't risk your health." He gave a wry laugh. "Sophia is mechanically inclined and I don't have a doubt in the world she can do it…but Suz, she has all those practice to meet. When would she help us?"

"Caroline would take off this last semester."

"No." Fire came into his eyes. "No, to all of it."

"Well, Mr. Preston. I'll be ready when the first picker rolls out the drive, I'll be behind it." She shut the door and he went around to his side. "Did you put that in your pipe and smoke it, Sir?" She teased.

"Yeah, I did." He gave a slight grin. "Barkley's the one will want to be out on the tractor, but we just can't chance it. Wait and see, that boy will put up a howl."

They were sitting in the outer office of Silverline Banks president Carlton Howell.. "This feels more demanding or what's the word? Intimidating?" Susan whispered to Hugh. "We have to be certain we can handle the payments. Ridgeline Farms will put us in deep water, debt wise. And I guess I want to understand why they're selling."

"They're all in their seventy and eighties and no one in the family wants to continue on with the farm. Their children all have degrees and live in the city. They like their life style." He was almost irritated. "Suz, we've been over this fifty times. With what we put down the land will make the yearly payment. Land's scarce. There won't be anymore; we have to jump on this, if we want to expand. It's close to us and that minimizes our machinery having to be out on the highway. It's a good deal."

"But…"she didn't want to say it wrong…"we can't purchase equipment if we buy land." She sighed. "Financially we will be strapped."

"That's why we're here." Hugh heard the secretary saying Mr. Howell would see them now. There was the customary handshake and settling Susan into a chair, being the lady present and the two men acting out a gentleman's role. Mr. Howell asked the questions, Hugh replied, "the crops coming along. We are a little behind but now we have the heat index in our favor. It's progressing and I feel optimistic."

Suz couldn't quite put her finger on why she felt ill at ease. Maybe the fact she'd not fully recovered, emotionally? She wondered. The whole visit with Silverline Banks was a blur, she heard what was said, registered the facts, but she felt that wait for the other shoe to drop syndrome. Although Hugh wore a smile on his face, it was a bit draining for him, too. They met Kane Alberson entering as they left; Hugh eyed the crutch under Kane's arm, and held the door open for him. Kane rolled his eyes and Susan wondered what that act signified, the upper hand or life's newest gift of the crutches.

At home Sophia had left for one of her practice. Barkley was holed up in the family room watching his favorite television program. Hugh helped set out leftovers, warming each plate in the microwave. He seemed happy and that it helped him to be near her. The loan was in the works, the seller agreed to sell them the land and mentally she reviewed the fact that the first set of papers was signed.

Evening dishes had been cleared when the call came in. Susan glanced at caller id. Why would anyone still be at that place of business? Silverline Banks. "Hello," she said. "Mr. Howell of Silverline wants to speak with you, Hugh."

Seeing her expression, Hugh laughed. "Honey, we signed papers. It's in the works. Ease up." Then he listened to Carlton Howell explain an unusual circumstance. "I see," he commented several times. "There's nothing we can do, me nor you? Well, it's completely unexpected."

"What's wrong?" If a man's expression was heartsick and disappointed, Hugh's was now.

"Mr. Howell apologized."

"For what?" She felt a sickness in the pit of her stomach.

"The family that owns the farm, backed out, another buyer with more money has come forward."

"After hours?" She sat down hard on the kitchen chair. "We met their price. How can they do this?"

"We have the option of hiring a lawyer but that could be money wasted if they pick the contract apart and fine a loophole." He stared at her. "He wouldn't say who, just that it's a new LLC company but I know he has the name of whoever is doing this."

"What about the money, the loan?" Suz put her arms around Hugh's neck. "Did he say?"

"All things will be corrected, every dotted I and crossed T according to Howell."

A few days later, Hugh came in to tell her, "I don't guess news of the sale of the land and the quick take back got out. I was several places picking up parts and it wasn't mentioned."

"That means it was in house, then," Susan replied.

"You mean Howell is responsible? He leaked it and someone else went over the price?"

"Exactly." A brief memory of meeting Kane Alberson flashed in her mind, but that was too quick.

Hugh leaned in watching the emotion in her eyes as she put the pieces of the puzzle together, but it was all too soon, wasn't it? He had wagered the facts, gathered information pertinent to the family's operation and decided to take the big step, they weren't kids, maybe it seemed a gamble but he had counted the cost and they could have made it. There was every reason to want that piece of land; it was close. No traveling miles with machinery on the road; it bordered their property.

"Whoever did this formed a new LLC and while it prevents disclosure for now, come next spring we will know who it is. Not that they had any conscience toward us, but it does keep it quiet awhile."

"Don't be bitter," she said. "Haven't we learned, the enemy, so to speak never feels the pain, we do."

"Sometimes, you wonder about it all. You do the best you can, someone else by passes all God and man's rules, they prosper and yourself...." He seemed to review the past. "In our case, we lost again."

"Did we really?" She grinned. "We still have each other and maybe we weren't ready for that kind of debt. Maybe we better cling to the scripture more that says God wants good and not bad for us."

"Jeremiah twenty nine, eleven." He set the hat back on his head, "I guess. Just wanted to see you a minute." Already his mind was taking in a dozen things that needed to be done before end of week. He drew her into his arms, bent to nuzzle there at the nape of her neck a second and worked his way around to her lips. He kissed her, soft, gentle and then again and again. "What would I do without you? Somehow when I'm troubled, just watching you work through things....gives me strength."

She pulled back, laughing, "So now you are Superman, right? Or, maybe I'm Super woman? I got the power." She was singing and doing a little dance, just for him. He left, grinning.

"Just hold that thought," he said, ready to close the door. "We'll take this up tonight."

But that night there was something different to talk over. "Caroline Dawn called," she said. He caught the tone of her voice. It had been a long day. He tucked her into the hollow of his body, waiting.

"Yeah, what's wrong?"

"She missed class, said she doesn't feel well. She's coming home this weekend."

"I thought there was something special going on at college."

"She said she doesn't feel up to it. She needs to come home to see us."

"Sounds serious."

"I know."

"Has she seen a doctor?"

"She's coming in Thursday night. I've made her an appointment Friday morning."

"That's good." Something jingled in the back of his mind; something to do with when his father became ill. But Dad was up in age when they found the problem. Caroline Dawn was twenty.

Susan awoke feeling the emptiness of the bed. They had fallen asleep spooned together, where he had pulled her into his body, his lips on her neck, his breath on her shoulder. She smiled, he did that every night. She often wondered how a tall man accomplished that feat with her being much shorter…but that was his way. She padded into the bathroom, then down the hall and found him, there in the shadows, his arms stretched up against the wall, his head bowed and she knew he was worried.

"Hugh?" She stepped under one of those outstretched arms, knowing he would bring that arm to rest around her. "Are you not feeling well?" She drew him over to the sofa. "What's wrong?"

"I couldn't sleep, Suz. For some reason, little things kept coming to me, Caroline bruising when the kids wrestle and she laughs it off saying she takes after your mother, but your mother's skin bruises because she's old. All the times Sophia acts up and Caroline heads her off and we don't have to. My mind just got busy and I started moving so I didn't want to bother you."

"I went through a question and search time myself after Caroline called. I didn't say anything to borrow trouble. Let's wait and see what the doctor says." This was Hugh, he could take the rebuff of many things but when it came to his family…that was where it hurt most, not something he could fix.

"Mom." Caroline fell into Susan's arms. "Mom," I've been so sick." The tears fell on Susan's shoulders.

"I'm glad you're home." She walked Caroline inside, holding her hand. "Tomorrow we'll see what's going on."

"We'll try doing this as an outpatient, Caroline," Dr. Jeffries said. "But if there's a need for more tests we will have to admit you into the hospital." Registering her expression, "I know," he continued, "Your Mother told me you have a bit of a drive back and forth to college. Still, you want to do this right. Think positive, do this now for later results. How about that?"

Four hours later, Caroline had been oohed, ahhed, prodded and seen the blood collected in many vials. Dr. Jeffries stopped by the room where she was waiting to hear from him. "From what I see, Caroline, there will be no reason for you to stay over next week, go on back to your college classes and we'll see you again next Friday with the results."

Susan handed Caroline her purse. "How are you feeling after all these tests?"

"Extremely tired. I told Sophia I'd go to the ball game but I'm so tired I think I'll cancel."

"She'll be disappointed."

"I know, Mom, but whether it's a bug or something more serious, I am just zapped."

They arrived home with Caroline going to her old room, removing her shoes she climbed up on the bed and when Sophia came in that night she was still asleep. "Since around four," Susan nodded. "It's like the life's gone out of her."

"We won. The cheerleading was great tonight, I wish Caroline could've been there."

Barkley, sensing something wrong, was like a guard dog going and looking in to where Caroline slept. "Do you think she'll go to church with us tomorrow?"

"Yes. I feel pretty sure she will, Barkley. She'll want to sit by you."

Chapter 7

*H*ugh felt a sense of pride, he had his whole family in church. The week had been rough, first the excitement of the loan going through and signing the papers to acquire the ground next to the farm, but then the call saying the seller changed their mine, in fact reneged on the contract and gave first rights to buy to another entity. The worst was Caroline sick and having the test. He sat there by his family praying it was nothing more than a virus but like a spasm of chill through the body, something had him on edge, little prism of fear running through his veins.

It was a day of the old hymns. Songs of my youth, he thought. *When peace like a river attendeth my way, when sorrows like sea billows roll, whatever my lot, thou hast taught me to say, it is well, it is well, with my soul..*

Following prayer, their pastor took the Pulpit. "Horatio Spafford wrote the beautiful hymn we just sang… after suffering the loss of his children," he began. "When Peace like a river attendeth my way," almost gives the impression he had many peaceful days, no problems…but it's anything but that. He was a lawyer. In the year eighteen seventy one, he invested in property. That same year, the great fire of Chicago wiped him out. His holdings were ashes. The same year, his four year old son died of Scarlet fever. Skip two years; in eighteen seventy three his wife and four daughters set sail for England. There ship was struck by another vessel and Spafford's four daughters drown at sea, but his wife survived. Listen to verse two, "Though Satan should buffet, though trials should come, let the blest assurance control, that Christ hath regarded my helpless estate and shed his own blood for my soul…It is well, it is well with my soul."

"Today is the second selection from the Guard Your Heart series. Proverbs twenty three, verse seventeen reads "For as a man thinks in his heart, so is he." Mark seven, verses twenty one through twenty three tells us what comes from the inside of a man is what makes him unclean, to break that down... your thoughts define you. You are defined by your thoughts. Remember Proverbs twenty three, verse seventeen, For as a man thinks in his heart, so is he." Who do you want to be? We have to guard our thoughts...who do we want to be when we are old? We start now, before we grow old."

"This past week, perhaps it was a really good week, or perhaps it was not. Perhaps someone wronged you, perhaps someone you love became ill, or the person died to this world to take a seat in Heaven. Think about the consequence of dwelling on the ugly part, once you've dealt with it, try hard to let it go, don't let it rob you of your serenity, the bond of love between you and the Father. Remember, the first scripture? For as a man thinketh, so is he. We have to work at being the best person we can be. What we harbor in our heart affects our soul. For as a man thinks in his heart, so is he."

Hugh remembered those words later, he had become engrossed in his own week, his own thoughts, how does one let go of the injustice another inflicts on them? He was a big man, carried himself well, he wasn't the largest farmer in his area, by any means, but he'd tried to build life on the grounds his father taught him, honesty and hard work, watch over your family, don't shirk that task it's the most important task God gives a man. Family. And now he glanced down the row, Susan by his side, then Barkley, Caroline and Sophia. On his left, his mother, stiff and unbending as always. He sighed. What would it take for her to turn loose and show honest emotion?

"Maybe she's unable to," Susan had once committed. "Maybe that inner part of her holds such strict expectations of herself, she can't bend, because she certainly holds all of us to..." He had laughed, yes, she did hold them to the highest. Wasn't there a book on that, giving your ultimate? But that was for God. He could only wonder what God was asking of them, if Caroline was seriously ill. Under her mother's care the last two days she'd blossomed a bit, the color coming back into her cheeks. He wanted to hug them all so hard they'd squeak. My boy, too, he'd thought, Barkley;

amused at what his mother once said about Barkley's name. "It sounds like a law firm." Truth was Barkley had been conceived when they were on a weekend trip and they'd viewed the workings of that dam.

It had taken Susan awhile to recover from having Sophia, then one day she said, "It's time we try for your boy." Sadness flit across his mind, they'd buried the little one Barkley named Joshua. Just the family and grandparents, but his mother didn't come, she thought it foolishness, he guessed. When does a child become a living person, Mother?" Silently, he wondered her answer, but then maybe he was wrong how she felt. He reached for Susan's hand. She was coming out from under the loss and he suspected she had laid guilt at her own feet but Susan could not have helped the fact the baby was outside the womb. He leaned over and brushed a kiss on her hair. She turned and smiled, meeting the stern eyes of his mother.

So it went, in his own way, Hugh was giving thanks for Susan and his kids. Working on forgiveness for the business aspects of their life was a bit harder. He knew their banker had let the information slip, but he didn't know with whom that slip occurred. They would know once the new owner started working the land next to their own farm. He prayed to God it wasn't anyone that would be troublesome. There was always the matter of turn rows, blocking entrance, letting water run onto the neighbor's farm. Farming was a business and you better treat it with sincerity and integrity or you'd have enemies. Most had a give and take philosophy, but occasionally there would be the rabble-rousers that just wanted trouble. Few profited if that were the case.

"Bless be the tie that binds, our hearts in Christian love." The music began, the people stood and joined in the age old message. "The fellowship of kindred hearts is likened to that above." His little family was singing; for this minute in time they were all in one accord. He listened as his mother's strong alto voice picked up the chorus. "When we asunder part it gives us keenest pain but we shall still be joined in heart and hope to meet again."

"Let us all rise for the benediction," the pastor said, leading in prayer and then the congregation joined in. "May the Lord bless you and keep you; The Lord make His face shine upon you and be gracious to you; The Lord lift up His countenance upon you and give you peace."

"So have you decided?" Hugh and Caroline were left sitting in the swing while the others changed clothes. "Sit and talk to Caroline, Susan had said, Sophia and I will bring the food and we'll eat lunch out in the screened porch." Hugh had both fans moving the air. "We couldn't be out here if the temperature hadn't dropped after that little shower. What do you think are you cool enough?"

Caroline nodded. "What should I do, Dad?" She shrugged, "At least I won't be behind in studies if I go on back, but if I stay even two days I have work to make up and with my little job at the college, I have very little time off, as it is. I had to come home, I was so sick and I needed to see Dr. Jeffries to find out what's wrong."

"You do what you think's best for you. Your mother and I are not going to pressure you either way. If you return, the doctor will call you and discuss the test results, I'm sure, and he can call your mother if you are agreeable to that." His eyes held with hers. "You're an adult now, sweetheart. You can make decisions without our interference but where it's your health, of course, we are very concerned."

"Dad," there was something in her voice made Hugh's insides quake. "Dad, I don't feel good about the test results. I think there's something wrong, more than just a virus or maybe an infection. But don't tell Mom, she's had enough sadness this year."

"I know." He wrapped an arm around Caroline's shoulders, "But I believe she'll know soon enough if there is something wrong."

"Dad, I think sometimes when it's serious we have this feeling. I think God is preparing me."

Hugh was alone when Susan's call came. He glanced at the clock on the shop wall, thinking it would be one of the employees calling to tell him about an irrigation motor needing repair, or a tube that had blown. He had a lot on his mind and in the back; simmering like a pot on the stove was the fact today they would hear Caroline's test results. She had left early that morning to be in an eight o'clock class. Susan would receive the call that afternoon and then she and Caroline would discuss it. That was how Caroline request the doctor handle it.

"Hugh?"

"Yes." It wasn't even ten o'clock. "Is something wrong, Suz?"

"Where are you?"

"I'm still at the shop. I had some welding to do on that old mower. It's falling apart."

"I'll be right there."

She must have run the two hundred and fifty feet to the shop. She was there by the time he opened the door for her to fall into his arms. He just held her while she let her breathing settle. "You all right, Babe?" It was obvious she wasn't. He led her over to two old saw horses where they'd cut board to fit into a ditch that was eroding badly from the irrigation water's flow through a rusted culvert.

"They didn't wait, Hugh. They called before ten o'clock and he said they would call probably two. That means it's serious. Caroline has leukemia, Hugh." Her beautiful eyes ebbed into a violet blue where they were usually bright as the summer sky beneath that wisp of sun streaked hair. Her shoulders sunk until her head sit down in their center cave. "I can't understand why, Hugh. Caroline of all people takes care of herself."

"What exactly did the doctor say?"

"They're not positive which kind it is though they've put a name on it, Chronic Lymphocytic leukemia. She has all the symptoms, swollen lympnodes in the neck and her armpits and remember how she said she had skin like my mom, always bruising?"

"And we said, but your mother is old." He nodded. "Is it hereditary?" He thought of his dad as he glanced around at the totes of chemicals waiting to be used before summer's end. "Or did the doctor say environmental, like what we are exposed to on the farm?"

"I don't think he would be that callous, it being our occupation. What he said was it's an unknown factor, it happens. It starts when the body makes too many white blood cells and they build up slowly and affect the blood."

"What does that mean, Suz? With Dad they repeatedly mentioned the lymphnodes and the bone marrow. I never understood. They thought he had it a number of years but it was slow in progressing. That wasn't what killed him but it served to weaken his body when the other problem occurred."

"Dr. Jeffries doesn't know if this will go slow. His words were, "Suz, Caroline's a sick pup and leukemia differs in each person. He said she can begin treatment here or he knows an oncologist at St. Francis in Memphis. If the doctor decides she will have high dose chemo, it will kill out the cancer cells in her blood and start her on the road to remission. But it seems, every oncologist handles it different.""

"Have you called Caroline?"

"No," her bottom lip trembled. "We need to go, go to tell her, she can't be alone when she hears and Dr. Jeffries thought it best she hear it from us. Can you go?"

"I want to but with our being two men short, how can I?"

"I'll go if you can hold down the fort, keep Sophia settled and Barkley fed." Already she was making plans, her shoulders were squared once more but her eyes were pools of sadness. "I'll fix a few dishes and leave in the frig, but Hugh, I may spend the whole week with her and we'll come home on the weekend. I don't know how this is going to affect her studies. Dr. Jeffries called in prescriptions. New medicines..." her words trailed off, "Who knows how her body will handle them along with radiation."

"I'll fill the tank with gas and check the car tires. Do you have cash?" She shook her head. He opened his wallet. "One of the guys paid me what he borrowed a couple weeks ago when he'd been out on a drinking spree and hadn't paid his electric bill. Here's all I have." He handed her two hundred dollars. "Use your card, but you need cash when you travel in case you need help on the road."

"I know." They were subdued. "We are never apart," she whispered as he took her in his arms. "I don't know how to be away from you, Hugh."

He felt the same, but he rubbed his chin against her forehead and then kissed the spot, "Just think how glad we will be to see each other when you get back."

She left shortly before noon. He saw her leave as he was driving the North field checking the pumps. The men were away on other farms. The impact of what they were facing hit him now. He'd tried to hold up for Susan. Finished, he drove back, got out of the truck, went into the shop and shut the door behind him. To his left there was a walled off room, they'd installed a sink and commode and a shower in case the men suffered a chemical spill. Arms raised he splayed his hands above his head leaning into that wall as a sob rose up and escaped his chest. He'd tried to keep the memory away, but how it claimed him, full blast, reminding him the most peaceful day could be shattered by pain.

It was a similar day, two years back, one of the chemical reps stopped by. They'd exchanged hand shakes. Kevin Johnson was a handsome young man, twenty four years old. "You're looking a little peaked, Kevin," he'd said. "You had that virus I hear's going around?" Kevin had stubbed the toe of his boot on a grease spot on the shop floor. "No, Sir, Mr. Preston, that's why I stopped by. I'm going to be out of circulation awhile and someone else may be taking my customers." Hugh remembered giving Kevin a sharp look. "I hope it's a good reason, Kevin We have a pleasant relation. You've been a great help." Again, Kevin seemed to be studying the grease spot on the floor. "Yes and No, Mr. Preston. I have leukemia and my twin sister is a good enough match they're going to do a stem cell procedure on me that they hope will help overcome the cancer in my blood." They'd shook hands, as the young man was leaving and then for some reason, Hugh reached out and hugged Kevin. In that moment, the young man seemed to crumble into his arms. "It's scary, Mr. Preston. My family and I hope for the best."

Two months later, Hugh heard Kevin died. He would have attended the funeral, but he hadn't known. The procedure didn't take, even though it was from his twin sister, that handsome young man was gone. Now, Hugh cried, unashamed, he cried for Kevin and for Caroline. They didn't know each other but there was the leukemia tied them together. His sobs could have been heard and his body did feel the effects as he slid to the floor on his knees. For a moment his fears owned him. "Lord," he whispered.

"Dad, why's Mom gone?" Barkley looked up from the history book he'd brought to the table that Hugh usually told him to put away until he was finished eating. But tonight, lost in his own thoughts Hugh allowed it. Glancing at Sophia, Barkley asked, "Is there something you're not telling me?"

"You just as well tell him, Dad." Sophia pushed her own plate back. "I'm not hungry tonight."

"Son, your sister, Caroline's got a health issue. It's more serious than usual."

Barkley looked from one to the other. "Dad, is she going to die?" His eyes had the same effect as Susan's; they'd turned that deep violet blue of worry. "I mean, Dad, what's wrong...if Mom's gone to see her?"

"Barkley, we don't know yet. The test just came today and Mom thought it best to be with Caroline."

"She'll come back though, won't she Dad." Tears welled up in his eyes and he scrubbed them away.

"Yes, she'll be back this weekend, so will you two help me keep the house and the dishes clean?"

"Mom," Caroline's voice broke, "I can't go home this weekend."

"Why, not, Sweetheart?" Susan stopped folding the laundry piled on the table. She glanced around at Caroline's tiny apartment, once a hotel; the chain had deed the building to the college when it built in a different area. The rooms were much as any hotel with a small kitchenette and sitting room, then the one bedroom area and bath, but it worked and was within Susan and Hugh's budget. She and Caroline had shared the same bed all week, with ample room to spare in the middle as they were both edge huggers and barely moved during the night. "Honey, I have to go home, your dad's struggling to keep things going with me gone since he has to be out on the farm; it's running two men short for the jobs."

"I know, Mom, but if words got out and you know it has if Sophie or Barkley mentioned it to anyone, then there's the nurses who have seen my records." She sit on one of the stools at the mini divider that served as a counter top large enough that four plates fit if you lined them up right. "Mom, I can't face people coming up to me asking questions and wanting to know what we are going to do."

"They're good people, Caroline. You need them in your prayer corner. That may be what you need most."

"I know good people, Mom. Just like I've known something was wrong awhile now. I actually wondered when I signed up for second year if maybe I shouldn't, that feeling..." She sighed. "Our family friends, Mom, I know their hearts. It's like you sense God is in charge of their lives, they have that look."

"What look is that?" Susan studied her daughter. "Are we so easily recognized, us peculiar people?"

"I mean it as a compliment, Mom. It's like they know something other people don't and they're willing to share it if anyone will listen. It's kind of self-assurance, a dot of pride and a whole lot of humbleness and maybe willingness to share what's on their heart."

"You'd miss that?" Susan asked, a smile on her lips and hope in her eyes. "You need it .l-I need it."

"Mom, you'll be driving home alone. I'm sorry that I'm tired already, I just can't do it. I'll try to rest through this next week so I can come home the weekend," she repeated softly. "O.k.?"

"its okay, Caroline. I'll finish these, you can put them away and then I'll head home."

"Mom? I'm going to try to work next week. I can't afford to lose my job."

"Your health comes first, if I have to get a job to get you through this; right now you take care of yourself for later."

"So I'll be here, right?" Tears welled up in her eyes. "We haven't said that out loud, Mom."

"Right." Susan sat on the stool next to Caroline. "We need our children, and you are our number one concern right now."

"Hug Barkley for me, Sophia, too," Caroline said in parting, "But Barkley's afraid I'm going to die." Susan was backing up when she realized Caroline was alongside her window. "Mom, if I die, it's all right. God has given me peace. At first, like Barkley I was scared, but I told dad I knew something was wrong."

"And you still feel peace?" Susan studied Caroline's pale face as she nodded. "I know God will take care of you, Caroline. I've never doubted you are in God's hands but as your mother, the thought of losing you sends me into such sadness I cannot explain the pain in my heart." Tears filled Susan's eyes.

"You and Dad always told us not to borrow trouble. So that's my advice to you." Caroline grinned. "Bye. Before you get too caught up in kissing dad, tell him I love him and I'm sending a hug for him with you."

"What do you mean, there's water flooding the lower field?" Hugh's voice carried to the back door as she carried her suitcase inside. The faucet was running water into the sink filled with dishes, ready to run over the rim if she hadn't turned if off. "I told you to turn that pump off first of the week. Those are early beans; we can start with them and progress on to the later varieties." There was silence, except a foot movement on the floor, which meant Hugh was pacing as he talked. "I'll be down to see it as soon as we hang up." He came around the corner fast, bumping into her, his surprise obvious. "Babe?" He righted her before pulling her into a fierce bear hug. "God alone knows how glad I am to see you."

"Whatever that phone conversation was about, it sounded serious." She pecked a kiss on his lips. "It seems you were ready to do dishes? Hmmm?" She reveled in the smell of the man, laundry clean shirt, a few wrinkles she noticed, his hair curling around the collar, the tan above absolutely beguiling as she felt him kiss her again, strong and demanding, taking ownership. "Wowzie, wowzie," she quipped, a grin spreading across her face until his eyes met hers, lit up, and his own smile appeared. "I've missed you, Mr. Preston."

"Not half way as much as I've missed you, Mrs. Preston." He pulled her toward his old leather chair and down onto his lap. "So, how's our girl?"

"Strong," she replied and told him of their week together. "And," she said in finishing, "there's this young man, Oliver, called each day to check on her. She wasn't up to seeing him but she always smiled when he called. I'm thinking maybe this Oliver has added new meaning to our daughter's life."

"They sent enough down for Caroline to begin medication? I want to know the details. Her treatment?"

"Only the prescriptions for now." With her arms around his neck, she said, "Oliver's kind of an old fashioned name, isn't it? I kind of got the feeling he is usually there....maybe all the time."

"Yeah, I hope Oliver doesn't have any plans for Caroline right now, with her illness?"

"Caroline's not one to rush into anything, Hugh. You know that but she does like him. I can tell." She stood up, "So where were you headed when I walked in?"

"Whether it's the previous owner or the new, there's been a breach of that ditch; you know where the gate keeps the water off of us and running where he needs it? Well, someone's carelessness has flooded our beans ready for harvest in about two weeks. You want to ride with me to see the damage?" Glancing at the clock, he continued, "Sophia is at practice, I don't know if its cheer or dance and she was dropping Barkley off at the field. You're free, if you're up to it."

After working by Hugh's side and watching the operational activities of her father's farm growing up, it was obvious the damage to the beans was significant. Hugh stood on the raised ground of the road, looking down through water that had run until it was clear, at the culvert and the mechanism that opened. "Why would anyone do this?" She walked over to study the gate. It was built on the same precept as the larger flood gates but required manual operation. "It wasn't shut at all, I thought maybe it had possibly moved a few feet, but that…as you can see, the fasteners are intact, no rusted out openers, it's more like someone took the time to go down into the ditch, remove the bolts that held it to each side, then they removed the gate completely and put the bolts back on."

"Yes, I see, they've just left the gate lying on the side." Susan was judging the depth of the ditch. "They did it between rains, because that ditch is six, eight feet deep, isn't it? And that let the water from the drainage ditch fill, but Hugh, the other end of this secondary ditch would have to be blocked or the water would have kept on flowing."

"Get in; let's go see what's been done on the other end." They were quick, the dust flying behind the truck on the field road. His adrenalin was pumping. "This is deliberate even if its careless neglect." She was right; someone had damned up the ditch on the end which allowed the water to build up and overrun on to his beans, the road rising above as it ran alongside the ditch made a natural barrier. "Where else could the water go, but back up in the field. I thought it would be just the low end, but look at this, Susan, its half way through."

"Do we have enemies, Hugh? This is terrible?"

"You tell me."

Word spread fast in the sleepy little town, population eight thousand. Hugh and Susan were shaken thinking someone disliked them that much, to try sabotaging their crop. They were suspicious of the new landowners next door. But life moved on. Caroline was taking the prescribed medication, trying to rest between work and classes and it seemed falling in love, all at the same time.

A month since being diagnosed, Caroline was home for the weekend and brought Oliver. "Dad," she introduced him, "Oliver and I have a wonderful friendship; I just wanted you to meet him."

"Are we supposed to do anything?" Hugh followed Susan into the utility room. "I don't know what to say to him or Caroline."

"Don't do anything," Susan offered. "Just be yourself and all things will be added unto you."

"That's what I'm afraid of," he whispered. "I think there's a romance here."

"Maybe it's seeing Caroline's health threatened and he's showing compassion."

"No, there's more." Hugh had blocked her way out of the room, intense as he leaned across the dryer.

"Hugh." Susan laughed. "It's too soon; you're reading more into this than there is, now how can I finish supper if you have me cornered in this room?" She reached up, pulling his face where she could place a kiss on his lips. "Now, move it mister, or you can finish the meal."

"She's our daughter, Susan and I want what's best for her, especially now. It's not a good time."

Stifling genuine laughter, Susan clasp one hand over her mouth, the other over his. "Shh, it'll be okay."

But it wasn't okay. "Sir," Oliver said to Hugh. "I don't know any other way to ask this than to just come right out in the open.

Hugh had agreed to take a walk around the house and shop with Oliver, now as he glanced at the tires on the car they'd come in, he thought he understood, the tires were thread bare. "Oliver, are you trying to ask for a loan to buy tires for your vehicle? I can see it badly needs them. Yes, I..."

"No, Sir," Oliver practically gulped, his Adam's apple bobbin up and down in his skinny throat. "No, Sir, I'm asking your permission to ask Caroline to marry me." If a man could instantly pale three shades, Oliver did while the blood rushed to Hugh's face and his complexion went a sickening red.

Hugh stopped short, his feet stirring a bit of dust. Emotions played across his features, shock tinged with unwanted, unbridled anger being the one that last. "Do you realize how sick she is?"

"Yes, Sir. I do and that's part of it. I already knew I loved Caroline but when she told me, I said I want us to marry, now, so I can help take care of you."

"What do you think, Oliver?" Hugh scratched his head. "You haven't been part of our vocabulary, Caroline has kept you secret. And now you come home with her one weekend and say can I marry Caroline, or are you saying something else, Oliver."

"No, I mean, yes, just that she feels the same way, she doesn't want to disturb you and Mrs. Preston."

"Well, I'm disturbed. I love my wife and children more than anything and sudden disruptions to my family create a great deal of havoc in my system."

"I understand. Caroline said you'd say something, like that...some what." He mumbled the last words, "I work ER, Sir. I plan to be a doctor but right now, I cover a diversified range of ailments that E.R presents." Oliver pulled his shoulders back from the droop they'd gone into. "I've been reading up on Caroline's symptoms and all and I believe the doctor has diagnosed correctly. It is leukemia."

"Yes," Hugh replied, softly. "Any change to her life can magnify the problem. Right now she doesn't have to cater to the whims of a demanding young husband, no preparing meals, house cleaning, laundry, etcetera. You get the picture?"

"Not quite, Sir, other than I don't think you like me, or perhaps think I'm good enough for Caroline."

A sudden flash of memory made Hugh remember his courtship days. "I was rather.." He blinked, gave Oliver a scathing glance and ask, "Can we finish this subject later, I'm sure there's other things for now."

"Yes, Sir," Oliver felt relief on one hand and on the other the fact Caroline was waiting to hear from him, made him wonder if he should have come on this trip home with her to ask permission to marry.

Chapter 8

"Daddy." Caroline shut the door behind, slipping out onto the porch where she knew her father escaped to. "Daddy, you have scared Oliver to death." She sighed as she sat down beside him. "That's not you."

"Yes, it is very much me." Hugh cast troubled eyes on his daughter. "I don't even know your Oliver and he's asking for your hand in marriage. Is that what you want?"

"He thinks you feel he's not good enough for me. He's in the bathroom puking his head off." She tried for a smile, but it was instead a wistful plea for understanding. "It may be too soon, Daddy, but I love him. He has been nothing but kind during the time I've been sick and not knowing what was wrong."

"Has he told his parents?"

"No. They're wealthy folks, Dad. His father's an attorney, his mother is a psychiatrist."

"Well that might come in handy," Hugh muttered letting out a breath of pent up air. "Wealthy? What kind of wealth is that when their son's car tires are threadbare and dangerous? Did you notice?"

She shrugged. "They make their children pay their own way as much as they can, but they do step in when needed."

"Well, it's needed. Before you leave, go down to Pearson's and have them put new tires on. Four tires."

"Oliver may resist that offer."

Hugh rose from the swing. "Caroline Dawn, you might tell your young man it is in his best interest he has those tires before he leaves. This is not a test of who's the most stubborn. Let him figure that out."

Caroline left the swing, going to the kitchen to find her mother. "Daddy's really mad, Mom."

"No," Susan replied gently, "Daddy's upset losing his daughter this soon. It was unexpected. He'll be all right."

"But he says Oliver has to go down to Pearson's and get tires on the car before we leave."

Susan began laughing, "Then encourage him to do it, that means he's winning."

Caroline went to find Oliver and Susan stepped out onto the porch to find Hugh staring intently across the landscape. "Soaking it in, huh, big fellow?" She draped an arm around his waist, waiting. And then his arm came around her shoulder as he pulled her close. "Scary, isn't it? We'll put it in God's hands."

"Am I so wrong?" Hugh's gaze fixed on Susan. "She's got to do her best with this medicine, no side tracks, nothing to make her absent minded and forget to take it. Her classes are difficult as it is, if they marry there's more responsibility and less rest. I don't think I'm so wrong in my thinking."

Susan noted the defensiveness in his voice. "No, Hugh, you aren't wrong but they are in love and they're young. We can't put old heads of wisdom on them. If they are set on marriage we can offer encouragement rather than become a stumbling block that wears at their minds every day."

"I thought we'd stand together on this." A quiver to the muscle in his tightened jaw let her know he wasn't giving up easily.

"What do you really want, Hugh?"

"I want our girl back home where I can see if she's getting better. I want her well, Suz. God help me, I don't mean to be selfish, I just want to go back to last year when she seemed healthy. Forget the classes, the job to help with expenses, just bring her home. Is that me being too selfish for you?"

"No, Hugh. You are honest and a good daddy but we can't leave out what Caroline wants and she wants to finish what she has started and she wants to get married."

Hugh stomped away, his feet making sound on the hollow boards beneath their feet. The door slammed behind him. She saw him go down the hall to their bedroom. Hugh would be all right after he thought things over. His concern over Caroline's health out shadowed his concern for her happiness presently.

"Mother?" Caroline whispered. "Daddy wouldn't listen to Oliver when he wanted to ask his blessing on our getting married. What are we to do?"

"Can you give him a little time to accept your new development?" Susan studied her daughter. "If there's no reason to rush?" Caroline blushed and met her mother's eyes.

"We've not been together Mother, if that's what you're asking. We just know it's right. That's why we want to get married now. Didn't you and Daddy feel that way?"

For the first time Susan smiled. "Yes, we did, honey and I'm thinking in about an hour that will kick in on your father. Just for the fun of it tell me when you were thinking an appropriate wedding date."

"Well, Daddy's going to want to get the crop out of the field and we need time to plan it, Mother." For a moment she looked stricken. "I don't mean elaborate but still pretty, is that all right?"

Susan put her arms around Caroline and drew her near. "My darling girl, you shall have the wedding you desire. Next trip home, bring your plans all jotted down on paper so we can go over them and do tell Oliver to just be patient. Your Father is a very good man and it is quite evident he loves you dearly."

"But can he love Oliver?" The wistfulness returned to Caroline's voice. "That's what worries me."

"Shush," Susan quipped, "The man I know will love whoever loves his child. That's for sure."

"Christmas." Caroline whispered, "I want to be married Christmas when the church is decorated with all the greenery, the red bows and that red runner goes up the aisle over the hard wood floor. "Oh, Mother, it will be so beautiful."

"Yes, it will," Susan kissed Caroline's forehead. "And you will be prettiest of all, I have no doubt."

Chapter 9

"Hi, there, Hugh Preston, I was wondering if you could stop by? This afternoon would be good."

Hugh checked his watch. It was two already. He was to take Bert's place on the picker at three while Bert took his wife back to the doctor. "It would be after four o'clock." The voice on the other end of the phone agreed four would be fine. Three o'clock arrived as if in the blink of an eye.

Bert confided, "I'm afraid the test will reveal cancer, Hugh. She's not felt well in a while."

"Don't borrow trouble, Bert," he'd offered. "The good Lord knows we are all prone to do that."

"So how is Caroline Dawn?" Bert followed Hugh's thinking. He'd seen the turmoil the girl's illness had on his boss. "I know through Susan that she is on medication and they won't try anything else, yet."

Hugh scratched his head. "I can't rightly tell, Bert. Sometimes, I think the whole world keeps things from us. Young people are kind of like babies, you know how a baby will play when it's at its worst? Well, Caroline hasn't given up on anything, going on with classes, keeping her job and add to that…she thinks she's in love and planning a December wedding."

Bert laughed. "I kind of feel like I helped raise these kids, so I'm real partial to know what Caroline Dawn's goin' through. Leona asks me every day. One thing we do is keep all three of them in prayer; of course you and Susan, too."

"That's about all any of us have some day." Hugh thought about Leona. "You drive careful now, and I'll see you when you return. Give Leona a hug for me."

"Truly the fields are white to harvest." Hugh muttered the thought out loud as he put the machine in motion. Up high he could see the rows clearly. The top bolls had opened well and for the most part the cotton looked good. "Might not be three bale but I'll be happy if it's two and a half bale an acre." He glanced up to the heavens. "You know Lord, out here, just the two of us, you seem closer."

It was past five when Bert returned. There was a look of relief on his face. "Tell me," Hugh said.

Bert scratched his side whiskers. "I was scared to death, Hugh, when they said it could be cancerous. For now they're saying calcification, which could turn cancerous but they're watching it. As far the nausea, they think Leona got so worried over it she about gave herself an ulcer, not yet but on the way, so they gave her medicine for that." Bert gave a raspy laugh. "All we got's each other, no kids or nothing, I guess we get a bit carried away. Still, it made us pray more and seek the Master."

Hugh clasp Bert's shoulder. "I'll take you and Leona praying for me and my family any day, Bert. Your faith is walking evidence to me."

"Well, I might of let you down this time when I had those moments of self-doubt and I'm sorry about that. Those human moments come on us so quick we had to get down on our knees and ask forgiveness." He was climbing the ladder up to the driver's cab. "You go on, now. I got this."

Hugh left him wearing the biggest smile he'd seen on Bert's face the last month. And somewhere in his own mind, he wished Caroline had received as good a news at her young age, but Bert and Leona were right, they just had each other and he rejoiced in their good news that the doctors would be watchful.

"Hello, Hugh." Dolly William's Harpo Kirkland met him at the door, "Won't you step inside out of the heat?" She opened the screen door enough to reveal long tanned legs in short shorts and an upper halter. "I reckon you and I know each other well enough for you to do that and not cause gossip."

"If it's all the same to you, Dolly, let's just talk right here. It won't take long will it? I really don't know why I'm here. Can I do something to help you?"

Dolly laughed. "Same old Hugh. Ever a gentleman. Actually, I was wondering if you had any kind of equipment that would dig a hole for a new septic tank in the back yard." She stepped outside the screened door now. "Evidently when a house sits empty small things begin to happen from lack of use and in this case, I'm told there's need for a new tank. There's problems we don't have to discuss, I'm sure you know already." She laughed. "I, on the other hand, being used to city sewers that I never see underground," she paused, "well, I'm new at this. I will be back and forth, time to time staying here, so I need to get it fixed so we don't have any more back up to the house. Lord, what a mess."

"I hate to hear that. Did you want this done immediately?" Hugh was considering the fact he was already two men short, and the cotton harvest was in full swing. He really couldn't pull away, himself. Someone had to keep things going and that was his job. She was nodding, yes, immediately. "I tell you what, Dolly, I'll think on this overnight and hopefully by day after tomorrow we'll have an answer."

"You can see to it, Hugh?" Dolly came off the porch, down the steps and motioned for him to follow. She stopped once and stooped to pick up a small digging tool, the shorts showing more than Hugh needed to see. He suddenly felt compromised as if some part of this little walk had been preplanned, there was no evidence the tool had been used. They were coming to a turn in the path and he was getting nervous.

"You don't want to fall into the old septic tank, it's been here for years, so I'm thinking find another way around the back of the house." She came to the end of stepping stones which had led to an iron gate, with a rusty device that wouldn't slide. "You see where the old tank is, Hugh? You can dig it out and put a new one there. Shall I order it, or will you?" Bending down, completely oblivious to where he was standing, Dolly left exposure to her braless halter, her breast in Hugh's direct line of view. "I'm afraid I can't open this gate, Hugh, can you?" It was obvious she had no intention of moving away.

A bit clenched mouthed, Hugh turned away, "We'll take it from here, Dolly. I'll talk to you on Thursday." He started back across the stepping stones to the outer edge of the yard to his truck. "I'll make the order and have them send you the bill." He felt the sweat dripping off his forehead as he climbed into the truck. "So that's how easily it happens, could happen," he corrected. He took a deep breath. Usually Susan was with him and there were never any reasons for concern, but he thought, in today's world a woman scorned could cry wolf and he had better keep himself a chaste distance from this one. Evidently she had not changed from the reputation she had in high school. What would Susan say?

Her words came to memory, "you are so vulnerable, you wouldn't know if a woman made a pass at you." Was that what just happened when Molly made no effort to right her clothes? So Susan was wrong he did know but maybe in her present state of mind he shouldn't tell her. Instead he drew out his cell, touched a familiar number and said, "Hey, Jim, there's an immediate need for a new septic tank out at the William's place. When do you think you could get to it?" He listened as a smile broke across his face. "That's great, Jim, and have the missus handy in case you need extra supplies." He was laughing when Jim asked was that entirely necessary? "It might be," he replied. "It might be." Jim was another school mate. It wouldn't take long for him to understand the situation.

"How was your day?" Susan shut down the computer, going to the kitchen, ready to make supper for the family. "Seems like this office was closing in on me today. If you need me to disc ground, tomorrow, I think it would be a nice change of pace." Now she turned sensing he was on the verge of something.

"Alberson would never let his girlfriend be seen on a tractor; mainly you are not ready for that."

She eyed him curiously. "Who cares what Alberson does or does not do? This is Hugh and Susan and I'm sick of the books. So did you have anything interesting happen today? Unusual? Wonderful?" She grinned, twining her arms around his neck. "Run into any damsels in distress?"

"As a matter of fact, I did." He waited to see if she took the bait. She didn't, instead she giggled.

"Come sit down and help me get the kinks out of my neck from peering at those books trying to make money instead of spend it." Instead he was getting a glass for ice water from the frig. "You are leaving, aren't you?" He nodded. "I can always tell when you won't even sit for a minute."

"Got to be sure the fellows are moving the modules to the right place for pick up." He sighed. "Seems like it all has to be done at once. Usually, we have someone cutting stalks and disking right behind picking, but this year Alberson has our men. I can't put you or Barkley on the stalk cutter."

"Can't or won't?" The fact a neighbor had been working on a faulty stalk cutter and let it down accidently on his son, was ever in their minds. "We will never forget that accident, will we? And yet, any other piece of equipment puts the user at risk if they don't know how to use it."

"I just can't do it," Hugh replied, sitting the empty glass in the sink. "I may not be in until really late. Get some rest, okay?" He flicked strands of hair away from her eyes. "You got dark circles around your eyes."

She laughed. "Have you looked in the mirror lately?" He rolled his eyes. "Where you headed after you check on the modules?"

"To the gin to see our arch buddy, Alberson." He smacked a good one on her lips. "Be good."

"A man just can't have too much fun, can he?" She sighed. "I'll be here with your children, Sir."

"I'll tell you a bedtime story tonight," he replied. "How good little wives should always bake apple pies for their hard working husbands."

"I can't wait," she said, going all sultry eyed and pouty lips as she slid against the refrigerator door. "Good," she whispered as he went out laughing. "I can always loosen you up but it's a good thing Sophia didn't witness that, she'd be worried." Hearing him whistling, she whispered, "Thank you Lord."

Pulling the bottom drawer open to the frig she brought out two pie shells. "Now to peel those apples, all for the love of a good man."

The weeks rolled by, November saw the crops out of the field and now Bert and his helper were cutting stalk and disking the ground. Talk of next year's crop was the topic down at the coffee shop. Today, however, work in the fields had come to a halt. Light rain was falling outside and the group around the table seemed not to consider leaving it. Gossip was in full swing when they welcomed Hugh.

"You should join us, Hugh," the neighbors said. "We rehash this year's woes and build on next years."

"Man, we are getting ready to clean up the machinery. Then I'll know what we need next year."

"Are you thinking of trading equipment?" Heads at the table came up, all eyes on Hugh Preston.

"Weigh the cost," Hugh replied. "Down time could mean harsh weather and a crop left in the field. Don't you think the end justifies the means?"

"Well, I wouldn't say that, if you can't make payments."

With his neighbors shaking their heads and resigned to use old equipment another year, Hugh drove on home. He'd put the pencil to the paper. He had to purchase new equipment. He was one that counted down time as loss. If the corn fell on the ground, or the wind blew the cotton out of the burrs it cut profit. The next thing he had to worry about was paying taxes and taxes had been a yearly thing since he first began farming.

"Who do you want to be, Hugh?" Susan's daddy studied his son in law. "You want to prosper and pay taxes or be another one of those who will be going out completely in the next few years?"

It did seem too many of his neighbors were seeking outside jobs, some driving a hundred miles a day. That had to be tiring to the body. When he considered the amount of years those friends would be driving until retirement, Hugh shook his head even more determined to make it in farming. A few had changed from row crop to raising livestock, meaning when they returned from their day job they still had hours of work waiting and the early morning rise was a given. Livestock had to be fed.

One thing Hugh thought on as he drove home was, "I heard Alberson has taken over the old Smith farm, too. Bought it, is the word. Kane may be a cocky son of a gun but he's putting a lot of acreage under his belt." There were some careful eye contacts going on around the table. "Where do you suppose the money's coming from?"

A reply had been, "If its foreign investors, think what's going to happen to our country down the road."

There had been the slower thinking two who ask, "What do you mean?" And then the reply, "Well, now how will it affect the vote? Do we want to be the United States of America or the United States under so and so?"

He felt plain discouraged as he pulled in the drive. He wouldn't have gone in the coffee shop but for the fact the part time help hadn't picked up their checks and that's where they were having breakfast. He found Susan at the sewing machine.

"Haven't we played out this scene before?"

She glanced up and smiled. "Sophia has a dance this Saturday night. She's dropped the Langston boy for good, says she's going with Thorn Lanksy."

"How are you coming along on the bridesmaid dresses?"

"They're done but Oliver's little niece's dress needs fitting before the final seams are in. I haven't seen the child, only pictures, so I can't afford to finish it without a fitting."

"How do you propose to do that?"

Wrinkles furrowed Susan's brow. "There's only one way, send it home with Oliver. His mother can pin up the sides and then Oliver bring it back to me for finishing."

"I don't know how you stay so calm." Hugh slumped down into his recliner. "I heard down at the coffee shop Alberson bought the Smith place. There's speculation as to where the money comes from. The simple truth is, they take it from those who farm their land. I hope they don't skim the rest of us."

"I meant to tell you, I heard that yesterday. Laurie Johnson and I were talking and she said Jason thinks there's money under the table. Like when we lost out on the farm, due to our very own banker becoming involved and informing Kane what our per acre price was and Kane met it and added more, except for the families lack of integrity they took money under the table, trying to save face in a deal that had already been agreed on between them and us." Susan's eyes snapped remembering. "I couldn't believe our banker would do that. He knew we'd realize sooner or later what happened and Kane had it figured out when he entered the door. The thing is," she glanced up, "Laurie said Kane's getting his money from foreigners and they are calling him in. There's still something going on that no one understands or knows about."

Hugh shook his head. "Between our own son and your friend we do hear some weird stuff. Do you believe any of it?"

"Well, the grapevine says Kane's daddy, mainly his grandfather has lowered the boom on Kane, no more gambling, no more borrowing from foreigners and if he tries using their land holdings or the cotton gin as collateral, he's out. They will kick him out of their business enterprises permanently."

Hugh sighed. "That wouldn't look good for the Alberson's. I wish we didn't have to gin with them."

Susan stood to shake the dress free. All seams had been pressed open and flat. "I had hoped Caroline would choose a more full skirted pattern and maybe a material that had some crunch to it, for her brides maid dresses but I'll have to say what she did choose hug the girls figures and flow tea length beautifully. This one of Sophia's is not bad either and it fits perfectly.

"Are the girls Caroline chose for brides maid's all thin?"

"They are and that was a surprise, because Lindy Anna used to be heavier and you know, round, but now she's as slender as the rest and Hugh, they are all pretty girls. It's going to be a beautiful wedding."

"What about the six hundred dollar rental fee on the tux's?" Hugh had heard that story, too. Oliver was afraid to ask assistance from his parents and yet reluctant to let Caroline Dawn's parents foot that bill.

"Well, it seemed only right we pay for yours and Barkley's. That's another three hundred something."

Hugh groaned. "I've never worn a tuxedo. Is that necessary?"

"You will be handsome and Barkley is excited over his." She glanced up, "but you two have to polish your black shoes to a high shine." She laid the dress over a chair and came to where he sit. "What's wrong, Hugh? I can tell you are down."

"I don't know. I guess I had my mind all made up. I'd conquered any worries over the new equipment but the farmers sitting around the table at the coffee shop seemed to question my decision."

She sat on the low tufted bench next to his chair they used for extra company. "Honey, they don't pay our bills and you thought long and hard on this, don't question yourself now. We always said we'd sell off something if we had to."

"What would we sell? Our house?" She squeezed his hand. "Old machinery has no value around here." He took a deep breath. "Do you ever wish we'd have gone to the city, got higher paying jobs that weren't so stressful and raised our kids in a different atmosphere?"

"How do we know they would be less stressful? We might have lived on a street where there were shoot outs and teenagers were heavy into drugs." She thought for a minute. "No, I think I'm pretty happy and secure right here." Tilting her head she glanced across the room to where three pictures of their children sit on the sofa table. "Actually, a few of those parents in your mind might like where we live but we don't have reason to say there aren't great families and good children there, too."

"I know. I didn't mean to imply that."

The phone rang and Susan went to answer. She came back with sadness in her eyes. "Hugh, that was Doctor Jeffries. Caroline's last blood tests were not good. The Leukemia has taken a turn."

He reached for her hand and pulled her onto his lap. "Let's just sit here awhile and think on this and pray a bit." His head dropped down as he stared at Susan. "Things can always get worse, can't they?"

"They can also get better," she whispered but there were tears in her eyes. "He was calling her, next."

Within thirty minutes of the doctor's call, Caroline called home. "Mom?" When Susan replied, her daughter burst into tears. "Mom, I know Doctor Jeffries called you. It's going to be all right, Mom. Oliver and I are praying and I know you and Dad are, so God won't let anything go wrong." Susan was quiet. "Mom. It's going to be a beautiful wedding. The wedding I always wanted, at Christmas with all the red poinsettia's, the greenery at the church and our family sitting in the front. Grandmother Preston and Mom-maw and Pop-paw." Susan had the phone on speaker. Tears were streaming down her face and Hugh's and they couldn't speak, but Caroline Dawn had the conversation in control. "Mom. Tell Barkley and Sophia it's going to be all right. But Mom, tell everyone to keep praying."

It was the week before Thanksgiving when Oliver called. "Mrs. Preston, would you please put the phone on speaker and tell me if Mr. Preston is with you?"

Susan did as Oliver asked. "I've put it on speaker Oliver and yes Hugh is with me."

"Mrs. Preston, I'm calling to ask your permission to move in with Caroline and I promise you there won't be any sexual activity until we are married. She's not doing well, Mrs. Preston and she doesn't want you to know. If I'm with her, maybe I can help her with her studies. Even getting dressed is an ordeal this week."

They heard a catch in his voice. "Oliver, are you crying?" Susan asked, the tears now slipping down her own cheeks.

"Yes, ma'am. I am. I'm sorry about that but I didn't know what else to do but ask. She is determined to finish her classes and I know the shop owner, I've already spoken to him and he said he will give Caroline a job that she can do without having to be on her feet. I don't know what it is but I trust him because he is a friend to our family and he wouldn't lie." Oliver seemed to gulp for air. "He said when I'm off I can come in and do her job for her if it makes me feel better and I plan to do that."

"Oliver?" Hugh very gently took the phone out of Susan's hand. He cleared his throat. "Oliver, thank you. What you are proposing is very commendable. You have our blessing, if Susan agrees and she is nodding. Just please keep us posted."

"Mr. Preston, it is my hope with my being there Caroline will rest more."

Hanging up the phone, the two embraced. "Is she even going to last for the wedding?" Susan asked.

There was a buzz on the phones in the next days as the family discussed Caroline's health. "We have to go on with Thanksgiving," they all agreed, but it wouldn't be the same if Caroline wasn't with them. "We'll fix all our favorite foods and believe if she is able to be here at all that Oliver will bring her."

"But Susan," Mrs. Preston reminded. "Oliver may feel drawn to spend the holiday with his parents. And didn't you say he has a sister?"

"Yes, Kathryn and she and her husband have a little girl, the one who will be in the wedding."

"It will all be fine, dear." Susan's mother comforted. "You are an expert at putting things together."

"So, we will gather as usual," Hugh commented. There was nothing more to say, only hope.

Chapter 10

$\mathcal{B}$arkley was beside himself. "I just wanted Caroline and Oliver here, Mom."

For once, Sophia wrapped her arm around her brother's shoulder. "Caroline's too weak, Bub." Leaning down she nipped his ear between her teeth. "They'd be here if they could." Somehow, Sophia brought laughter to all the others sitting around the room when Barkley yelped.

"We'll be ready to say grace, any minute now," Susan informed them. "It's the gravy, too thin and we've made the same gravy every year for our lifetime together," she grinned suddenly, "well except for those years we were at Mrs. Preston's or Mom and Dad's." Bert and Leona snickered as the rest joined together joking. "Well," Kathryn Preston announced, "I think we've got it. It just needed a bit of flour."

Everyone circled the table trying not to stare at the two empty places as they waited for Hugh to clear his throat and say grace and just as he bowed his head the door bell rang. Sophia broke loose and ran to answer it. Susan's face was white with dread, she felt as though her knees would buckle and Hugh had stepped back hoping no one was seeing his face. It could not be good, someone coming at this hour.

Sophia returned wide eyed and then a smile broke across her features. She was carrying a huge dome lidded cake container. "It's from Oliver's parents; his mother's special Thanksgiving cake. But wait, just a minute there's something else." She hurried back, opening the door as Oliver carried Caroline inside, followed by an older couple Susan and Hugh had not met and behind them a pretty woman carrying a little girl about four years old.

Susan hurried to take another dish from the lady as Oliver announced, "everyone, this is my mother and father. My mother, Cecily, and father, Alistaire, my sister, Charlamaine and her little girl, we call Millie. Her name is really Millicent." He shrugged self-consciously, "forgive our arriving at this time, but it was about all we could do." Susan sprang into action while Hugh seemed to have developed paralysis.

"Oh, my you are so welcome to our home. Please, take off your wraps. Oliver lay Caroline on the sofa and Charlamaine, do come take this chair at the table and we will find a taller chair for Milly."

Charlamaine laughed. "Please, everyone calls me Charlie and somewhere between your front door and our car my husband will be bringing up the rear. He has a hamper full of food, but we couldn't press mother's cake into it." She laughed again. "He couldn't have carried it. It is quite heavy all ready."

Suddenly there were fifteen people in the room, Susan had thrown a cloth over the table in front of the window and the stack of plates had grown on the serving table. No one would have guessed the original plan had not known the number of guests. Charlamaine's husband arrived laden with a bulging food carrier, met everyone and joined his in laws washing their hands for dinner. The dining room and sitting area had precipitately become a welcoming diner for all. Laughter and unexpected delight had settled into hearts that had previously felt the pain of absence. Hugh began the prayer of thanksgiving; his heart breaking in happiness, unable to go on and to his amazement, when no one else picked up the prayer, Barkley took the place by his dad and to everyone's delight began to pray.

"Heavenly Father, thank you that Caroline Dawn has come home with Oliver and his mother and dad, his sister and her husband and Millie. I don't know Charlie's husband's name but we are happy they are here with us and we will make them as welcome as we know how. You are our heavenly father and we love you and we love each other. Now thank you for this good food, the thin gravy too, and let us eat the turkey Momma fixed and the food Miss Cecily and Mr. Alistaire brought and be happy. Amen."

"Young man," Charlie's husband offered his hand, "My name is Howard and I'm called Howie by my friends. Alistaire's name we shorten to Al, but maybe you should call him Mr. Al, for your parent's benefit." Howie laughed, "and thank you all for making us welcome. We are starved."

"I think," Barkley said, "It's a good thing you are a big tall guy and could carry all that food by yourself."

Howie rubbed his stomach. "Son, if you only knew. We didn't stop for breakfast hoping to arrive in time."

Barkley grinned. "Well, I'm glad you are here. I have wondered about Oliver's family, a lot."

"Wonder no more," Howie replied. "We even have reservations at that motel on the edge of town."

"Starlight Motel," Barkley announced. "It has a glassed top roof, and you can watch the stars."

Hugh caught Susan's eye. He was dumbstruck. He had never experienced such a startling experience. Susan winked and he grinned. This woman, he thought, silently, can handle anything and that boy, my boy, is showing he can pick up the reins if needed. "Thank you Jesus."

The meal was a great festivity, becoming acquainted, enjoying the food and Cecily's cake. "What all does this heavenly concoction contain?" Susan asked. "My word, I recognize whipped crème, dream whip, pineapple, lemon sauce and what else? I will have gained ten pounds it is so enjoyable."

Cecily laughed with pleasure. "I'm so happy you like it. I only make it for special occasion. We love it."

"We could quit our jobs if she would go into baking this one dessert," Mr. Al confided, "But she won't.

Everyone laughed, even Kathryn Preston. "It certainly is delicious," she said and they all agreed.

The afternoon ended before they were ready, "Anyone wanting a second go round, please feel free," Susan encouraged when she heard the clock strike six. "I've set the dishes on the table again and you can warm your plate in the microwave. Just feel at home. There's drinks and Cecily's dessert left."

Caroline had made her way to the evening table. "I just have to sit with family," she said. "It's Thanksgiving and I am so thankful for each of you." She turned to Millie who had been laying by her on the sofa, "I think, Millie, that mother would like for you to try on your dress for the wedding. Would you like that? Your mother can help and the rest of us will watch. Okay?" Millie nodded.

"Oh, my," Charlie was in awe. "You are so talented, Susan. The sewmanship is beautifully done. I think seam down the side and you will have a perfect fit. What do you think?" Millie was busy admiring herself in the portable mirror Hugh brought in from their bedroom. "You're a miniature bride."

"I like it." Caroline had looped a strand of pearls through the curly updo of Millie's hair. Now she hugged Millie. "Do you like it, Caroline?"

"I love it. We will be twins. You are beautiful." Everyone clapped hands.

"Well, Barkley," Howie said, "I think we'll be heading toward the hotel. I want to see those stars when it gets dark." He glanced at his watch. "My goodness, it's eight o'clock." Howie yawned. "That turkey has done its job, I'm as sleepy as a baby." He and Barkley did the hand shake, knuckle ending. Howie bowed before Susan. "You are a wonderful hostess for strangers bursting in on you. Next time, come to our home. I can visualize years of friendship and I just want to thank you for today. Both you and Hugh."

"You made our day," Susan replied. She and Cecily and Charlie hugged while Millie gave them a kiss. The men were busy shaking hands. Susan heard Bert saying, "We should've let you folks have family time," to which Caroline overruled.

"Oh, no, Uncle Bert, you don't get out of it that easy. We always expect you and Aunt Leona."

When all the dishes were put away and in the dish washer, Susan turned to Caroline. "I guess you will be going to see Doctor Jeffries, tomorrow?"

"Yes, ma'm, Oliver's going with me. Doctor Jeffries has brought in another specialist. I'll let you know..." Her words drift away. "Surely it will be all right, Mom, don't you think?"

"Yes, Caroline, there are so many prayers with you, it has to be. Our hope is based on nothing less than God's mercy in finding cure for you."

"Thanks for today, Mom. I didn't warn you because I wasn't sure we'd make it here. You did great, Mom. Oliver's parents are so good to me, but Mom they're not Christians. Charlie and Howie are, though." A wistfulness had crept into Caroline's voice as she spoke. "I pray they will be, soon."

"What time shall I prepare breakfast for you and Oliver?"

"My appointment is at nine thirty, Mom. I think if it's all right with you we'll skip breakfast and eat left overs with you for dinner before we leave to go back to my apartment." She sighed, wistfully. "I wish we could stay another night but the trip is so tiring for me, I need to rest as much as possible before Monday. Sunday, Oliver and I will watch the church service on television. It's what I have to do right now"

"I'm happy to know you realize that, dear. Some don't and they create more problems in their illness."

Hugh had left the next morning when Oliver came from the guest room and Caroline from her old room. It was obvious she was having difficulty walking. "Morning, Mom." She pointed toward her feet. "I must have eaten too much dressing or something; I could hardly get my shoes on." She tried to smile. "Every morning, Oliver helps me squeeze my feet into my shoes but today's probably the worst."

Oliver studied her feet. "Yeah, I think maybe this morning gets the prize."

"Oliver sleeps on the sofa, I'm not sure he rests but he says he does." She leaned over to press a kiss on Oliver's lips. "I don't know what I'd do without him. I'm not sitting down because it's too hard to get up. If we're going to stop and tell your folks goodbye lets go and I'll just stay in the car."

Pressing her cheek against Caroline's Susan hugged her daughter. "Sweetheart, if I did something in your years of life that had a hand in causing this, I'm sorry." Caroline kissed her mother's cheek.

"You didn't Mom, it's just one of those things. If the pain doesn't get any worse we'll be all right."

"I think it's the medicine, Mrs. Preston," Oliver offered. "She's got all the symptoms, the swelling," He took a deep breath as if coasting into Caroline's health issues tired him, too. "We think, Mrs. Preston the medicine is breaking up the cancer cells in her blood and causing all these symptoms, and if that's true the company who makes the drug has been in touch and their hope is she is the stage before going into remission," A slight smile crossed his face, "and if that's true, maybe she can enjoy the wedding. Because that's what's keeping her going right now."

Caroline grinned. "Silly. It's not. But it is a girl's dream to plan her wedding, and Mom and Dad have been wonderful. You saw Millie's dress. Wasn't she sweet, Mom?" Oliver was helping Caroline into her jacket. "She looked like I hope I will. Beautiful." Oliver kissed the top of her head. His eyes straying to Caroline's mother.

"Do you think she will be beautiful? Mrs. Preston? I don't think we have any worries."

No, Susan thought as she saw the door close behind them and then the sound of the car leaving the drive. No worries. Please, dear Lord, if it's possible, let remission come and Caroline have good health at the wedding. She will be beautiful Lord, and I thank you for her and Oliver. He is good to her. Thank you." Still, it worried her the doctor said her test results were at their worst.

Susan was putting away the china and good silverware when the phone rang. It was Hugh.

"Any word, yet?"

"No. But Oliver says the swelling and fever Caroline's experiencing are due to the medicines. Evidently it's been worse than we know. I saw a little tablet laying by Oliver's bed that said she had been having nausea and vomiting too, which would make her tired. He had listed fever and chills on a daily basis. It sounds terrible." She listened to Hugh's labored breathing. "You don't sound so good yourself."

"I'm okay, I've been shoveling a ditch there by the pavement where the tractor can't run. I'll let you go, babe. I was just wondering what the doctor said. I guess that boy, Oliver's going to be all right."

Susan knew any reservations they'd thought had long since passed. Oliver had already assumed the phrases through sickness and health until death do we part. Any stigma attached to the two living together had passed along with the reservations. Oliver was doing what they would have found difficult trying to care for their daughter and maintain their own life. If those outside the family cast doubt on the celibacy of the couple then it was their own sin, Hugh and Susan had accepted in this life there are often circumstance we thought unacceptable that rearrange themselves to real life. This was one of them.

The couples return from the doctor was somber. "It is as Oliver suspected," Caroline began. "Dr. Jeffries thinks the next stage is remission but he has no time table as to when or how long. If it doesn't happen, then Doctor Jeffries wants to try transplanting stem cells to help restore my immune system by harvesting and using my own cells."

"We hope for the best," Mrs. Preston." Oliver's heart was in his voice. He was as intent on Caroline's welfare as his own and certainly as her parents. Susan's heart filled with thanksgiving. She was seeing God's plan for her child revealed. It was a holy moment, that God would show her, yes your child is suffering but she is such a sweet child, there has been no denial, nor resentments, instead a child who has hope and believes in God. Still, Susan's heart ached as she saw Caroline hobble to the room to finish packing for leaving. That was not what you thought would happen in your child's life.

"Thank you, Oliver, for loving Caroline."

Oliver's chin quivered as tears filled his eyes. "I do, Mrs. Preston. I do."

Again the car rolled out the driveway and Susan text Hugh. "Dr. Jeffries hopes remission is on its way due to the severity of present issues. Perhaps it means the cancer medicine is at work destroying bad cells and if it doesn't, the next plan is to harvest Caroline's own stem cells and inject into her body hoping to restore her immune system to its intended use. I love you my darling husband."

Hugh returned to his truck. He had picked up parts. He and Barkley had plans to work on the Four Wheeler. Barkley was a happy lad walking along by his father's side.

"Let me check my phone, Son. I think it's probably Mom with information concerning Caroline's doctor visit." He read the message out loud. His voice breaking as he saw how Susan closed the text.

"Is it bad? I thought remission is good. But I don't know if the other is or not."

"It's good, Son. All we can do is hope Caroline goes into remission and let God take care of the rest."

"Then we need to find a quiet place and thank God, don't we, Dad?"

"Yes, we do, son and I want to thank you for yesterday. You stepped right up and took over."

Barkley watched as Hugh swung out into traffic. "Dad, if you want to pray, there's a place down the road I see every morning when me and Sophia go to school, someone put a bench there and there's a cove of trees. It's real pretty. We could go there. It's not far."

Chapter 11

*H*e saw her through the window, placing gifts under the tree. Susan was smiling. Hugh slipped quietly into the house. He could watch her all day when she was doing the things she loved, because she smiled. It seemed the doctor was right. Maybe their daughter's remission was going to happen. That would make him and Susan smile. Caroline seemed to be gaining strength and the wedding was a week away. The house was as festive as the church they attended. The only part he had in the decorating was the star on top of the tree and that had required a ladder.

"We're going to have a twelve foot tree," she'd said, matter of factly and he'd winced. The wedding was costing a bit more than they'd expected because the caterers convinced them both for the wedding reception two kinds of meat were necessary; then if a person didn't like beef there was pork. He'd taken a deep breath and agreed. He heard himself saying I thought we were going to use last year and the years before that tree, to which she'd replied. "There will be so many people here, Hugh, I think we need to use the slim nine foot tree, instead, but make it taller. No cost, Honey. You'll see." He was confused. "I know it will work if we use part of the old one, for the bottom and the slim one on top. I feel certain it will slip together and no one will ever know once it's covered in decorations."

Women seemed to know those things. The bottom of the old tree had been too wide, but the middle part worked well. He had actually spent two nights the week following Thanksgiving when it rained helping separate the non-breakable balls. "We want all white," she informed him and Barkley. "Put the red ones aside for another room. "It's a wedding.

Get it? White." There it stood, in all its glory, he had suggested why hadn't they just spray painted the tree white and avoided her tedious hours of adornment? But she was having the time of her life and the artificial ornaments did look like glass.

He slipped up behind her. She jumped as his arms went around her. Nuzzling her neck, he tasted the saltiness of her skin. "Must be some other lady putting gifts under the family tree. My gal don't sweat."

"Oh, Rhett, is that you darlin'," she crooned in her best southern accent. "And here I was expecting that fuddy duddy old Hugh any minute." He turned her to face him as she did the customary giggle.

"Scarlett would never giggle," he scolded. "So what are you doing, now?" She blew out a puff of hair that had strayed into her eyes. "Looks good, but I thought you were through."

"Well," she said, studying where the tree set under the tallest part of the ceiling, the only fifteen foot raise to the architect on the ranch style home. "I was actually placing the gifts and wondering if it would be better to put them in the family room next to the kitchen where our red ball tree is." She chewed her lip thinking, "You know, not have the mess in here and the kids like the comfort where there's nothing precious and the comfortable sofas are. Things in here are a bit posh, even if they're ten years old and need replacing." She sighed. "Kids will be in tonight, so we'll see what they have to say."

"Do you have the energy to undertake that job?" He shook his head. "Babe, we're just drawing this year to a close and you've worked as hard as anyone making it happen; I'd think you need a rest. Seems to me decorating's a hard task." The room was elegant and the tall tree was a statement with the white glass balls, the red velvet bows she'd made herself and the stems of red berries all topped off with the silvered angel wings Caroline had brought home Thanksgiving. She had been excited to show them.

"Mr. Bartlett said they used these last year, but this year's tree will have a new theme, and when he asked if I wanted them, I was thrilled. He knew I'd been admiring them. Three dozen, Dad. Aren't they beautiful?" She seemed to enjoy touching each one. "And look, Daddy, they match the star you put on top." This year, Hugh found himself reliving moments with his children, it was like tasting something good and yet there were those bittersweet moments. Seeing Caroline handicapped was a scar on his heart. For a moment he had turned off Susan's conversation.

"Yeah, I've decided," Susan said, "Help me, we are going to reroute these babies." Her arms were already full. "There you go, Rhett, darlin', grab as many gifts as you can. I want to straighten the skirt around the tree, finish the mantel and we're done."

"Completely? Are you sure? You always decorate right up to Christmas morning and if someone gives you an ornament that has to find a home, too. No waiting until next year. You sure about this?" She rolled her eyes, leading the way to the open room that joined the kitchen.

"You know, this room showed its true worth when Oliver's family showed up for Thanksgiving. I must say that was an unexpected event."

"You know what I found unexpected?" Hugh was unloading the gifts onto the floor. "You'll have to place them; I'd just get it all wrong." He sit on the nearest sofa arm, watching her, again. "It was completely unexpected that Oliver's family would be so down to earth and enjoy a regular family day with their son's fiancée."

"Honey, there's nothing regular about a holiday that brings family together, and I'll admit I was a bit concerned they'd be all uppercrust, high society folks. But they love their kids just like we do and thank the Lord they seem to love our daughter." She paused from placing the smaller gifts into the branches, "We really have had to step back and realize our time together as family is the most important part of life. It is a given, work prevents us doing more, but we have to make the most of time when we can."

"You mean, Caroline's health and the fear she might not be able to walk down the aisle for her wedding." As usual he felt the somberness overtake him, "we never know what the next day will bring. The good Lord knows I've had my own concerns on Barkley learning to operate the machinery. One mistake could bring him harm or Sophia's impulsiveness, Susan. Does that girl have to be in every school activity? She may have the energy but I worry about you having to keep up with her and help me too."

"How do you feel about her and Thorn?"

"The question we can't address is the fact Thorn is actually Kane Alberson's son and Kane has a way of trying to stay abreast of our lives and what we're doing so he can try to make us miserable. Does that make any sense to you?"

Susan shook her head. "Doesn't the bible say life is a great mystery? That's one for the books, but what about Thorn? I think they're getting serious and Sophia will be going off to college next fall."

"I don't think Sophia would let us have a final say about Thorn," Hugh replied. "I like the boy, well enough and that, I take it, is due to Emily and Sam's raising him. Emily was always a quiet lady type girl and no one finds fault with Sam Lansky. Now, if it were the Langston kid I might have to say different." He scratched the stubble of beard on his chin. "The question is does Kane ever intend to make his being the boy's daddy a problem to the Lansky's or Thorn. I wouldn't want Sophia mixed up in that mess."

They were both quiet for a minute, until Hugh said, "My word, Susan, Kane could be Sophia's father-in-law if it's true she and Thorn are becoming serious. There's something else, you'll be surprised."

"By the way," Susan said, "I thought you were going to Tolison's farm sale. Did it end this early?"

"No, I left it in full swing but had a piece of news to share with you. I thought Tolison had already rent out his farm, but his son, the one that works in the city, kind of a nerdy type fellow. Anyway he said, "You're Mr. Preston, aren't you?" I nodded, a bit surprised he'd know me, but he said his father asked him to watch for me and he came right up to me. Susan, Mr. Tolison's land is for sale. He hasn't let word out yet, but he'd like to see it stay in the hands of a local farmer and not the city conglomerate."

"You're remembering Kane buying the last piece of land out from under us, when the agreement was already made?" Her hands were still, the placing of gifts forgotten momentarily. "What's to keep that from happening again? We do all the work, ready to sign and Kane comes into the picture. We've been hearing that over and over." She rose up, out of the floor, the gifts under the tree forgotten.

"I hope this is different if the son came to us first, possibly Kane won't have the chance."

"That hurt. We lost trust in people we'd known all our life and Kane left a public sting. What kind of man touts his victory publicly? I felt he was ridiculing us, when he knew very well he purchased that land with money under the table; which we have no reserve funds as he does. He has a whole family backing him." She stared across the room, beyond the window where the fields lay fallow in winter. "You decide and I'll stand with you but Hugh," she cast troubled eyes on him. "Money always speaks."

"I know, but maybe we learned something last time. In the future we won't put time between it."

"You know what I don't understand? Why is Kane so bent on knowing about our lives?"

"Mother and I were talking about that, she remembered in school Kane wanted to compete but I didn't have the financial means to keep up with his crowd, she said it seemed to her he was jealous of the fact my dad was always interested in what I was doing but Kane's father was busy building his empire. When a child takes second place to his father's business...maybe he redirects that unrest and in Kane's case it landed on me."

"That wasn't fair. Did you realize it? We've never touched on that before."

"Nah, I was too caught up in you and being an only child I'm sure I had all the attention I needed."

Hugh found himself out of bed around midnight. He was sitting in the dark when Caroline opened the refrigerator door and the line splayed across to where he sit. "Don't let me scare you," he said.

"Oh, Dad. Are you all right?" She flipped the switch and light flooded the room.

"Yeah, just couldn't sleep but I didn't know you had arrived. Is Oliver with you?"

"No, he's coming in tomorrow with his parents. I just wanted to spend time with you and Mom."

"Barkley and Sophia will be glad, too." He watched Caroline pour a glass of milk and come to join him. "Can't you sleep either?"

She smiled. "I think I'm excited. I want to see the church and from what I can see here, the house is beautiful. Mother has done a good job. Did you help?"

"Yeah, I put the star on top of the tree and the ornaments at the top. That's about it, though."

She scoot close to him, just like she did as a little girl. "Thanks Dad. Everything you do is special and I appreciate it." She turned to look into his face. "Dad, I love you. No girl could be more proud of her father."

"Same here, little girl. I love you in an almost unbelievable way. As a man, I didn't know this kind of love until I got you kids and became a dad."

"I remember you explaining the love between you and Mom to Sophia. Do you remember? After Mom miscarried and Sophia was embarrassed?" She was quiet a few minutes, the silence not uncomfortable but stretching for more words to come. "Dad? I think Oliver and I will have a love like yours and Mom's."

He found her hand. "I'm glad to hear that, Caroline. Our love with God's help has got us through a lot of situations." He took a deep breath. "One of those situations was recent when Sophia forgot to come home and I went out looking for her. She didn't call before a group of the kids decided to go to the lake. We didn't know where she was and maybe we'd never have known except a part of the group was in a second car and the driver, they call him Bumper, well, he lost control and hit a boulder on the side of the road. The wheel flew off and hit the jeep Caroline was in and one of the girls fell out and broke her arm."

"Was Thorn in the group, Dad? That doesn't sound like him, at all."

"No, Sophia was with the girls that cheer and supposedly this Bumper was interested in her that night. But when the accident occurred, that ended most of their reckless plans and they had to call for help because of the girl being hurt. I was in town where they hatched their plan when the police got the call."

"Bumper is the Caraway boy, Dad. He's pretty wild. His parents travel a lot and they are completely unsuspicious of what he does while they're away or maybe they don't care, I don't really know."

"I worry about your sister."

"I worry about you, Dad."

He pulled her close. "Why would you say that?"

"You're driven, Dad. You work hard and you'd just as soon work as play, if it wasn't for Mom and us kids, I know you'd work all the time. I can always tell when something's going on, by how you breathe."

"Really? Breathe?" He chuckled. "What do I do make sounds?"

"No, you are just more intense. Mom can bring you out of it, but she notices it too."

"Sweetheart, I've seen our world nearly turn upside down this year, with your illness, and the farm."

"I know but Dad you've got to slow down. Things happen to men your age."

"Hey, I'm fine. With your progress, life is getting better. I just hate to see you leave us."

"I'm not leaving, Dad, just changing my name. If you ever need me, I'll be here."

They had the family gift opening that weekend because the next week would be Caroline Dawn and Oliver's wedding. Everyone helped put the house back in order to lighten Susan's load. "How many are

coming?" Barkley's enthusiasm was on a high. "I hope I don't drop the ring."

"If you do, that cute little niece of Oliver's can pick it up." Hugh teased.

"No, she can't, Dad. She walks in front of me, throwing out flower petals."

"Strewing them gently," Sophia corrected.

"Christmas has never been so good," Barkley quipped. "It's just double fun."

And then it was the day everyone was looking forward too.

"Mom?" Barkley called from the next room. "Mom. I think you need to look at something."

"What's that, Barkley?" Susan was trying to apply her make up. The house was full of family that had come in from other towns and needed a place to stop off before the wedding. She was nearly run ragged trying to see to everyone's needs. It wasn't like Barkley to wait until last minute. She shrugged into a summer house coat, peeped down the hall to see if she'd encounter any of the relatives and hurried to his room. "What is it?" He was dressed, the white shirt immaculate, the black vest fitting, but in his hand was a roll of silver tape and he was pointing at the side seam of the trousers.

"Look, Mom. What do we do about this?" The season's fashion was smaller legs in men's wear as well as women's and Barkley carried it off well enough, except evidently whoever rented the tux before had not. The ripped open at the seam leg of the pant in the trousers had made it through whatever kind of cleaning the clothes went through on return to the company. "I can tape it together, if you want me to."

"Barkley, slip your pants off, put on a pair of shorts and go into the closet where I keep the portable sewing machine. There's a box beneath it has all colors of thread, find the black spool and bring them both to my and dad's room and I'll stitch those back together. I think that will be better than taping." She stood silent for a minute thinking. "That friend of Oliver's, what's his name, Jensen? I'm thinking there will be another problem...and Oliver and his friends are getting dressed at the church."

"Yeah, Mom, we better take this roll of tape. They're bound to need it."

A few minutes later the phone rang. It was Oliver's mother. "Susan, this is Ceciley, we have a problem here. Oliver's friend's tux pant either needs sewing up or...well, I just wondered what you think we should do? Wherever they came from, this pair made it through inspection with the side seam ripped open."

"Barkley's was the same, Ceciley. We'll be there within a few minutes and I'll sew them up, too."

Hugh came into the room as she hung up the phone. "Hon, it's time to go, I've cleared the house of the relatives and everyone's on their way." He appeared puzzled. "Why did I see Barkley putting your machine in the back of the car?"

Susan was slipping her dress over her head. Hugh zipped it up the back. "Wow, Mrs. Preston, you look like a bride, yourself." She smiled back from the mirror as he placed a strand of hair in place. "I want the first dance with you, ma'am."

"You look pretty handsome, yourself, sir." She wasn't surprised when he turned her around and kissed her. There were tears in her eyes. "We are making it to Caroline Dawn's wedding, my love. This is a milestone."

"In more ways than one," he replied. "I love you, Susan."

"I love you, Hugh." She sighed. "Get me to the church. Oliver's friend's trousers need stitching up."

"What?" Hugh chuckled. "Bless be the mother of the bride who can sew, huh?"

"Yeah, bless be the tie that binds two families together with a memory to last a life time."

Kathryn Preston in the back seat with Barkley said, "Susan, you have done this very well."

In the candlelit room, the ceremony was well underway. Caroline Dawn had walked the aisle with her dad's hand firm on her elbow. Few realized the importance of that walk. Hugh's pride in his daughters was evident. Sophia smiled from the front in line with friends Caroline had chosen and Barkley and Oliver's little niece were a cute pair as they led the way down the aisle before Hugh and Caroline.

It is well, Hugh thought, It is well with my soul. Thank you, Heavenly Father, for this blessing. His eyes met Susan's. In a room filled with loved friends and relatives, they knew their daughter's hope was shining bright on this special day. When the minister said, "in your life it will be the small things that make or break you, the big situations will automatically be done, and the small ones will be your curse or blessing for they are always with you. Remember, to handle them together with love and stay strong in the Lord."

The reception was held on the outer skirts of town in an old barn, newly renovated for special occasions. Oliver's parents had insisted they provide the musicians and there they sit dressed in black suits, wearing sparkling white T shirts with a message peeping through their opened jackets, which they removed promptly once the bride and groom had the first dance across the floor. Now visible on the shirts was a picture of Caroline and Oliver kissing, on the back their wedding date in formal script. "Now the grandparents," the Bass called out and as Al and Cecily prepared to step onto the floor, Hugh offered his hand to Susan, the musicians flowed into a slower rhythm and all eyes were on the parents of the bride and groom. "May I say you look especially enticing, tonight, Mrs. Preston," Hugh said. "How did I ever win your heart?" He tilt his head just so and kissed the top of her hair. "My lovely bride, we've lasted." The music ebbed into The Rose. "How appropriate," Hugh whispered into her ear. "My rose." The champagne folds of Susan's dress glowed in the dim light and her dark hair framed the luminescence of her skin. Pressing her close, "May our God be merciful to us," he said and she whispered, "Always."

"Your parents are love in motion," Oliver whispered in Caroline's ear. Tears brightened her eyes.

"Yes, they are, and to think Mother wasn't sure about wearing that dress. It's perfect. They're perfect."

The drummer was on a roll as young people spilled out onto the floor and the music gained momentum. Ceciley and Al were grinning ear to ear as they whirled around the floor. "Let's make this a night to remember," Cecily challenged Susan and Hugh. "Our kids have started life together and we want them to have every blessing." In the center of the floor, the loves of their lives were dancing. "That is what we've prayed together, for," Ceciley said. "Your daughter explained our need for the Lord. We accepted Him into our hearts last night. Somehow it just seemed right and our hearts are full to bursting."

"It seems kind of strange to receive that news and be in a barn dancing, doesn't it?" Susan whispered.

"The bible is filled with people dancing for joy," Hugh replied, "I think it's as good a way to rejoice as any." His eyes sought out Sophia across the way but she ignored him. "I am concerned, though, I notice Thorn is here but Sophia's not paying any attention to him, what gives?"

Susan gave a strange laugh. "She's playing a game. She better watch it, it could back fire. You notice one of Caroline's friends is staying pretty close by Thorn's side. I think our girl will come around, soon."

As always, Susan was right. Hugh observed, by the time the evening had worn down and one of the musicians had taken charge of the microphone singing Ed Sheeran's song, Perfect, Sophia was moving toward Thorn. The words of the song cut through to hearts young and old, Caroline had pressed on, in spite of swollen joints, fever and days void of energy, with Oliver encouraging her they had made it and whatever the future held they would face it together. Hugh saw Caroline lay her head against Oliver's chest as they were alone out on the floor. "She's tired," he said, "But happy." His and and Susan's hands tightened as they stood watching. Across from them, Cecily and Al's eyes were bright with tears. "They will be good to our daughter," Susan whispered, glancing up. "Thank you, Jesus."

It was following Hugh's dance with his mother, when the musicians seeing Caroline was tiring stood in honor of the bride and groom, allowing the pianist to go solo as around the room the guests joined in singing "When You walk through a storm, hold your head up high." Hands raised toward the ceiling on those precious words, "You will Never Walk Alone."

Hugh felt someone pressing his arm and looked down. Sophia with Thorn stood by his side. Barkley was secure with Susan's arm around him to Hugh's left. It is well, his mind replayed, silently. It is well, it is well with my soul.

It was three o'clock in the morning. Hugh slipped quietly out onto the porch and settled into the swing. His first born had left the nest. He'd felt Susan's tears on his arm as they'd gone to bed, trying to let their tired bodies fall into needed sleep. No words were necessary. A mother's love was tied up in her own prayers for her daughter just as his were, but he'd awakened needing to stretch his frame and slipped into his denims with a need to sit in the swing outside and think of Caroline's sweetness.

"Dad?' Sophia stepped through the door. "Can I sit with you?"

"Come on." He waited for her to scoot in close, his arm going around her. "What's that you got a blanket?"

"Yeah." He heard the huskiness in her voice.

"You been crying?"

Sophia took a deep breath. "Yes. I needed too. Seems like a chapter of our lives has ended. Caroline's really left us, now."

"Maybe not," Hugh's chin settled on top of Sophia's hair. "Maybe it's a new chapter where she comes home with a new need for all of us. When

I left home I didn't have any siblings to go back to and I always wondered what it'd be like having brothers and sisters. Caroline has you and Barkley."

"I'm going to be nicer to Barkley. He will really miss Caroline. They love each other more."

"Not more than you."

"Yes, they do, Dad. It's my fault. Sometimes I'm mean to people. I've got this selfish streak, if I want something I make up my mind and go after it and I forget to be nice."

"What?" Hugh chuckled. "I can't believe you said that."

"Caroline says I'm like Grandmother Kathryn."

"My mother does have her ways," Hugh conceded.

"But she'd never let anything hurt us, either, Dad. She just sees things different and I do too."

"I'm speechless."

Sophia snuggled closer. "It's cold out here. But Dad, I was thinking tonight about the time you told me you hoped someday I found the kind of love you and Mom have. I had to make up with Thorn tonight. I think I hurt him pretty bad and he really likes me. I may have a future with Thorn, some day. But I'm going to college, first. I just can't tie myself down, for a while. Do you understand, Dad?"

"I can't honestly say I really understand, Sophia, but sounds like you're trying to commit yourself to better ways and I'm for that...I have to take stock of myself now and then. Your Mom's got her hands full and too many times I let a lot of my baggage slide over on her. She's going to miss your sister. How about we both try together to be nicer, starting with Mom?"

Sophia was trembling with the cold. "I will, Dad, but I got to go in. You better, too. Don't get sick." He kissed the top of her head. "I love you, Dad."

"Love you, too, Sophia." He watched her slide back inside, shaking his head. "Wonders never cease," he whispered. He could only wonder what the years ahead would bring and his mind flit to the possibility of buying the Tolison place. That, too would be a milestone but Kane Alberson would be after it, too. In the back of his mind, he wondered that Sophia was dating a young man who was in reality Kane Alberson's son.

Chapter 12

"*I* ran into Dr. Jeffries," Susan was saying as she put away the groceries. "I always wondered if doctors went to Walmart like regular people. I guess they do, anyway, he said Caroline's medicine is a type of chemo and the doctor in Memphis has put Caroline through the radiation blasts. That is why he thinks remission is in effect. He asked how the wedding went." She sighed. "We should have invited him."

"We tried not to prevail on people." Hugh glanced up from sitting at the table studying the ledger. "Does it seem to you our labor expense was heavier this last month, I don't mean just the fact we were out more hours but there's something I'm missing here."

"Let me look at it, I could have made a mistake." She studied the print out. "I'll compare it to the bank statements. A voided check could explain it all."

"We did hire the extra worker," Hugh agreed. "Picking up the extra land required we take him on."

"I hate to admit it, but I've not been as sharp with the paperwork, with Caroline's health issue pulling me a different direction and that has concerned me, that I'd miss something." She was pulling bank statements, examining the copies of checks. "I don't know why but I feel it's in the new guys paperwork. The others are weekly pay being the same, but his was based on hours that varied by the week."

"Oh," her breath caught. "Here's a huge error. Mine or the banks. Robert could never have made that much in a week. Why that's more than our salaried guys." She riffled through the remaining statements.

"He worked through August until first of November. There's one check each month that cleared the bank with an amount different than what was printed. Now how could that be?"

"Let me see." Hugh studied the copied checks on back pages of the statements. Bending closer to try to solve the mystery, "Look, Susan, there's a smudge around the numbers. As though someone changed the amounts. You don't do that, do you? I would think you'd just draw another check."

Her breath caught. "Four thousand, instead of four hundred. Why that threw the whole account off balance." She sit back, staring at Hugh. "I can't believe I missed that, the balance was off and in my rush I didn't catch it. Hugh…" She shook her head. "I can't believe he'd do this…but worse that I didn't catch it immediately." Putting her arms on the table, she rest her head in her hands, her fingers threading through the strands of hair that fell around her face. "I knew there were moments I was brittle…. but this….?" Slowly she raised her head and began to search for other high number amounts on the employee checks. "They're all his," she said, finally. "It amounts to Eight thousand more than it should have; Eight thousand, three hundred dollars to be exact."

"What could he have needed that amount of money for? He seemed like a trustworthy fellow."

"He appears pretty wholesome, not on drugs." She tried to think. "I can't pinpoint any distrust."

"But here it is," Hugh held up the ledger. These figures and those on the checks are completely different." He sat staring across the room. "Now, what do we do? We have to face him about this."

"What do you know about him?"

Hugh thought a minute. "Not much, the other fellows recommended him, brought him out, even, and we were desperate for another hand. He said he was married, a new baby and needing a job."

"Usually, you have me do a search, but due to needing him that day you put him right out there." Her voice trailed away lost with her thoughts. "If we take it to the prosecutor, not knowing his personal life we could ruin him. If we don't do it quickly, it looks like pure negligence on our part, which…." Her voice was troubled now as her expression, "It is my fault. My only excuse is it happened during the time I was so caught up in Caroline and Oliver's wedding, not to mention her health and Christmas on us."

"It could just as easily have been me, but, this brings to mind a few other things…we have tools missing out in the shop." He pushed back his chair, taking a deep breath as he did so, "I rode the guys pretty hard, their only defense was did I consider the two that left might have them riding around in the back of their car where they'd forgot to return them and I didn't think so, but now this. A man that will steal from you one way will another."

"What kind of tools?" Through the years Hugh had worked hard at reminding the men when they used a wrench, not to walk away and leave it on the tool bar of a piece of equipment, they might not return and then the next person wasn't aware it was left behind to be lost when it bounced off in the field. A lot of tools went into the ground and had to be replaced. It was a small thing but the little things were what ate away at profit.

"Well, you won't believe it, but something as large as an air tank or as small as a meter we use to check the electrical wiring. Each guy has his own tool chest, or a box, whatever they choose and they've made their own rule you don't borrow unless you ask first and put it back later but that became a problem this fall, too. It seemed to mostly center round the new guy not having his own tools."

"That causes distrust among the workers."

"Yeah and sometimes they've been near fist fights. Not a good over all working condition for any of us." He felt nervous agitation descending on the calm he'd felt until he'd discovered this problem. "Now, what do we do?"

"I think you go see the new guy, first, and then you'll know how to proceed from there."

"How about you go?" He stood up. "Just kidding, it's my job, but not one I wanted." He scratched his head. "Wouldn't you have thought the bank would have caught those smeared numbers?"

"It matters most to us, and we didn't until now." She felt the need to move and stood. "It really irritates me that I didn't and yes, they know I don't do that…but I can't believe they'd take credit for it and if they did, for sure our employee would be in deep trouble."

"Well, he didn't sign on for next year as he's hoping to find work he's accustomed to."

"I never knew what he did before; he just told me he was raised on a farm. So what was his work?"

"He was an accountant. Didn't have his own office, but worked for one of the best in the area."

Their eyes met and they were both shaking their heads. "So he knew what to do," Susan said.

"Fraid so. I guess they call that premeditated. I'm just glad it wasn't more than eight thousand." He started out the door and turned. "That should have been my tip off, why he wasn't still working there."

The address Shane Boyer had given had a for rent sign in the window. Hugh's next stop was Shane's previous place of employment. Frank Mitchell shook his head, a rueful expression on his face. "So he got you, too." Now he rubbed his chin, briskly. "I guess I taught him well and he used it wrong." Hugh was almost out the door when Frank spoke suddenly. "You might check out at Dolly Williams, I forget her last name now. She married that Harpo guy from St. Louis, then a Kirkland I believe but that's who Shane was dating when he was here."

"He told me he was married."

"Yeah, well he was, maybe still is, but him and Dolly have a thing going on." Putting his hands up in defense, Frank declared, "She stops in now and then, her daddy did business with me but Dolly can't decide what she wants to do. I figure by end of February she'll make up her mind."

Back tracking, Hugh wondered how he'd missed the signs. Shane Boyer's new black pickup truck was parked in Dolly's front yard at the Old Williams homestead. He knocked on the door and Shane answered. "Could I speak with you outside?" Hugh asked. Shane reached for a coat from the rack by the door and stepped out onto the porch.

"Shane, we've found your discrepancies with your pay check. What do you plan to do about it?"

"Nothing."

Hugh tilted his head studying the man. "Nothing?"

"Nope." Shane put his hands in his pockets and met Hugh's stare. "I figure you got more to lose than me."

"How's that?"

"Well, me and Dolly got a thing going on. That's how I came to work for you. She said, Hugh Preston farms my land I bet he'd give you a job and you were pretty much in need of my help, weren't you?"

"Yeah, but you were paid a weekly salary."

"I needed more."

Hugh was taken back by Shane's brazen line of thought. "I can't see as I was responsible for your need."

"That woman in there," Shane pointed back to the door. "I can twist and bend her to my will. You mess with me, I'll see that you lose the land your farming that belonged to her daddy and then how will that affect you?"

Hugh's blood boiled. His eyes drew into slits as he stared harder at Shane Boyer. "It won't do you much good, whatever your plans, if the prosecuting attorney becomes involved in this little fiasco."

"No, but Kane Alberson will be farming this land and you'll be looking straight ahead when you pass by."

Hugh turned and went down the steps. He'd had his say and now he'd made up his mind what to do. His first stop would be at J.W. Halsop's office of law. On the way to where he'd parked, he glanced into the back of Shane's truck. There sit the air tank with Preston on the handle practically invisible where someone had tried to erase it. Hugh reached over the tailgate and lift it out. Shane watched him put it into his own truck. He knew within his heart, the men's tools were probably inside the cab.

"I have a contract for five years," he told J.W. "What does that mean if Boyer makes waves and Kane Alberson tries to take the land out from under me."

"It means you have the land rented for five more years but it doesn't say anything about protecting you from Boyer or Alberson. I hear tell they're drinking buddies and that particular association can wreak havoc with a good man's life. I mean yours, Hugh, if they have a vendetta against you."

"This is utterly ridiculous."

"That's what law suits are made of, my friend."

"How'd it go?" Susan was still sitting at the table, books spread across and spilling into one chair. Hugh threw his hat across the room. "That bad, huh?"

"We just as well prepare for trouble. That fellow knows no scruples. I've got to work on my hiring skills." Something else was gnawing at his conscience. It shouldn't matter, but what if it did? "Susan?" She glanced his way. "You remember that bill that came from Jim's Excavating?"

"Your friend from school?" She waited, pencil poised in air. "Is he all right? You seem worried."

"Remember it said overdue and I said go ahead and pay it, it was on the William's place?"

"Yes." She was puzzled. "I did, are you going to tell me now that I shouldn't have?" She had left the books and was in the kitchen now, opening two cans of corn and drawing a package of frozen green beans from the refrigerator. "Go ahead, I'm listening but the kids will come home starved. We can eat early since you're home. You said pay it. Now, I shouldn't have?"

"No. But I had thought I'd tell you the weird situation that day and we got busy and I didn't."

"Is it important?"

"It might be. When I received the call to come to the William's place, it was Dolly answered the door; in fact she made the call. "He drew out a long breath. "Well, she wasn't really dressed appropriate and she did invite me in."

Susan's face blanched, white. "Did you go inside Hugh Preston?" Warning signals were going off in her head. "I hope not, the stories circulating what's going on there at that house are not nice."

"I haven't heard any stories." Hugh replied, warily. "Just let me tell the story in my defense." He grimaced. "I wish I hadn't even started this." Susan's eyes were bordering on enemy distrust. "I didn't go in; in fact I said I'd take care of the problem, while in truth I was backing off the porch."

"I haven't heard the problem, yet. Do be clear in the telling of this story, please."

"I don't like your tone."

"And I don't like the fact you waited…what…three months to tell me? Whatever it is…."

"Well, in view of today's encounter with her boyfriend who was our summer employee that embezzled money from the farm account, I just want to say, she was wearing shorts that showed her behind and a halter that she stooped low enough for me to see everything she has and I think I was being set up for a trollop in the hay." He huffed a big puff of air. "There, I said it and the fact is you told me I was so vulnerable I wouldn't know if a woman made a pass at me and I do believe I did know."

"Trollop in the hay?" Susan circled where he stood. "Aren't you the elegant one? If I wasn't so mad, I'd laugh." She had emptied the two cans of corn into a pan on the stove and was still holding the green beans.

"Why are you mad? Because a woman thought to make a pass at me?" He scratched his head. "Is that what she did? Just by showing off her body?" Now he was as confused as she seemed in the beginning. Susan wasn't looking at all friendly. "I mean, for heaven's sakes, Susan, what do you call that?"

"I think you described it pretty well, yourself. Now, why am I angry?" She was counting on her fingers; August, September, October, November, December and now January. Six months, Hugh Preston and now you decide to tell me." She went to the door and threw the pan of corn out and slapped the green beans in his hand. "Here's the way I see it, if you thought it was important enough to keep six months, maybe I think it was important enough to tell me. I don't know if the stories are true, but it is said, and I don't carry this tale to anyone else but you, that she doesn't mind dating other women's husbands."

"You didn't tell me." He wasn't being entirely truthful, Dolly had always been promiscuous.

Susan gave him a scathing look. "You can think this one over, Mr. Macho. I'm going to take a ride by myself and meditate on this and see if I feel there's any reason for us to worry over such an insignificant little ploy that you kept to yourself and why suddenly it might be important."

He felt stone cold, his body had gone numb. Finally he said, "Shane Boyer threatened saying he could twist her around his finger and if she told him about that day, he just might enlarge on the story."

"Then we have reason to pray that day never crosses her mind and you won't be brought to task."

"You're not mad, then?" He took the nearest chair, his long legs sticking straight out in front of him as he studied the tip of the toe of his boots as though they had suddenly been gold dipped. "Right?"

When he glanced up, Susan had her purse in her hand, a jacket around her shoulders and was getting in his truck. He went to the door and opened it. The kids were coming up the drive and Barkley was picking up the pan. "Where's Mom going and why's the pan outside on the ground, Dad?"

"Don't ask," Hugh replied. He was still clutching the package of green beans. "Sophia, what goes with green beans?" Sophia stopped digging in the frig for a snack and stared at her father. "Do you know how to cook?"

Chapter 13

Susan pulled in to a grove of trees, laid her head on the steering wheel and cried. Once in the truck she'd glanced down to see she was wearing a blouse with a slight tear in the sleeve and even if she covered that with her jacket, a tomato stain was on the button line from the last time she'd made spaghetti.

"Stupid," she berated herself. "The whole thing was without merit." Yes, Hugh forgot to tell her, or maybe Dolly looked so good he didn't want to tell her. Three babies later, a lot of days spent in the field helping Hugh, she was not a fashion model. Her figure was still good and she did apply night crème, but she often felt lack of assurance when it came to her handsome husband who seemed to catch the eye of other women. "Sister," she whispered, "you got a bad case of feeling sorry for yourself."

A knock on the window brought her up, fast. She wiped spittle from the corner of her mouth before turning. Lord have mercy, she thought, I actually fell asleep sitting in somebody's grove of trees. It was the evening shadows of the trees splaying across the hood of the truck and the dimness of the night prevented her knowing who was standing just outside her vehicle. Rolling the window down a few cracks she said "hello."

"You all right, in there, Ma'am?" She recognized that voice. Talk about not wanting to face someone?

"Hello. Yes, I'm fine. I feel a bit foolish telling you this, but I got so sleepy I had to pull over. You know, other people on the road, I couldn't risk hurting someone else. Am I in your way, or something?"

"No, no," Kane Alberson was standing peering in. "Why, it's Susan, isn't it? Susan Preston, Hugh's wife?"

She grinned. "Yeah, that seems to be the way we're known, Hugh's wife or Barkley and Sophia's mother."

"Tough, huh?" He was scanning the truck, "just sleepy, no flat tire I could fix?"

Susan yawned. "Fraid not, on my way home. Guess you are calling it a day?"

"Not really, "Kane replied, "Have a call from Dolly Kirkland and her new boyfriend, something about a job done in August…"He laughed, "Why that's last year now and I'm wondering why they'd call me?"

Susan put the truck in gear, starting to back away. "Have a good night, Kane. I'll be seeing you. Thanks for stopping to see if I was having problems."

"My pleasure." Kane tipped his hat. "Have a good evening."

For a split second she wondered that he seemed nice and then her thoughts returned to Hugh's story. Wasn't it every woman's dread that someone prettier, thinner, would come along and take her man? Well, to be honest, she thought, I never have but this, that woman even considering my man ticks me off. She didn't know which one she had the most hostility towards but for now she suspected Hugh. She sat there another hour; the worst person in the world to see her had already made appearance.

The lights were off, she supposed they were all in bed and wondered why a loaded can of trash was sitting by the door but then carrying the trash to the garage she found the car was gone. She turned the light on in the kitchen and gasp. It was a mess, obviously they'd tried to make spaghetti and let it boil over on the stove, and then from the conglomerated mass in the largest pan she owned she saw the noodles, mushy and congealed. Dishes remained on the table, a pile of spaghetti strings in the middle of each plate sticking out from under a spoonful of ground beef and cheese topping. But why were the noodles uneaten and where were her children? It was past bedtime for Barkley. She checked the calendar, there were no ballgames scheduled and it wasn't church night. She considered cleaning the kitchen and then decided she was completely not responsible for the kitchen and decided to go to bed.

Hugh, coming in would be a disturbance. Susan showered, donned her mother hubbard gown and crawled into the guest room bed.

Cool, reserved and handsome as ever, Hugh met her in the kitchen the next morning, taking his plate of scrambled eggs, bacon and toast from her. Pouring a cup of coffee he sat staring as she moved around the room, fixing Barkley's lunch box, Sophia's slice of bread in the toaster and finally her own cup of coffee to sit opposite him.

"You know this is the day for us to sign papers on the Tolison land?"

"Yeah, I'll be dressed and ready to go by eight fifteen. Is that good enough?"

"I guess it has to be. You're in charge, aren't you?" He sounded every bit as disdainful as intended.

"Whoa, whoa, whoa." He was preparing to leave the table. "I'm not understanding your tone of voice."

"Well, aren't you? We have a little discussion, you get upset and leave. Do you suppose you'll stay if we take on this new property and a heck of a lot more debt than we already have?"

"Do you want me to?" she almost whispered.

"I guess that depends on you," he replied.

Susan made a buzzer sound. "Wrong answer, my friend. Wrong answer."

Hugh spread his arms and shrugged. "It seems I'm good at that. I'll be in the truck. Eight o'clock."

"You really aren't helping your case, Mr. Macho," she muttered. "Last night's kitchen and now leaving the breakfast I cooked for you." Glancing at the clock, she pulled his plate across the table as Barkley joined her wearing his cap and carrying his plate. "Remove your cap, please, as a courteous young man."

"Are you eating out of Dad's plate? That's gross."

"Not really. He hadn't touched it." She grinned, "Besides that I only had enough eggs for you and him."

"Is Dad sick or are you two fighting?"

"What makes you think that?" She tapped his shoulder. "I believe I said remove your cap, please."

"Well I know you slept in the guest room and I don't think you've ever done that before, have you?"

Susan giggled, "maybe once when we were first married."

"What's that all about? Maybe I'll need to know for when I'm married."

"That's not anytime soon, is it?" She stood, taking her plate to the sink for a rinse and then into the dishwasher. "Well, Son, I've gotta run, Dad's waiting in the truck and I'm not dressed, but I will be."

"Mom?" Sophia came flying through the hall. "Did you sleep in the guest room?"

"Long story, short. Yes." She smiled, handing Sophia the slice of toast with jelly. "Be sweet." She stepped back to kiss Barkley's cheek. "Sophia thinks kissing is gross."

"I don't think that applies to Thorn."

"Barkley, get in the car," Sophia demanded. And to her Mom, "I hope your story is good."

Susan bowed. "It is." The door closed behind Sophia and Susan hurried to get dressed. Applying the usual matte foundation, the light brown eye shadow and the dark brown mascara, she left the coral lipstick until last. Her clothes were laid out on the guest room bed and she was slipping on her shoes when Hugh came storming down the hall. "My, my, my," she muttered. "that hall's taking a beating."

He came to a halt when he saw she was fully dressed. "I thought you were dilly dallying."

"No," she said sweetly, "I never dilly dally. I leave the dilly dallying up to other folks."

Hugh studied this sultry piece of clay standing before him. Unusually fetching, he thought and in high spirits it seemed, not at all as upset as he'd thought she'd be when she saw the kitchen last night.

"Let's roll," she called out, sauntering down the hall and Hugh followed, thinking Susan's behind was much nicer than the one he hadn't even thought of viewing that got him in trouble in the first place, when he followed her down the path that led to where the old septic tank was located. How was he to know he needed blinders on that day? Now he realized coming clean with his story wasn't the thing to do.

She felt like a million when Hugh rushed to open the door for her. "Thank you," she said. "It's nice to know there's a gentleman around."

They had no idea a surprise was in store for them arriving at the First National Bank. Not only was Mr. Tolison present but Kane Alberson was there, also. Hugh was a bit bullish in his greeting Mr. Tolison.

"If you don't mind, Hugh, Kane will meet with us the first few minutes and then if all goes well he will be moving along. There's just something I want to set straight. Shall we meet in your private room, Alex?"

The President of the First National Bank took charge. "Come right this way and make yourself comfortable." It was an all mahogany room with pictures of past presidents on the walls. "I don't see your photo, Alex," Tolison remarked. "Does that mean you move on one way or another, first?"

Alex grinned uncomfortably. "Something like that. Now, Mr. Tolison do you want to lead off?"

Tolison sat directly across from Hugh and Susan. "There's a very simple matter in play, here, Hugh. It has come to my attention my best friend's daughter is raising a question as to you being the better man to purchase my property. Me and James Williams were best friends, so I kind of look out for Dolly." He took a deep breath and cleared his throat. "Now, yesterday, Dolly and her fiancée' came to speak with me. It seems Dolly ask you to oversee work for a new underground tank in her backyard, which you did hire, who was it, Frank's Excavating to do the job? But she declares while you were there you made a sexual advance towards her and she wants to break the contract her daddy made with you to farm his land even in the likelihood of his dying before it expired. You follow me?"

Hugh rose to his feet. "I don't appreciate you bringing Kane in to hear your friends lies toward my conduct, Mr. Tolison. I did not come here to be insulted and have those lies strewn throughout the community. Mr. Williams rent his ground to me in good faith and I've honored that commitment. You agreed I could purchase your farm and gave your word." Hugh lay emphasis heavily on the word your. "Let's go, Susan. This is a Kangaroo Court and we will have no part of it." Susan arose immediately.

Mr. Tolison was on his feet. "Sit down, Hugh. I want to hear your version. Please, sit down."

Susan laid a hand on Hugh's. "Tell them, Honey. Tell them exactly as you told me."

The three men seemed to register surprise that Susan knew.

Hugh told them the story of the day he stopped by due to Dolly's request for help. How he did not enter her house and last, how she was dressed and what she did. Then from start to finish he began and ended the truth about Dolly's fiancée, how he had come to work for them, re-written the amount on checks and embezzled over eight thousand dollars, how when confronted he warned he would see Hugh lose Dolly's rented land and encourage her to rent the land to his buddy, Kane Alberson.

"Shane Boyer looked me straight in the eye when I asked him what he intended to do about the stolen funds and said, "nothing." He said I had far more to lose than him, meaning Dolly's farm I rent, but I had no idea you would come in to this picture, Mr. Tolison and if my integrity is on the line, I have done nothing wrong and it is now time my wife and I leave this meeting that switched from my purchasing your farm to being called up on lewd acts I neither considered doing and certainly did not do."

Tolison's face flushed red, Hugh's countenance was a sickish white. For once Kane Alberson was an observer with the good sense to keep his mouth shut. He was learning the mettle of three men.

Tolison was standing. "I understand what you are saying, Hugh. Now Kane wanted consideration as to purchasing the land if you chose to back out on the deal. I understand what you are saying about Boyer is truth and I believe he has to be accountable and return the money and if he does not, it is up to Aaron to look into the matter. Last time I checked, each account is insured by the Federal Government up to a certain amount and I know that eight thousand plus figure is covered." He turned to Kane. "I'm sorry, Kane that I brought you into Hugh's personal business but you two are the same age, have the same interest and you both know these things happen and a man has to stay on his game to control them."

Kane grinned good naturedly at his number one encourager and client to the ginning industry. "I just wanted to buy your land, Tolly."

"Well," Tolison replied, "Looks like Hugh beat you to it. I'm sure he'll bring his produce to you, anyway."

Kane reached across and took Susan's hand. "Good to see you, Susan. You look lovely and aging gracefully." He shook Hugh's hand, their eyes sending a message; we're letting it rest for now. "See you later, Tolly, Aaron."

An hour later, Susan and Hugh left the bank with the deed to the Tollison Farm a promise. The back of Hugh's jacket was soaking wet and Susan's posture was more rigid than when she first arrived. In the truck, Hugh said, "I feel like I've been run over by a train, every car tearing away a piece of my flesh." He pushed a button and felt heat on his cold body. "there's bound to be more reason to life than this."

"That was a frightening experience that an old man would go that far, bringing in Kane when he must know Kane is a threat to every man in this community, pushing his way through, intimidating, bullying." If I were a man I'd feel like punching Mr. Tolison and Kane Alberson."

Mr. Tolison came down the steps of the bank, waving to them as though they'd not just undergone his personal questions. Before thinking it through, Susan was out of the truck, walking fast to catch up with him. "Mr. Tolison, may I ask you a few questions, Sir?"

"Of course, Susan, may I call you that?" He waited for Susan's nod. "Here, come sit in my car, I've had it running a few minutes. This air is cutting, isn't it and the cold seeps through our bones." He motioned and she accepted. Even in old age he was a gentleman intending to open the door for her but she denied that courtesy. They were seated, with him leaning across the steering wheel peering into her face. "Now, what would you like to discuss?"

"Mr. Tolison, you always seemed to be a dignified upright gentleman of our community and yet you took it on yourself to question my husband's accountability; a man who is equally respectful of others and you questioned his integrity before a man who counters what he does every step of the way. Are you aware Kane Alberson demands certain rights to the lives of the men he rents his ground to whether it's his own family holdings or perhaps yours? Everything is done to further his wealth, with no thought to others. That's what happens to your holdings if he takes over."

"Susan," Mr. Tolison said her name gently, reaching across to touch her hand, briefly. "Do you know what lies beneath the statement you just made?" He thought out his words before uttering one. "Those men make the decision to abide by Kane's rules."

"They have no choice, they know land is scarce and someone else will take it if they don't agree to buy all their chemicals and seed from Kane, which is profit in his pocket and he charges above regular price."

"Let me say it again, Susan, they choose to go along with him. If they choose then who can go against it?" He gave a weary sigh. "My dear, there's power in number. Those men should unite and discuss the impropriety of Kane's actions but they don't, I think it's easier to fold up and go along with him, no matter how greedy he becomes. Understand this, people have a choice. Your husband had a choice and he chose the right one. I know Dolly is a handful. She has been all her life."

"But you would have gone along with Kane's rules?" Susan was preparing to leave the car.

"No," Mr. Tolison smiled. "Kane and I would have had a discussion. Now, Susan, I've enjoyed our talk. When you and Hugh purchase the acreage, don't dismiss me and neglect to come see me."

Susan's smile flashed as she opened the door. "You are a gentleman, Mr. Tolison. Thanks for listening."

He nodded. "You are quite a lady, Susan Preston. Tell Hugh I said you do him proud."

"Was that wise, your talk with Mr. Tolison? Hugh asked once she was settled back into the truck.

"There was no harm in it. I felt you were ready to turn your offer to buy back in, based on the rudeness of the situation. If I'm going to sign my name on the dotted line and be responsible for half the cost of the land purchase I feel I have a right to my questions."

"I wouldn't have it any other way. We've always stood together. We're a team." He seemed weary beyond the hour of the day's demand. "Do you want to catch a bite or just go home?"

"Let's pick up something." They were quiet, picking up food and riding home. "I'm so drained there's nothing I want to do the rest of the day," she said. "My mind and my body are exhausted."

Changing from the dress slacks, Susan glanced longingly at the bed, the spread pulled to the top, the pillows covered by matching shams and she wanted to crawl into that haven. She and Hugh had allowed themselves to become estranged, they had forgotten the 'whither thou goest I will go in their hearts' though in the confines of the bank on a business deal they had stood together. Right now she longed for Hugh's arms around her, the comfort she counted on when all else went wrong.

Her jeans lay on the chair, a simple thing to call her husband. He would sense her need but the rift between them had deepened to a chasm deeper than they'd expected and neither was wont to climb out first. Tears welled up to be wiped away but the stream would not stop. Had she been jealous? She couldn't say but frustrated that Hugh waited until he feared a backlash to tell her of a time he had done nothing wrong but might be used against him. Would Kane or Alex spread the story that could unravel a good man's future, especially now in his run for the school board position?

"Susan," Hugh opened the bedroom door, "everything's on the table, are you ready to eat?" And then he saw her standing between the bed and the bathroom, tears flooding down her face, her jeans in her hand. "What's wrong?" He came into the room, took the jeans, tossing them as he pulled her roughly against his body. "It's going to be all right," he whispered into her ear, as he began to rock her; just a small movement, as one would a sleeping child in a cradle that whimpered in the night. "We've made it through some hurdles before and this is just one more. We've just learned another lesson, that's all. We can never let go of each other because that and God's love is what pulls us through."

With a sweep of one hand, he managed to throw the spread back onto the pillows, sinking onto the bed, kicking off his boots as he pulled her down beside him. "I've missed you, Susan. Missed the honey in your voice that touch you lay on me each morning when it's time to get up and knowing every night you are mine; for a time I don't have to share you with your Mom, our kids, no one. You are mine."

He was removing every shred of her clothing as he whispered in her ear from that spooning position; she was liquid in his arms completely unaware how he untangled from his own clothes to make love to her. She only knew the hours had been few they were estranged in spirit but seemed an eternity. He did not hurry, she did not want him to, and when their love was consummated still they lay there for a time, sated and content promising silently to not let small things get in the way of their love, again.

Chapter 14

*S*chool Board Election the papers touted, Who Are You Going To Vote For? Pictures of Hugh and Kane circulated the small country town and the contest was on. If Kane or Alex had told anyone about the day in the bank with Tolison, Susan or Hugh had not heard. "Maybe Kane's saving it until last minute," Susan whispered into Hugh's ear. They were riding a float with the Senior Citizens. The school band was marching in front of the float and between their trailer and Kane's was another area band. Kane's float read Veterans of Foreign Wars. "He's throwing out candy," Susan whispered again. "That's a good idea." Hugh groaned.

"I need to be in the field, not sitting here on a bale of hay soliciting votes."

Susan smiled as though he'd said the most beguiling words of his life. "Smile," she said between clenched teeth, "public image is everything. Your platform is children are the continuation of our lives; Kane's is I can love your children, because he can't claim one of his own. Now, if you smile I think you have a greater chance of winning."

She thought he groaned again. "Was that groan audible or am I now hearing your spirit speak?"

"I don't know how I got into this?"

"Your friends say they admire your relationship with your own children and with that said they know you will keep their interest at heart concerning the education of all children in this school district."

"Who tells you such things?"

She smiled. "You know who tells me, the same one's that asked you to run and stayed with the issue until you gave in." She poked him in the ribs. "You know you will do your best and they do, too."

"This is it." Susan's smile spread across her face, lighting her eyes and making her appear younger. "Today is history for the Preston's. Old Dad's going to gain a seat on the local school board."

"I sure hope you don't have to eat crow," Hugh teased. "Now, what am I supposed to do?"

"Word has it Kane's already down at the precinct, meeting the voters and trying to swing things his way. What do you suppose his goal is, not having a child he can call his own, why does he want to win?"

"Whatever Kane does is to further his agenda in the community, to look good, a man of essence and integrity. May I ask who is feeding you such tidbits as to Kane's presence and trying to win the voters?"

"For one, your son," Susan replied. "Barkley saw him on the way to school. Sophia checked it out and said it's true, Dad better get down there and not to linger." Susan laughed. "At least the kids are for you."

"I don't know what I could do to change anything, Susan. This is all new to me."

"Maybe go down to the coffee shop, shake hands with those fellows, then step out on the street and encourage those you meet to vote. Tell them it's important no matter who they vote for to let the children know they care."

He shook his head, a weariness settling into his body. "I think they've ask the wrong Preston to run."

End of day, Hugh was declared the winner. He and Kane had shook hands in front of the school early that morning and Hugh had returned home. Kane had spent the day canvassing the voters. Hugh had ignored everyone's suggestions and spent his day on the farm. But the cameras in the hands of the local news tracked him down. "What've you got to say, Mr. Preston?"

Pausing from his work, sweat on his brow and a shovel in his hand, Hugh smiled and said, "I want to thank the people who voted for me. I will strive to keep their interest in first place as I serve in the position they've elected me to. As I said before, our children are our legacy. What we do today has an intricate bearing on their future. Training a child does begin at home but then we entrust them to the school system for twelve years of their formative life, we must see that it is always structured according to their needs to live in a fast changing world. Thank you again for all who have faith in me."

"Well said, Mr. Preston." The camera faded away with the interviewing reporter shaking Hugh's hand.

The phone rang at six that evening. An excited Caroline congratulated her dad on his winning the empty chair on the school board. "It carries a lot of weight and responsibility, Dad," she said. "Who knows, they might even elect you president."

Hugh winced. "I believe that position is filled, Caroline and I'm very grateful it is."

"Well, Dad, we're working on giving you another title, anyway." Caroline was laughing and Oliver in the background could be heard joining in. "Is Mom, handy, Dad? If she is put the phone on speaker."

"I'm here," Susan said, "listening to the joy in your laughter. It sounds good."

"What do you think about Dad's title, Mom?"

Susan glanced at Hugh, eyebrows raised as she shrugged. "I'm not sure what that is."

"Well, Mom, Dad, how does Grandpa sound, or Grand daddy? Whatever dad prefers and Mom-Maw or Grandmother? Are you all okay with that?"

"What?" There was an instant look of concern on Susan's face but she masked it with a lilt in her voice. "Are you saying you are pregnant?" She gripped Hugh's hand. "You should see Dad's expression."

"Are you happy for us? We are just over the moon," Caroline chortled. "We are pregnant."

Sophia came into the room in time to hear the news. "Two scores for the Preston-Devoe families. Or should I say that differently, Devoe-Preston.

Congratulations. Our parents are speechless." Sophia laughed, "They probably think they're too young to be gramma and grampa."

Barkley heard the commotion and came down the hall from his room. "What's going on?"

"Is that Barkley," Caroline asked from the phone. "Let me tell him."

Barkley took the phone. "Tell me what?"

"I'm going to have a little baby, Bub. What do you think of that?"

"Did you check with Doctor Jeffries, Caroline. Should you be having a baby?" Barkley, ever mindful of Caroline's health issue had asked the question circling Susan and Hugh's mind. They listened for the answer.

"Oh, Bub, why would doctor Jeffries care. Oliver and I are so happy. Just think, you'll be an uncle."

Barkley hand the phone to Sophia and escaped back to his room before the tears welled up in his eyes overran their basin. "Don't let her get sick over this," he whispered a prayer to God. "Please."

"I just found out today, guys and you're the first to know. Oliver's family is next. Isn't it great?"

"Didn't anyone tell you to use protection?" Sophia giggled as she ask. "Better watch that stuff next time."

"Only you, Sophia," her sister chortled. "We are so happy. It must have happened immediately."

Embarrassed, Hugh backed away. "I'm leaving you on that one, Caroline. I love you. You all take care."

"See you soon, Dad. Love you."

Later, they all came together for the evening meal, due to the election there were no activities.

"Why's everyone so gloomy?" Sophia asked. "I keep waiting for something, somebody to say what fun a baby will be but there's a death dirge at this table." No one spoke. Barkley's head was down as he studied his hands in his lap. "Bub, for heaven's sakes. Caroline is not going to die. Women have babies every day and she wants this one so badly. Can't you all be happy for her, for Heaven's sakes?"

"I went to Internet and googled women with leukemia having babies." Barkley whispered. "What if she isn't pregnant? The article says women with leukemia who have received treatment like Caroline has probably are infertile and can't have a baby. What if it's something else?" Tears slipped from Barkley's eyes, falling onto his clenched hands. "It said in a case study twelve out of thirty seven women died and if she makes it through at some time in the pregnancy she might have severe bleeding which would cause spontaneous abortion."

Sophia's attention now riveted on Barkley. "What else. You are holding something back."

Reluctant, Barkley whispered, "The consequence of Caroline's treatment could cause damage to the baby. The words were potential fetal problems with required termination of the pregnancy."

"I feel horrible,"Sophia muttered. "I wish I'd never said anything. I'm sorry, Mom, Dad, Barkley."

Hugh cleared his throat. "There's only one thing we can do and it is the utmost important thing we will do today. We have to take this to God in our prayers. Each day, every night, we will ask God to cover Caroline's pregnancy, if there's danger or harm to the baby or Caroline we will ask him to remove the problem. Now, let us pray believing and remember there's never an earnest prayer been said but that the devil moves in and tries to take away our faith and put doubt in place of God's mercy and our hope." He opened his hand to receive Susan's on one side and Barkley's on the other. Sophia's hands were joined to Barkley's and her mother's.

"Heavenly Father," Hugh's voice broke. "We come to you with fear in our hearts. Lord, we wait for you to replace that fear with hope as we ask your mercy to cover Caroline with your hand, to hold her close that no disease or side effect will touch her through this time of pregnancy. Lord, we ask you to strengthen her body and in so doing make the little baby that grows there strong; strength to stand against any harm the chemicals used against Caroline's leukemia might have left. In the name of Jesus we ask all that could be harmful be removed from her body and only healthy tissue and cell take over. Lord we really don't know how to pray but you know our hearts and you know the need, we give these to you now, Lord, for this one we love. Let your blessing reign over Caroline, the baby and Oliver; For we ask this in your Holy name as we give you praise and honor, Lord, and we love you. Amen."

The months progressed along with Caroline's expanding belly. She was delighted with every movement. "The first time, Dad," she said reaching to take his hand on an early spring day when they were sitting in the swing. "The first time it was like a butterfly movement. I couldn't believe it, that soon?" Even now her voice rose in happiness, "the fact our baby was a living being swimming around in there, just blew my mind. I remembered that verse of scripture where God said I knew you before I formed you in your mother's womb. Before you were born, I set you apart." Caroline laid her head against her dad's shoulder. Hugh shifted and brought his arm around her.

"Don't guess Oliver minds old dad sitting with his first born, does he?"

Caroline giggled. "Dad, his mother still sits as close to him and holds his hand when they talk and he likes it, so, no, he doesn't care, besides that he's trying to beat Barkley on some Big Box game they're playing, whatever that is." They both chuckled. "I hope Barkley lets him win at least one game."

"So you have no fears?" He had to hear it from her.

"Well Dad, Oliver and I gave it to the Lord. We can't take it back, besides that there's all kinds of people praying for us and this baby." She leaned over to kiss his cheek. "I need to see if they'll let me set the table. They ran me out. They said, "Your Dad is probably waiting for you, were you Dad?""

"Yes, Babe, I was. I'm glad you took the time. I've missed you, but so have the rest."

"You're the best, Dad." Tears shined bright in Caroline's eyes. "Anymore, I even cry when I'm happy."

It was farming time again. A new man had signed on taking the place of Shane Boyer. If word was right, the gossip vine said he'd had to take a few months away, seemed he'd not only embezzled from Hugh and Susan's farm account but once that became public, three former employees came forward. Boyer had been living high on other people's money a good while. Tolison didn't bother Hugh, the papers were signed and the land was now under Preston Farms. Dolly made a few appearances, wanting to break the rent lease Hugh had on her ground, but Tolison being friend to Dolly's daddy and somewhat of a benefactor to Dolly spoke with Susan. "Tell your husband to keep the contract entact. Dolly will be breaking contract with the next person she chooses and if it's Kane Alberson she'll just step out of the fryin' pan into the fire, so to speak. At least with her farm under Hugh's belt she's dealing with an honest man. I like Kane Alberson but he does play under the table and I don't like that."

"So there you have it," Susan said, "I'm just relaying the message." She grinned, "But, I'm very watchful, I catch that half naked woman too close to my man and I'll scratch her eyes out."

"Would that be Tolison?" Hugh replied. "I never thought a filly like you to be seeing an older man."

Susan snorted. "You tell me why he calls me to relay messages when he could speak with you."

"I don't know there's something about you; I even heard through Frank that Kane Alberson thinks you are a fine woman. So if anyone's eyes are open and watching, little filly, that would be me. Be careful." To make the words stick, Hugh reached out and pulled her to him. "Never forget who you belong to, woman."

"No, sir, Rhett, darling, kiss a girl like that she ain't likely to forget." She started toward the house and then came back to where he was checking something on the tractor. "Why would Kane Alberson make that remark about me, Hugh? We don't travel the same circles and about all I know of him is his name."

"Do you ever take time to look in the mirror, Susan?" His eyes were warm as honey, delighted in stopping to study his wife. "You make me proud. You're a lady and my love. I don't ever want to share what we have with another person. I love you; God gave you to me and I'm happy and blessed. When I say my wife, it means everything."

"I don't think you've ever said anything that nice to me before, Hugh." Tears brightened her eyes.

"Then shame on me," Hugh replied. "I'm ashamed of myself." He grinned. "I'll try to do better."

On tip-toe she kissed his cheek. "It goes both ways, Hugh, but I tell you all the time."

"Yes, you do. I have taken it for granted in the past thinking you knew how I felt and I apologize."

"Yeah?"

"Yeah," he said, with a gentle slap on her behind. "You better go in the house before we get in trouble."

It was the first of June. Sweat trickled down Hugh's cheeks, ran onto his shirt collar and his back. Farming was in full swing, the crops were up and looking good. To think only weeks back they were turning the earth, soil glistening beneath the sun just waiting for seed to go in the ground. Now, Hugh watched the tubing come to life as water rushed from the well to the end of the line where the tubing was tied off ready for holes to be punched to feed rows of plants. They had watched the sky, listened to the weather forecast and finally decided to start irrigating when the forecast was without rain.

In the distance he saw Kane's men doing the same, punching holes. He listened to the sound of the motors for the irrigation equipment, a solid drone from field to field as far as eye could see. No one admitted to drowning his beans the year before, but he had a strong suspicion it was Kane's men. Who else would be near his field, now that it was public the land he'd sought Kane had undermined and gained control but it hadn't worked with Tolison. To this day, Hugh decided only God had whispered in Tolison's ear. The question was why Alberson would drown out his neighbor's crop.

April and May had enough rain to save on irrigating but he had a feeling from here on out that would not be the case. There had been some replant on lower ends due to the constant spring rains, which was a headache in harvest but you worked with what you got and this time it was rain that stopped and apparently now could turn to drought.

They were ready to move to the William's place and he always had an uneasy feeling going there. The Kirkland kid no longer spent evenings with Sophia. Sophia said she and Thorn were a couple, whatever that meant. He hadn't seen the kids mother since August of last year but the backlash of that visit to say he'd have Frank take care of the need for a new septic tank had backfired on him when Boyer set the wheels in motion saying Hugh had sexually harassed Dolly. Actually, Hugh guessed it was the other way round. Maybe he wouldn't even set foot on that land today, there were other task ahead.

A neighbor to the South had asked if he'd stop by. Hugh turned the punching of holes in the tubing over to the men. It was a good time to make the visit. This was the only field they'd had to replace tubing due to the fault of the manufacturer. The remaining had come from another supplier and apparently was without flaw. For a minute he wondered if Kane had received some of the inferior product, too.

He didn't know why their lives kept bumping into each other. Now with Sophia and Thorn dating it couldn't get any better even if Kane had no part in raising the boy. As far as Thorn was concerned his last name was Lansky and Sam was his father. It was not discussed, it was assumed everyone agreed.

The day after Hugh was elected to the school board it was said Herm James was stepping down as President of the school board due to health reasons and the first runner up, which was Kane Alberson, would now take the empty seat on the school board rather than the community go through another local election.

Aaron Copeland came out of his shop, having seen Hugh driving down the lane. Extending his hand, he said, "Come on in. Can I get you something to drink?" Hugh shook his head no and waited for Mr. Copeland to begin the conversation. The man cleared his throat. "Son, you're a lot younger than me, but I hear tell, through that infernal grape vine that you've had a number of run ins with Kane Alberson and usually you come out the victor. Now I have this problem." He was motioning as they walked for Hugh to come into the inner office and have a seat. "Here's what it is. I don't know if you are aware Kane owns land in our area, lot of land. Sometimes though, down here, our drainage system has cut our land into divisions we didn't really want but we do need the drainage our big ditches afford." Hmm. He cleared his throat, "Just as we need our turn rows and roads along the ditch banks that access our land." Hmm. He cleared his throat again. "This is difficult, what I'm going to say."

Hugh leaned forward, "Mr. Copeland, if you are worried I'll pass this conversation on to other farmers you can drop that concern. And I might add there's probably nothing you say that hasn't been said before or happened to me personally. "Three times Kane Alberson tried to purchase acreage that I'd already made a deal on. Twice he succeeded but the third time, the older gentleman wasn't having his two handed ways."

"So you don't like him either?"

"I didn't say that, what I'm saying is I don't trust him. We'll never be best friends so that might answer your question."

"Well, it makes me hot under the collar his disregard for my land with my crop on it when I allow his men to drive through on our ditch bank because there's no other way to get into his fields. What they've done is brought something wide enough to knock down crop and run over it. Ever so often he brings in equipment and disc it good but there again is a problem. If it rains we have erosion."

Copeland seemed to want to say more but the two were new acquaintance and sharing a road to property, he stood more to lose if what he said got back to Alberson. "I don't like having to tip-toe around someone when they actually have no rights but I'm trying to allow the man to get to his field." He took a deep breath, "I might as well tell you, he bragged about gaining those first two pieces of land. He said he paid money under the table. Something we all don't have and if I did, you can bet the government would be down on me in a minute."

"I can't figure out why he's always finding ways to try to upset my progress."

Copeland studied Hugh a moment. "I've just met you and you strike me as an even natured man, taking care of what yours and not infringing on another man, but Alberson is out for himself, he'll use you or me to climb higher and he's a man with wealth behind his name, his daddy and Granddad. It's greed, there's always someone out there to get us."

Hugh stuck out his hand, "I'll be going, Mr. Copeland." Hugh crossed the floor to the doorway.

"Son?" Copeland lingered, letting his voice carry to the door where Hugh had his hand on the door knob. "I've had a bit of bad luck come my way in the last few days, my cancer markers came back with a certain degree of serious problem and I'm going to have to start treatment again, what do you think about renting my land, cash rent next year and if I can't hold up to get this year's crop out, do you think maybe you could oversee it, help get it done." At that the man's face crumbled.

Alarmed, Hugh hurried to his side. "Back up there and sit down, Mr. Copeland." Hugh shook his head, "I apologize I had no idea you were having health issues, you're the picture of health. How old are you?"

"I'll be seventy, come December twenty first this year. I should've retired when cancer first hit me but I was strong in body and decided I could beat it, but the treatment slowed me down and weakened my system. That's my opinion." He gave a deep sigh of melancholy. "You probably know my son was killed in a car accident last year and that's worse on a body than anything I could ever have imagined. With that happening, he left no teenage sons or daughters and our family has no one to carry on in farming. I've heard good things about you, Hugh, and I wanted to get a feel about you before I ask."

"Sir, I would be happy; I'd be honored to farm your land and I'll help you whenever you need help, starting today. You just call me and give me time to work in whatever is needed, but if it's a dire need I'll come immediately.

"That's how it happened," he was telling Susan two hours later. "Are you all right with it?" He waited for her to consider the miles, the need for another tractor and another employee. "I told him I'd see what you thought and if you're against it then we will break our verbal agreement of today and he agreed." He waited but she seemed to be thinking something over. "What is it, Susan? Spit it out."

"Sounds like you'll be right in Kane Alberson's path, even on Mr. Copeland's land." She sighed. "That field road could become a well of contention. I know you've heard it before, Hugh. Kane has skimmed too many farmers around here, taking their land, not being careful with his farming practices, charging his own people higher prices. It's becoming an unhealthy atmosphere. They're hurting. Someday he's going to push one of those farmers too far and in haste there could even be bloodshed."

"I heard it, but if anything," he studied the problem, his mind trying to wrap around what she was saying, it was true, he'd heard it but he was already too far into the deal with a man who had health issues to back out now. "How about if we think of killing him," he tried for a teasing tone, "we do it with kindness, no weapon except the fruit of the spirit, maybe that's what Kane needs more than anything. Honestly, I want to help Mr. Copeland and in helping him it also helps us. Is that wrong?"

"I just pray this is God's will, Hugh. I know we're supposed to help others but we already have a lot to deal with and I can't imagine Kane will make our lives any easier, as it seems he's always in the picture."

Looking back, Hugh realized Susan's opinion hit too close to home. There was no avoiding the truth. They hadn't even discussed it further. When Sophia graduated in May, Thorn was there, in the pictures made outside the school building and afterwards at home helping her pack a hamper of food to take to the lake for an all-night celebration. And in one picture, Kane Alberson was standing on the fringe watching Thorn. Hugh had left the field early to join in all of the festivities but he was none too happy to think a class of seventeen and eighteen year olds were going to the lake unchaperoned.

"Sophia, I don't like this one bit. Why aren't there adults supervising this event?"

"Why they are, Dad. The teachers wouldn't let us go alone."

"Thorn, is that true?" He watched the boy shuffle around before answering. "You don't seem to know, now do you?" Hugh realized he was making the young man uncomfortable. "So what's the answer?"

"As far as I know, there was no mention of chaperones until Wendy Shief and Morgan Dillard's fathers heard about it and they put their foot down. Now this just happened a couple hours ago and what I heard was they will be there." Embarrassed he added, "I also heard a few teachers are going."

"Dad, it will be all right." Sophia was giving him that look that said please don't say anymore.

"Yes, it will because your mother and I will be there, too, once Barkley's with the grandparents."

"Well, maybe the school board can attend," Sophia quipped. Thorn had turned aside unnoticed by Sophia but Hugh made the connection and he'd already embarrassed the boy enough.

"Young lady," Hugh's feathers were immediately ruffled, "That tone of voice will keep you home."

"Dad, you're treating me like a child."

"No, I'm treating you like a daughter I value and don't want anything happening to. I'll see you later."

It appeared there were surprises for all, in a hasty last minute decision, the school board had been notified and three out of the six staunch board members and wives had made an appearance plus Kane Alberson was in attendance with the pretty little Sherry Newell from Memphis. Susan and one other wife had been intimidated in the beginning by her title, Miss Cotton, but she had proven to be a worthy friend to the small town community, especially interested in Susan's outlook on cotton's future as she said, "I work for the Cotton council and I'm always looking for another woman's views."

"Do you and Kane plan to be married?" Dorothy Albrighton was neither shy nor intimidated by anyone. "You do know his history with women is not so great, don't you? You seem to be a nice person."

"Honey, Kane Alberson and me?" Sherry practically giggled. "We are like oil and water. If that should happen, it would surprise us both. What we are, is this, we are friends that don't lie to each other. He's made a mess of his life too many times and he keeps trying to sate his granddaddy's expectations of him but sometimes I think he's just diggin' the hole deeper. I just don't want to get married, yet."

Together again, Susan thought, her eyes meeting Hugh's across the mammoth bon fire. Again.

Chapter 15

$\mathcal{S}$eptember rolled onto the calendar. Summer rains had been few. They'd ended up having to irrigate more than anticipated. The drought was opening the cotton early. The men were worn and ready for a rest when the sky turned gray on the twenty seventh day of the month. Bert grinned, taking his straw hat from his head and rounding it in his hands as the first drops fell. "Lord a mercy," he chortled, "that rain does feel good." Glancing Hugh's way, he said, "Sorry 'bout that, Hugh, but we're all about tuckered out. I just want to go home and sit down and look at Leonie." They watched together as the other hands drove their equipment into the farm headquarters'.

"So you say, we're going to get old man Copeland's crop out, for him? Heard he has cancer."

"We've kept it quiet, Bert, but we'll be farming his ground next year." Bert nodded but Hugh saw the wheels turnin' in his friend and employees head. "Yeah, I know, Alberson uses that road to get to his fields. We'll have to talk to the younger ones, talk some patience in their heads, no foolishness from us." Three of the fellows were walking toward them. "But we'll wait til closer to time for that talk."

"Well, I'm glad Tab and Grant came back. At least they know their way round what we farm."

"Everybody help lock up, be sure everything's turned off and we're leaving the shop in good order. Susan's got the pay checks ready and we'll knock off until Monday and then we'll hit it hard. If the reports believable, we're not supposed to have heavy rain, just enough to slow us down and let us rest."

It was after four by the time they cleared the lot. Barkley had arrived home from school in time to have his daily chit-chat with Tab and Grant. "Dad," he said as rain spattered the dust and they were walking to the house. "Tab said word has it you're going to farm Mr. Copeland's ground, how would he know?"

Hugh groaned. There could be only one way. Mr. Copeland had said he'd be going to the farm office signing papers as to Hugh renting the ground, "just in case anything should go wrong with my treatment," he'd said. "Well, Son, I meant to tell you but I guess Mr. Copeland's had to do some legal work and the word got out before I had a chance."

"What's the difference in cash rent and crop rent, Dad?" Hugh winced and stared hard at his son.

"Is nothing sacred? How in the world does everything hit the grapevine so soon?" Barkley shrugged, waiting. "Cash rent is when a farmer pays the one he rents the land from a set amount of money per acre and Crop rent is when the one who owns the land pays a percentage of what it takes to produce the crop. In crop rent there's other incidentals like sharing the maintenance and upkeep of the ground."

"Can you afford to do Cash rent, Dad? That's a lot of money."

"In this case, Son, I can't afford not to. Mr. Copeland asked me to farm his land as he's got health problems. It's my hope it will all go smoothly."

"I know but Tab says you'll have to deal with Kane Alberson running through your fields."

"Tab said that, did he?" Hugh rubbed the back of his neck. "Man, I'm so ready to get a bath and sit."

"I know how to take care of Kane Alberson, Dad."

"Son, look at me." Hugh laid a hand on Barkley's shoulder. "We will have no problem with Mr. Alberson." Barkley muttered, yessir and walked away. It chafed Hugh's spirit people knowing his business. "I need a mini-vacation before we start harvest," he mumbled as he washed up. Susan was hanging up the house phone.

"Guess where we're headed, Rhett, darling?" She danced a little jig in front of him. "Our girl is headed to the hospital. Gramma's got the bag packed and we may be holding a little Preston-Devoe in our arms come morning." She saw the sag of Hugh's shoulders. "You look a little ragged there, Partner."

"Cut the stuff, Scarlet. I'm so tired I can't think and just found out the world knows my business."

Susan laughed. "Hurry up and eat, then you can get your shower while I pack Barkley's set of clothes and we'll be on our way. Maybe you can take a nap while I drive."

"How much older is Barkley than me, anyway?" Hugh sit down at the table, waited for her to be seated and studied Barkley's empty chair. "You'd think I delivered the worst ultimatum ever to him and don't ask." Now his eyes held hers. "Say grace, Susan. I'm thankful but I'm out of words."

An hour later, Susan had them on the Interstate, was calling Kathryn to tell her the news and her own parents to say Sophia would be staying with them the weekend, much as she wanted to be there for the birthing Sophia was committed to a school activity. Hugh leaned his seat back as far as it would go, marveling at the multi-tasking genie at the wheel. What would he do without her were his last thoughts as he closed his eyes and slept the two and a half hours drive with images of Caroline dancing behind his eyelids as a fear wrapped around his heart that she or the baby was in danger… and still he slept.

Barkley watched the scenery along the roadside. Today was either going to be the worst ever or maybe he'd hold the little baby and see Caroline's contented smile. The family had prayed in every prayer that both would come through; the baby being born with no ill effects and only happiness thereafter.

They had passed Alberson Holdings where it was said the patriarch of the family held tight to the purse strings. Barkley had no idea how old the man was but he looked ancient in his three piece black suit riding the streets in that long nosed Lincoln town car. Then there was the old man's son and his son, Kane Alberson. No one deserved the rights Alberson took away from others. Yeah, Tab told him some of the man's escapades. It irritated Barkley that his father always wanted to pass the olive leaf when devious deserved devious. He thought of Sophia's boyfriend, if rumor was right and Thorn was Kane Alberson's son, he pitied Thorn even if he carried another man's name.

Fourteen was a hard age. His voice had settled somewhere between baritone and bass and he hoped it didn't go into bass and stay. He could carry a tune as the saying went, but he didn't want the church people looking his way when the regular song leader was absent. That was not his calling. Caroline Dawn was the one made the people happy when she played piano but Sophia, though musically inclined had rather play her flute than the piano. That left Susan, his mother, glutton for punishment, he thought, she had no voice to say no. His father often reminded her, "Should I go before you, Susan, you are going to have to learn to say, "no." You can't be nice to everyone and be talked into loading yourself up for everyone else, including me."

"Don't go before me," she would say in that wispy soft voice. "I don't know what I'd do."

Barkley considered what he was hearing. He knew his mother was a strong woman and she knew it. She played second fiddle to the whole family, seeing that everything ran smoothly. They, meaning Hugh and Susan as he often labeled them when he was silently working through the family happenings; they kept a lot to themselves, but sometimes things like Sophia's escapades spilled over into their laps. Sophia was coming around and it was time. She'd be going to college next year. She graduated all right, but kept too many ties to school, helping the Cheer team, the theatre group and that one was Sophia, all right. Grand Diva, he labeled Sophia, while Caroline was the gentle warrior, yes, she led the pack but the pack didn't know it. By coming around, he meant Sophia was finally seeing Dad was not her enemy, Grandmother Kathryn was not her best ally and Thorn was a good person, she'd be lucky if she got him.

He hoped he didn't meet a girl he really liked until he got his head on straight whether he wanted to go to college or stay with Dad on the farm. Dad said if he stayed, they would need more land and land was scarce, "they just don't make more of it, Son, we've got to work with what's available." Available? Barkley's silent person snorted, with Kane Alberson scooping up every acre that came available, what was the chance of him farming alongside his dad?

Fourteen years old, thinking ahead and not knowing what life would bring, his thoughts came back around, to Caroline. He liked Oliver but if Caroline died, he might have to rethink why she died. Fervishly, Barkley began to pray, closing his eyes to the world around him. Please God he whispered, take care of Caroline and the baby and don't let anything happen to either one. Thank you. Amen. Barkley slipped into a voidless sleep.

From the visor mirror, Susan saw Barkley nod off and in the front, Hugh's gentle rustle of breathing now and then reminded her miles were slipping behind them and in front lay the fact Caroline was having their first grandchild. "Oh, Lord, my God," she whispered, "Let it all be good. I praise you, Lord."

"All right, troop, it's time to walk and roll. Our Sweet Caroline is probably waiting for us to pop that baby right out into the open and begin life as Mommie. Come on, hop out, let's go." She watched her two men unwind their long legs, stretch and get out of the car. "Lord, help us, you two are slow."

"Can it, woman." Hugh wondered that she could have such enthusiasm. "You're gonna be a gramma. That means you're too old for all that clatter and laughter. Just think they'll call you Gramma."

The two hours seemed twenty until the doctor appeared to call "Devoe family?" Allistar and Ceciley had arrived and came to their feet; Ceciley holding tightly to Susan's hand. The doctor's smile enveloped the family. With a sigh of relief it was quite visible on their faces the strain they'd been under. "All went well," he said, and turned as if to leave, then as suddenly turned back, "hey, I bet you want to know what we've got in there, don't you?" He laughed, good naturedly. "Well, he's a perfect little boy, got all ten fingers and toes and arrived mad and hungry's my guess. He didn't just cry, he really cried."

There was a lot of hugging going on, but Hugh managed to say to the doctor, "Is Caroline all right?" The doctor feeling the intensity of the man's hand on his arm, stood perfectly still, studying the one he guessed to be Caroline's father.

"Yes, Caroline came through fine. God has been with her through *this* pregnancy."

Barkley, old soul that he was waited behind the grandparents, listening to their comments, as he watched his mother's face. What was she thinking?

Once she had a little boy that did not live? Mentally he came to grips with himself. Susan would be overjoyed for Caroline but somewhere in there, a moment would come when pain hit her heart...and Susan would replace the pain with gladness, that's who she was.

"Oh, Daddy," Caroline waited for Hugh's kiss on her forehead. "Daddy, we've named him Oliver James Devoe. How do you feel about that?" Caroline's eyes were luminous with unshed tears. "Daddy, I feel like I'm going to cry, I'm so happy." She waited for the nurse to return with her baby. The little bed would be rolled in and she and Oliver could keep him by their side.

"Oliver James," From behind, Ceciley said the name. "It flows, doesn't it, Susan? And Caroline told us that is Hugh's father?" She turned to Hugh. "Isn't it an honor, Hugh? I'm so happy to know part of little Ollie's name will come from you and his grandfather. Oliver James Devo, oh yes, it does flow."

Caroline's eyes were on Hugh. "I loved granddad so much. He was kind and good to all of us. Wasn't he?" Overcome, with this unexpected news, Hugh simply gripped Caroline's hand.

"Now, I feel like I'm going to cry," he said.

Life changed. Susan couldn't put her finger on why, but the moment was when Oliver was born. They had their children and now they were falling in love with their grandchild. Hugh met each day wondering what Caroline was doing and thanking God for bringing her through safely, for Barkley growing into a fine young man and Sophia becoming the sweet young lady he knew was beneath all that desire to do this and that, which sometimes strained them the limit.

Then there were the appointments, the financial needs met and Susan's yearly check up. 'How'd it go?"

"As usual they ran me through a second time, something about the density of tissue. A second mammogram when our insurance probably only pays for one."

"At least we have insurance, some don't but stay healthy, babe. I don't want to see you sick."

"I know."

They went through all the steps. Being grandparents was not that unlike being a parent. Loving a child was easy. Seeing him only on weekends was the hard part. That October the rains came; the drought had ended but the concern of applying chemicals was real, the ground was wet and farmers did not like rutting the ground. Still it was time to harvest the crop they'd worked on all year.

Susan saw the flecks of gray in Hugh's hair and stood before the mirror examining her own.

"Something wrong with you?" Hugh had sit on the bed, watching. "I mean you don't usually stand that long in front of a mirror. "Got a headache?" He pat the bed beside him. "Come over here."

"No, I guess the title, Grammaw fits." She sighed. "We are turning gray. That means age."

Hugh laughed. "I prefer to think it means wisdom. Didn't we hear a sermon preached on that?" He lay back, pulling his feet to the edge of the bed, letting his shoes drop to the floor. "You hear that, it's raining again." He sighed. "I've been out to the shop since six, thinking whether to let the men off or not."

"And you did." Susan grinned. "So what's on the agenda for today, other than our meeting at four?"

"Well, I thought maybe I'd wine and dine my best gal."

"Wish I could go with you. Lucky girl, that one." Hugh's arm went around her and she snuggled close to his side, yawning. "I don't know why but rain on the windows makes you want to go back to bed."

"If I didn't have to take my clothes off, I'd settle for that, but this rainy weather, having to search for fields dry enough to do our work, it's about wore us out. I think the men will appreciate a day off with pay."

Susan was reaching for a throw at the end of the bed, pulling it over their bodies. "How do you feel about the Cotton Boll Ball?" Rising on one elbow she waited for his reply. "I would never have expected the committee to put me in charge, but this far the results have been good. The community has responded and the outer fringe of farmers who bring their produce into our little town have come across in a way that surprised me and we've invited our medical community and they are responding."

"So they want a little excitement in their lives." Hugh hid a yawn behind his hand. "You're right, we are likely to go to sleep and I'll miss my date with that cute little filly I mentioned." Susan kicked at his leg. "Ouch. Well, anyway, it's not often we have the Memphis Philharmonic playing soft music while we dance, now is it? Didn't you say they are providing the music?"

"Rootie and the Hoppers are not exactly the Philharmonic, though I did understand they are exceptional." She giggled. "I was worried a hundred dollars just to attend would stop people from coming, but they have embraced the event. I can't think of a family farm that's not come by and paid the admittance fee, and you should hear the talk of dresses ordered, tux, mind you for the men. It's the event of the year and it has gone beyond our fair city to those tied to our city in some strange way."

"They should be interested and attend, at least contribute, if we don't get the community center repaired and this time have insurance on the building, then the community has no place to meet. I can't believe that was forgotten by the mayor and his aldermen to let that piece of business slip by."

"We are camouflaging the ceiling's leak stains by draping white sheets in those spots. It will look great."

"You are a hit, Mrs. Preston, no one else would have poured their self into seeing the Ball exceeds."

"Well, if it interest you to know this at all, Sherry Newell has been a wealth of information on what to do to make it work. This is part of what she does for the Cotton industry and they are supplying a lot of the back drop that will make this real to those attending."

Hugh yawned. "Why hasn't she married Alberson? Maybe if he was married, she could shape him into a real individual that saw other people have rights and those rights don't all fall under his last name."

"She says they are just good friends but if they married they'd be like oil and water."

"Does he come around for those meetings?"

"No, he doesn't and I've been to every one but since we were asked by Sherry to bring our spouse or significant other to today's meeting, he might be there. I think we need more muscle power for setting up and don't be surprised if there's a more extensive job comes up. It's in the works."

"I did wonder about that, there's usually a reason." He listened to the rain growing stronger on the window pane. "I hope the wind doesn't get too strong and knock the cotton out of the bolls. That's all we need, our crop on the ground." He shut his eyes tight; as if he could shut out that sound…it was fear of losing the crop and not making payments. High wind at this time of year was a dire threat.

"Well, so much for treating you to a nice dinner," Hugh remarked as they walked into the community building. "At least we are on time, aren't we? Is there a reason we aren't unloading the cotton, yet?"

"I can't believe we slept with our feet hanging off the bed, like that. I have a crick in my neck, too." She grinned. "You thought I pulled a lot of cotton in the stalk, but wait til you see what it becomes."

Hugh reached across, his hand massaging her neck, pulling her close when a voice from behind said, "All right, you two, go get a room." Susan laughed but Hugh turned to see Sherry coming through the entrance with Kane right behind. She extended a hand, "Hello, Hugh. I guess the rain brought you in without a problem?" She was nodding to Kane, "Just sit that box of vases over in the corner if you will." And to Hugh, "I'm glad you could make it. Hopefully a few other guys will show up."

Sherry walked to the front of the building, speaking to different ones seated in the first rows. "Hey, everyone, we have lots of work to do. Hey, James, Benny, and Jeremy. Glad you guys came. We have a huge job for you all if you will join Hugh and Kane at the back, I'll let you in on it while Susan starts with what has to be done up here." She motioned to the men, "Come on, let's get this show on the road."

To Susan, she whispered, "Looks like our plan will work. Kane agreed. Now if the men can do the muscle work, we are in business. Did you tell Hugh?" Susan shook her head as Sherry passed on by.

"Here's the deal. You all know a number of years back one of the Alberson homes burned to the ground but for some reason it left those wonderful tall columns standing intact. Well, they will be the back drop for our Cotton Boll ball, sort of a Gone With The Wind theme setting, and we measured to be sure they will fit. It just so happens at the far end where

Susan and the ladies are organizing the decorating of our building, there where the roof was raised architecturally, it is twenty three feet in height."

There were murmurs of why that had been done. "I'm sure the only person who could give us that information would be J.T. Alberson, and I've not gotten him still long enough to hear the story. Anyway, the Alberson's have given permission to use those columns but the problem we were having was how to get them here, today, without having to spend part of our money on moving fees and muscle power." She clapped her hands. "Now, we have you and Kane has a long trailer outside, if you all can get them here, and please, please, please air out the hollow core of those wonders so there's no snakes, please."

The men's expression belied the fact they didn't have a clue as to what was expected, but if Kane did, then they would follow his lead. "Shooo," Sherry was motioning them towards the door, "and hurry back."

Sherry hurried back to where Susan and the ladies were examining the stage, a raised area of some two feet with no step up. "I'm thinking instead of a short step, let's make it two long ones all the way across so that when we have special singings or those theater presentations the steps will be put to good use. And don't worry, I've already ask the lumber company about the wood and they are supplying it."

"Great. Another job for our men. If they work together, we can be finished by night."

"In your dreams," one of the older women called out, "It always takes longer than you think. And we have a question, Kane Alberson never helps with anything. What's he doing here?"

Susan ignored the remark and turned to Sherry, "What do you think about the columns?"

"What's your plan?"

"If we install them, say eight or ten feet apart, they won't be in the way of movement if we should leave them permanently and for theatre, they could become the front entrance with props."

"Sounds good. Let see what the men think." She smiled seeing Mattie and Grace with paint buckets and brushes, "I'm so glad you thought of that. Is the lumber company supplying paint, too?"

"No," Susan grinned. "Hugh is supplying that. We are only painting those bare spots hoping for a match in the paint. Otherwise we'd be here tomorrow and the paint would cost a fortune for this building."

"Well, I brought those vases to wrap, and the burlap too, from another project so they're free."

They were well underway with the decorating when the men returned with the columns.

"Aired and delivered," Jeremy exclaimed. "After we jack sawed them out of Alberson's own museum. I tell you there's history in that building. I think J.T. saved every car he ever owned. They're all there."

"Oh, they're magnificent." Sherry was thrilled to see there were no burn marks, just white columns. "Tell them the plan, Susan." But Susan heard the women whispering "she didn't answer our question."

For some reason the three men stepped behind Hugh and Kane while Susan ask their opinion on the location. Then Jeremy and Benny being the youngest went up into the attic, vouched for the placement of the rafters, reinforced their stability and directed the placement of the columns. Hugh and Kane strained under the weight of each until Hugh made a call to two of his men asking if any were free to come to the community center for an hour's job and he would gladly pay for their time.. To his amazement, all arrived and in two hours the columns were set firmly in place and the men denied payment for their time saying it was good to be of help.

It was midnight when Susan and Hugh finished their showers and climbed into bed. "I can't believe this," Hugh stared at the hands on the clock. "The work was hard but working with the people from the community was worth it all. You'll never believe Kane even spoke decently to me before leaving."

"What did he say? I was so busy trying to direct what had to be done, I didn't hear."

"I quote, he said, "Preston, a man's employees must think highly of their boss to give of their time freely." Hugh grinned, "Of course by that he was thinking he'd steal them away, if possible."

"They did stay, didn't they? I thanked them for painting the columns. Of course when Bert came, Leona was with him. She is fantastic with how to sit up tables and the arrangements of cotton in the stalk in burlap wrapped vases for the center of each table. She showed the other ladies what to do and bragged on them." Susan slid beneath the sheets. "Oh, that feels good. But listen to that wind, Hugh. It will dry out the cotton but I pray it doesn't put it on the ground."

"Babe, I've been listening to the wind all day, and it's not good. On the way out to Alberson's storage, we saw the damage it is doing. I'm very fearful we are losing pounds of cotton by the acre."

"No, that's not good. I love you Hugh. Thank you for today and the help at the center." She felt his arm reach for her and pull her into the hollow of his body. "I hope we are always spoons," she whispered with his chin on her shoulder as she heard his words.

"I love you, Susan. Forever." He heard her sigh. "Were our children in their beds?"

"Yes, I checked. Sound asleep. Good night, my love." He knew she was fading out and like magic she was asleep, but Hugh heard the wind.

"Lord, be with us," he prayed, "In family, in health in the crops that make our living. For all, I thank you."

Chapter 16

"Mom, we're coming home if you think you can stand our being there when you are so busy."

"Darling, we wouldn't have it any other way. But you know children under thirteen aren't allowed at the ball. The committee decided it would be a good social experience for the teens but not good if there was a younger bunch running around playing tag when it's supposed to be the social event of the year."

"I know, Mom. I called Leona and she is happy to keep Ollie while we attend but she did say, right on the last, she might sneak him in to show him off. Would that upset you, Mom?"

Susan laughed. "No, I'm hearing a lot of people are sneaking in at last minute. So that's what Bert meant when I ask if he was going, he said, "Nope, Suz, I'll be having more fun at home that night." Susan's laughter was catching, Caroline joined her. "I was afraid to ask what he meant. Now, I know."

"I sent our money in and told Miss Carrie Newsome to not tell you til last minute we are coming."

"I noticed we are having a few anonymous attenders."

"Al and Ceciley are dying to attend, Mom, but I didn't know what to tell them."

"I tell you what, I'll make an executive decision, tell them to sign in as guest from Memphis. No doubt the locals will think they are part of the cotton board. It's a funny thing, there's more excitement over this little shindig than I'd ever have imagined."

"Mom," Sophia called from down the hall. "Please, come see what you think about this dress."

"I've got to go, your sister is calling. Bye and be careful driving home. Love you." But the phone rang again. "Yes, this is Susan. Today? What time? Yes, I did forget. No, I didn't get the text. Okay. Three."

"What's at three," Sophia asked. "Aren't you supposed to be at the center by five?"

"I'll have plenty of time. I have to have another mammogram."

"But you had that last week."

"There was a blur." Susan sighed. "I have to run over, anyway. We are using those little cotton bales for decoration, too, and Alberson Gin Company has several, so that's close to the hospital where they do the mammograms. Sherry was to pick them up, but she's coming in late from Memphis."

"So why didn't the fair Kane Alberson deliver them?"

"Sophia, you sound just like your brother. If Dad and I can keep it under control, why can't you?"

"Mom, the man has insulted Dad way too many times. I'd like to see Dad punch him, just once."

"Sophia, is this what we are teaching you?" Threading a needle, Susan began to shorten the strap.

Sophia grinned. "No, I learned this all on my own. It's a survivor skill. Keep your eye on the enemy."

"Have you heard the old idiom, Keep your enemies close?"

"Yeah, it's got more words to it than that, but I know the meaning. So that's what Dad does? Cool."

"How's Thorn handling things?" Susan finished the first strap and examined the second.

Sophia shrugged. "He prefers not to discuss his biological father, it would be unfair to the one raising him and he loves Sam Lansky dearly. I do, too, Mom. He is a very kind man and he adores Thorn."

It had never struck Susan, before, the meaning of a name or the fact many times in life one's name gave perfect understanding to a person. Thorn. She wondered that Kane Alberson was the boy's real father and had come back to the town of his youth to live out life when he could have lived anywhere in the world. The Albersons may have begun life in the rural community as did all other families but whether fate or hard work they had prospered and were more financially set than most. She and Hugh had to work hard to continue progress while Kane Alberson seemed to come to wealth through his family.

But she would not change a thing about their life. Together they faced whatever life brought their way. She was so thankful God allowed them to fall in love and in love meant the same today as yesterday or twenty years past, she believed more, in that they had also grown. Now she had things to do and the weariness of her bones would not leave. This project for the community had proven tiring and hour consuming.

She arrived at the women's facility three minutes until appointment and they took her right in.

"How are you feeling, Susan?" Jennifer was taking her vitals when Doctor Jeffries peeked in from the hallway. "How's my patient?"

"I was fine, but now that you are here, I'm wondering if this is coincidental or a planned appearance?"

"May I?" Doctor Jeffries accepted Jennifer's nod and came into the room. "Susan, Dr. Borders called me since you listed me as your doctor to be notified if there was any problem. Since he left town for a convention he asked if I was around would I come in and talk with you."

"Is there a problem?"

"As you know, this is his field, and he did call you back in for a second mammogram, and there is something there," Dr. Jeffries pointed to the monitor showing Susan's mammogram. "He feels you need to have a biopsy." While she collected her wits, he spoke of treatment after surgery, named the surgeons available to the hospital and listened while she calmly asked questions in case those services were needed. "After the biopsy, if it's cancerous, the next step is a lumpectomy or mastectomy."

It was a lot to digest. Caroline listened but it came to her ears, ethereal. "When am I to do this?"

"As soon as possible. I know through the buzz in town you are tied up with the Ball right now and it's the greatest grandest thing to hit our community since the hospital came in, so how about next week when the dust clears?"

Susan choked down the sudden anxiety she was feeling. "Are you attending? We have asked all our town leaders to join us."

Dr. Jeffries was rising from the stool he'd taken and smiled at Susan. "I wouldn't miss it."

"Shall I make the appointment?" Jennifer asked and Susan nodded.

"But neither of you tell anyone until this thing is over and I have time to tell Hugh. Right now, he has his hands full, the strong winds created havoc with our cotton fields and even though the fields have dried out, the wind is still a problem. Have we ever had this kind of wind before?"

Driving home, Susan felt the whiplash of the last report. She had rattled on about the wind when in reality her mind was asking a thousand questions. She had no symptoms except tiredness, but attributed the weariness of her body to the hours she was keeping and the additional work of the social event. It was going to be a success. She felt it. Then why hadn't she felt a problem in her body?

She was a failure. She hadn't known she was carrying a child and now this, her family, her poor family. But she had a mammogram every year and they always ran her through twice. It was probably a mistake. When Dr. Borders returned, she would have him review the x-rays and he would see.

Caroline called at last, "Mom, we won't be able to attend. Ollie has a cold." It was a disappointment. Barkley was allowed to leave early for the ball with Sophia to pick up Thorn since there was a problem with Thorn's truck. Unlike the rest of the young men, Thorn did not drive the latest year model.

"You okay, Susan?" Hugh was dressed except for his shoes. Now, as he zipped Susan's dress from the back he watched her expression in the mirror. "I love you, Mrs. Preston, if I'm not mistaken you look even more ravishing tonight than you did for Caroline's wedding and that was pretty smashing."

"Smashing, huh?" Susan forced a laugh. "I'm fine. A bit out of breath, maybe, but then again the dress may be too tight, you think?" She studied her fingernails, lest he see the truth in her expression.

Hugh laughed. "No, I think it has to fit that way, who wants sagging around the waist when you got that figure?" He pecked a kiss on her shoulder. "I'm pretty proud of you."

She picked up a small sequined purse that held a comb, a tissue and her lipstick. "You look pretty smashing yourself, Mr. Preston." For a moment she wanted to just drink in the moment, her eyes filling with tears. "We can never relive this moment, Hugh. It's mind boggling. Right now, feels perfect. We may be tired but we have each other and it is as if blessing wraps around us and we'll never have it again."

He faced her, his hands reaching for hers, purse and all, his eyes locked on this woman who was his bride; who stood by him when life was hard. "You are engraved on my heart." For a moment the intensity of what she meant to him thundered through his mind. "So many accidents can happen, things we would never plan," his arms tightened, forgetting he wanted to be careful not to muss her dress. His voice became a whisper, "if ever I should leave you, if you have to look back, remember this moment I love you more than life its self and living life together has brought me more happiness than anything else in this world."

She felt safe in his arms, her own wrapped around his body, her cheek against his shoulder. "Yes, we are engraved on each other's heart," she agreed but sadness came unwanted, unfolding its face permeating their bodies. "What do you feel, Hugh?" Surely he did not feel her sadness.

"It's heavy, Suz, whatever it is, it's love, our love for each other, if there's pain we stand together, if there's joy you are there and when there's hurt we grieve, our hearts become one. I think its love."

He stepped back, again her hands were in his, the little purse dangling from a golden chain on her wrist, "Hey, aren't we going to a ball?" He tipped her chin, leaning in to place a kiss on her lips. "Cotton Boll Ball, where the cute little filly's dance all night and the clumsy fellows try to keep up. Sorry no rhymes here." He was laughing that infectious laugh she loved. "Let's go, little Suz," he said and she followed him to the car pulling the wrap close as the wind whipped at the long skirt of her dress.

Within thirty minutes of their early arrival the room was filled with jubilant teens, weary farmers and their wives worrying over the wind that settled but still gave an occasional stir. They heard it in the creak of the boards on the outside of the building and the gentle swing of the huge lighted ball that hung from the center of the room's ceiling. "What is this?" Jim Toomey filled his glass with more punch and caught Hugh's attention with his next words, "Did you get the weather report? We may get ice on

Wednesday; First the wind and turning cold and next an ice storm? It's almost unbelievable."

The musicians were tuning up, the leader saluting Susan and giving Hugh a thumbs up. "They have their own Master of Ceremony, so to speak," Susan explained. "He'll be calling the shots."

"It's beautiful, Susan," Jim's wife said. "I heard how hard you worked to do all this for us. Thank you."

Susan was overwhelmed. Gripping Laurie's hand, she replied, "I didn't think anyone would know, I mean we never expected gratitude, just our hope everyone would enjoy their self."

"Well, it's grand and I love the columns, kind of a Gone With the Wind effect, isn't it?"

And so it went, until Hugh noticed about an hour into the social several boys were slipping away to a darkened corner of the room where a small vestibule held the town's book of history, a few reward plaques and something he thought he should check out when he saw Barkley easing that way.

What he found was Kane Alberson grinning and looking proud as a couple of the senior boys followed his instructions. "Just tilt your head and take a shot. It will burn like hell, but you'll be all right."

"It's not like we haven't tried it before," Jimmy Stanley replied, as he tried to look worldly, "but it made me puick."

Barkley was on the edge, looking in when Hugh's hand claimed the collar of his shirt. Barkley's eyes went wide seeing his father but Hugh gave a slight nod to his right and Barkley understood. Now Hugh's eyes narrowed and his face flushed with anger. Hands and elbow, he pushed through the group of young boys. "Alberson," he said, "Maybe you didn't read the rules. The city doesn't allow alcohol on community property and this building is community property." Facing the boys, he said, "Young men, you came here to enjoy the community's first Cotton Boll ball, I'm going to ask you to find a girl and get out on that dance floor and make us all proud you are here. Let's not ruin this for the mothers and wives who worked so hard to make it happen."

"Wait a minute," Alberson sputtered. "They weren't drinking, only tasting to see if they could stand the burn as it went down their throat." Hands clenched, he was in Hugh's face. "Who do you think you are, I have as much right to these boys as you and I'm sick of looking at your sterling ways and holier than thou attitude toward me. I've won the last few matches we've been up against and I would have today. These are my boys, their father's and I are friends, not you."

"You don't win teaching young men about liquor. Your intention might have been one drink and that's it but we both know it doesn't work that way."

"I saw that little milk sop boy of yours back there, Preston. Looks like you aren't such an example after all. I believe five minutes more he'd been in here asking to try it."

"What was that you called him?"

Alberson grinned like a fein. "I called him a milk sop, you know, spineless, does nothing on his own."

To the laughter of the young men standing around and Alberson's taunting grin, Hugh clenched his fist. At the moment Alberson leered forward, his teeth shinning beneath the light, that evil grin spreading across his face. "I own these people, Preston. You can't win." Hugh's fist hit him square in the face, blood spewed from his nose and Alberson went down just as Susan and Laurie came running across the room. "What in the world?" They saw the blood and Hugh picking the man up off the floor.

"Hey, Kane," Hugh's voice was warm as honey, "Let's get you back on your feet. The night's just beginning." Susan was giving him a dagger edged look. "He's fine. He forgot his feet and fell on his nose. We'll clean him up and he'll be good as new." Sherry Newell stepped forward. Hugh grinned. "He's good. You women go on and we'll be there in a few minutes to dance you across the floor." They turned but Sophia and Thorn stood by Barkley's side taking it all in. Hugh released his hold on Alberson, as he bent low and whispered in Kane's ear. "You don't own me, Alberson."

Barkley waited until just the moment Alberson wiping blood on his white shirt sleeve walked by and turned just so that his right foot came into Alberson's path there above the man's shoe top. "This is from the milksop, Sir, meaning no disrespect," he said, and Kane Alberson with his following of young men whose father's farmed his land, stumbled and would have fallen except for a chair in his path.

"Son, that was not respectful, at all." Kane's eyes were mere slits as he studied Barkley.

"I'm not your son, Sir," Barkley replied. "In case you don't know Sir."

Barkley's eyes reminded Kane of his mother's, even if his demeanor was Hugh Preston's.

"A milksop is a weak person who is easily frightened," the boy said and Kane Alberson threw back his head and laughed as he reached out to tousle Barkley's full shock of hair.

"I like your putza," Alberson remarked glancing to his followers, "you know what that means? He's a bull dog." Barkley was fighting mad as the older boys laughed. "It's a compliment," Alberson said as he growled and Barkley was ready to pounce on the group. "I like you, young Preston."

"Come on," Sophia demanded. "Come with us, Barkley, you have no business here."

"She's got a point," Alberson agreed, his eyes on Thorn, wondering if the boy knew who he was. "We won't ruin this event. There were some good women put time into it." With that he turned to leave.

"Just for the record, Mr. Alberson, Sir." Barkley straightened his shoulders and stood tall. "I don't like you."

Kane turned, "I thought we were through, Boy. Let me tell you one thing. You don't have to like me. At this moment, I'm not so keen on you. But you'll learn to respect me as I will you."

"No, Sir," Barkley held his ground. "You keep on treating people the way you do, I won't ever respect you."

Sophia was literally pulling her brother by the arm. "Thorn," she entreated, "help me."

Across the room, Susan was watching the scene play out as Hugh arrived by her side. "I left when Kane began to talk," she whispered, "is everything all right."

"Right as rain," Hugh replied as the sound of fresh drops hit the building's roof and the Master of Ceremonies called out, "Time for photos, gents. Dance your little gal under the columns portico and the photographer will snap a couple and you can be on your way around the room. We intend to do a waltz first that will graduate into a good old fashioned broom dance." He brought the bow across the fiddle he held in one hand, called out, "Ye-haw," and the fun began.

Hugh and Susan's time came soon enough, when they lingered, for the photographer to adjust the camera, Hugh dropped his head and kissed

Susan, there, between the columns and not only was Sophia and Thorn with Barkley watching, across the room Kane Alberson felt a pain wrap around his heart, there was one thing he could never have, Hugh Preston held ownership. He turned away and went out the door but the rain was coming down hard.

They left the ball a few minutes past midnight, everyone agreed to meet the next day for clean up. Susan was glad; her energy was gone. The majority of people proclaimed it a wonderful event and she was happy. When Hugh pulled her to the center of the seat and wrapped his arm around her she lay her head on his shoulder and sighed with content. A mile down the road, she slid into unexpected sleep.

Later they heard activity in their children's rooms getting ready for bed. "All is well," Hugh whispered.

"Yes, it is," Susan replied, as he unzipped her dress and she slid into bed. But was it? Her mind questioned. Tonight amidst people she had wanted to confide in someone but with the rain Hugh had enough on his mind. Her secret was heavy to bear. Now he pulled her close and she slept.

The phone rang early Monday morning while Susan was outside telling Sophia and Barkley to be careful, the same message she gave them daily, but the message on the machine was different. "Susan, this is Dr. Borders. You left a request I review your last Mammogram. I feel you need to come in, meet with Dr. Jeffries and myself and let's talk about it. Please call the office at your convenience."

With trembling hands, Susan dialed back. The appointment was at ten. She arrived fearful of the news.

"There's only one way to find what's going on.." Dr. Borders saw Susan wince. "Susan would you like to have your husband with you? Don't you want to tell him...share this?"

"I will, after he is finished looking over the damage the rain and wind did to the crop. I felt he had enough on his plate at the moment." She sighed. "I don't keep things from him. I'll tell him tonight."

"I believe you and Dr. Jeffries had discussion of this concerning the fact cancer often begins in the milk ducts and spreads into the fatty tissue of the breast, so you already understand after biopsy, lumpectomy is first line of treatment, then further treatment will be decided; which sometimes is radiation and medication to prevent reoccurrence."

"When should I have the surgery or lumpectomy as you called it?"

"Soon. I'd say if Hugh can't get back into the fields and your choice of surgeon can meet the date you decide on, then do it now and have it behind you." Doctor Jefferies glanced to Dr. Border's nodding agreement. "Go home and discuss this with Hugh and call back in the morning what decision you've made. Dr. Jeffries tells me you've already chosen a surgeon."

"Yes, but I have to admit, it all seemed as though we were discussing someone else's needs, not mine." She gave a big sigh. "Dr. Borders, if you do the biopsy, why can't we do it now?"

"Well, of course," He was caught a little off guard. Dr. Jeffries had said she would want her husband present. "What about your husband's absence?"

"It's fine. Hugh is a calm man who seldom worries and today I don't want to add to his concerns."

"This is rather intimidating to many of our women," Jennifer explained as they stood in front of the padded board that reminded Susan of a piece of plywood. "You will lie on top of the board. I will have you strip to your waist and wear the cape that covers your body, but you will have to let the breast in question go through the hole and that is where the doctor takes biopsy after deadening the area."

"I think I'm beyond embarrassment. I have a feeling this is the beginning."

"Sorry to say, but I have to agree," Jennifer was collecting the paraphernalia Dr. Border's would need. "To the doctors we are probably just an object, they do this several times a day, but we don't."

She drove home, knowing Hugh would have wanted to be with her but he had other demanding tasks.

In the privacy of their room, Susan explained her day and the biopsy. Hugh sat on the edge of the bed, his head in his hands staring at the floor. "I should have been there," he said, "not looking at wet fields."

"Hugh, there was nothing you could do. I could either wait or get it over with and I chose the latter."

"How long before you know?"

"It could be by end of week." Now as she sat on the bed by Hugh she let her head drop, cradling her face with her hands, "I know it's cancer because of the depth of the doctor's discussion. I feel the biopsy is for the records, they already know."

Hugh pulled her to his side. "We will face it together, if that's what it is." For a while they were lost in the comfort of being close to each other. "Suz, there's a lot of cards on the dining room table; the ones I opened are thanking you for the Cotton Boll Ball. I'm hearing everywhere I go that it was the best thing happened in years and they hope you will head it next year, too."

She sighed. "We'll see what next year brings."

The weekend came as usual and she hadn't heard. No news is good news she was thinking when the phone rang on Saturday. "Hello, Susan, Dr. Jeffries here, I tried to reach you yesterday but my calls wouldn't go through. I'm afraid you are going to have to see your surgeon, the test reveal cancer is present. Do you want to go with the plan we discussed? If you do, your surgeon wants to see you on Monday. Could you make a four o'clock appointment?"

The next week was a whirlwind. Susan saw Cheryl Anthony. "Well, Susan, this is not what we women want but often it is what we get," the doctor closed Susan's gown, let her tie the front ties and stood studying her new patient. "We have an opening on this coming Thursday or the next week on a Thursday. Either date gives you time for pre-opt to surgery and the test we need beforehand."

"What kind of test, you've seen the biopsy and know the location."

"Yes, but there's the blood work and EKG not to mention we have this wonderful machine that shows pictures of your lymphatic system. That means," she smiled seeing Susan's expression of concern, "it identifies the node nearest to the breast tumor, the lymph node that watches out for a problem approaching, we inject a radioactive dye into the area and the machine tracks the flow. That's our road map, we don't just go in there blind, along with the marker from the biopsy we know the precise location." She patted Susan's shoulder, "I don't know if that gives you any comfort right now."

"As Hugh says, it is what it is," Susan replied. "Seems like there's been a lot of that, this year." Sliding off the table, she paused to gather her thoughts. "I don't suppose I could leave this alone and not have surgery but do the health thing, eat right, exercise, etcetera?"

Dr. Anthony's expression changed immediately, "Oh, Susan you can't chance that. This cancer can turn mean left untreated. For a woman, I'd say it's one of the worst in the way we think of cleanliness and care of our body; this one can come to the top, to the outside and it becomes runny and smelly. You don't want that." Concern was evident in her eyes. "I'll get with the surgeon and set up your surgery."

"No, I don't guess that route will work for me, but it just came over me, wondering if there was a possibility. You hear of people juicing and doing the health thing. Seems I just dread the cutting away."

She had planned to make the trip count but facing surgery was discouraging. She headed home.

Chapter 17

$\mathcal{S}$he was within five miles of home when she recognized a pickup truck on the side of the road, tilted an angle that wasn't normal she could see whoever was driving had tried to guide the truck off the highway, for some reason the tire was laying center of the road, still spinning, and the truck wheel bare to the axle.

She had been crying, in midst a pity party of one, now before stopping, she swiped a hand across her eyes as she searched for the driver. Feet on the ground she was rounding the truck and nearly run into Kane Alberson. He was carrying a beat up hubcap, his eyes on the tire that had quit spinning. Putting out his hands he stopped her before she buckled against him. "Whoa, there, we don't want another accident, do we?"

He studied her for a minute. "Susan, isn't it?" He nodded, "Hugh's wife. I was at the ball, remember?"

"Yes, I remember." She was catching her bearings, stepping back. "Are you all right?" He was nodding. "Do you need a ride home?"

"I tried calling my men but not one has answered. Yeah, I could use a ride, but let me get that tire out of the road first." He left her standing there while he manhandled the tire, returning to shake his head woefully at the looks of where the axle dug into the pavement. "Well, that's not good." He locked the truck and started toward her vehicle. "I appreciate the ride. Maybe with a little help I can get things fixed up and make it home." Removing his cap, he laid it to one side of his feet on the floorboard.

They were quiet for the most part. Somehow the animosity of the past lay as heavy as fog over them.

"I trust you all are doing well. I saw the tears when you first arrived. Anything terribly wrong, Susan?"

"Why would you use that word, terribly?"

"Because I know you are a strong woman and tears don't come easily."

She tried to laugh. "You know women, we cry happy or sad, when someone does something nice for us, or if someone displeases us."

"No, Susan, you don't." He paused and then added, "But maybe you should. My mother has been gone a long time but when I was a little boy, she said, "It's all right to cry, Son, it washes away the problem." He drew in a tired breath. "I said, No Momma, boys don't cry and she said sometimes little ones do."

"How old were you?"

He grinned, "I was seven and Jackie Green didn't like the shirt I was wearing and when he made fun of me, all the other kids laughed. I didn't cry in front of them but when I got home and thought no one was looking I cried."

She smiled, "and your Momma found you."

"Yeah, that's what Mom's do, isn't it? How's your daughter? I heard she went through a bad spell."

"Caroline Dawn. She'd doing well. We just pray remission holds."

"I hope it does." His voice was soft, thinking of his mother who died of cancer. "It seems like there's a lot of victims of that disease among us. Sometimes you wonder if it is because we are in an agricultural area; the chemicals we use and such. My Mom suffered. I thought I 'd never say I was ready to give her up but when the medicines wouldn't put down the pain, I finally told her it was okay to go because she'd hold on for me as long as she could and her pain had become intense."

Susan winced, the conversation was hitting close to home and Kane Alberson was the last person she could share her own problem with. "Well, there's your headquarters, do I drop you off there or home?"

Suddenly Kane was patting his pant pockets. "Lord have mercy. I left the key to the shop in the truck." He was embarrassed, his forehead wrinkled in a frown as he blew out hot air. "I know it's past your home but do you mind taking me to mine? I have a second set of everything there and I can go back and check out what I should've brought with me before anyone else does, I was just frustrated."

She laughed. "Sounds like something I would do. So don't fret anymore." Trying to ease his discomfort she said, "Tell me more about your mother. I feel like I would have liked her."

"She was the typical mom, I was her pride and joy because for some reason she had no other children. She said she guessed God knew I'd be a handful and thought she'd need all her strength raising me."

Teasing, Susan asked, "Was she right?"

"Pretty much. I came back when she became ill, leaving a lucrative job, to make about half of what I earned farming compared to where I had been." He rubbed the back of his neck, the tension of the evening tightening muscles that were reaching up and giving him a headache. "I don't really miss the city life but there was a whole lot more social functions but," he sighed, "Farming doesn't seem to go hand in hand with late night hours and carousing. I'll stick to my story though, that I did come back for Mother and I don't regret that one bit. Her last year, we spent a lot of time together."

"I treasure the hours with my parents. They're both slowing down with the years added on, and Mrs. Preston losing Hugh's father was a sad time for all of us."

"Mrs. Preston's a tough lady," Kane tilted his head to one side, "Considering she and my dad went to school together and remained friends, I can't say I know her personally but I've observed her and Dad talking on occasion and she is sharp. She watches the markets and she can explain hedging better than I could ever hope to. Yes, she's quite astute when it comes to the business of that farm."

"Yes, she is." Susan agreed but dared not elaborate on her mother in law as she pulled into the drive of Kane's home. "Well, have a good evening, Kane and I hope everything is intact with your vehicle."

He was climbing out of the truck. "Thanks, Susan, I'm glad you came along or I'd of been hoofing it."

She pulled into the garage wondering where Hugh and Barkley were. The day had worn her out. Removing the dress slacks and hanging them

up, she pulled on a terry robe and for a second lay across the bed before going in to prepare supper.

She awakened to Hugh's hand on her arm. "Babe, I'd let you sleep but it's been over an hour since Barkley and I arrived and I don't know how long you slept before that. I just want to know you're all right."

Pulling the light blanket around her shoulders, she asked, "Did you cover me?"

"I did, you seemed a bit uncomfortable drawn up in that knot and I thought maybe you were cold."

"Seems like I remember being cold but I was too tired to get up or even turn the covers down." She sat up, all of a sudden she remembered. "My goodness, is it dark outside? I have to fix supper."

"No, Hon, you don't. Barkley and I ate left overs and cleaned the kitchen behind us, do you want something?" He was rubbing her arm. "If you want I'll scramble eggs for you, or if you rather sleep."

"Have you already showered?" He nodded. "Then just lie down and hold me, then maybe I'll want something. Right now I just need you to hold me."

"Then let's turn the cover down. I'm a bit too long legged to lay across the bed like you are, but it does seem you managed pretty well. I don't think you even knew when I slipped the pillow under your head."

She yawned, "No, I didn't." She slid between the sheets, waiting for Hugh. He was slipping out of his denims and settling down beside her. His arms went around her and pulled her into the hollow of his body.

"You want to talk, or just lay here."

"Just lay here." He pulled her close. "Thank you." She turned to face him. "I love you."

He kissed her lips. "Thank you, Mrs. Preston. I love you, too. I'll hold you any time I can."

"Oh, Hugh, what's happening, to me, what will happen to us?" Her arms went around his neck.

"Are you scared?" His caring and the expression on his face was her undoing.

"I think anyone dreads hearing the C word." A tear slid out of the corner of her eye. "How about you?"

"Babe, don't worry about us, we will slide through this one, too. You'll see." His arms tightened around Suz. "I'd give you the world if I could but this is out of my hands," he whispered.

"If I wasn't so…it's not that I hurt, Hugh, I just have no energy and I can't understand…." She did not finish the sentence as her breathing became even and soft. Susan went back to sleep.

A few days later, Hugh saw the mud on Susan's vehicle, thinking to hose it off before it was tracked into the house. If Susan was having difficulty with chores, it was the least he could do. He was seated behind the wheel when he glanced down and saw the cap. The logo made him sit up straighter; Alberson Farms and Gin Company. What in the world was one of Alberson's caps doing in her vehicle. He forgot all about hosing off the mud, turned the key and was out the door by the time the motor came to a halt.

He found her in the kitchen. "Babe, what's an Alberson cap doing in your vehicle."

"Oh, that," she smiled, sitting an apple pie on the table. "Want a piece of hot pie? I just pulled it from the oven."

"No, not now," he answered, holding up the cap. "This puzzles me."

"Well, it shouldn't, it's just a cap. I picked Kane up, off the road, the day I was returning from the biopsy."

Hugh slumped down on to one of the kitchen chairs. "Consorting with the enemy, huh?" He tried to smile but the effort was wasted. "I don't like that, Susan. I always have a fear Kane might hurt my family."

She turned to face him, her expression one of unbelief. "You don't mean that, do you?"

Hugh thought a minute, and then nodded. "I believe I do. Don't forget I knew him as a boy. Kane seemed all right as a boy, but after his mother died…" Hugh shook his head. "Something changed. He became more ruthless, kind of like waging war against friend and foe." His eyes met hers. "Honestly, in the beginning, I was glad when he went off to college and then took employment in one of those posh companies. But life around here changed when the old man put Kane in charge of operations."

Susan settled into the chair opposite Hugh. "He had to grow up, Hugh. Maybe he was angry over losing his mother, after all he'd had to have been away awhile, he told me he came back the last year of her life in order to be with her when they realized she was dying." She was trying to absorb Hugh's fears. "He seems mellow."

"Yes, he does and all the while he's cutting deals under the table with money the rest of us don't have."

"That, too," she nodded, "but that doesn't make him a serial killer, does it?"

"Well, no, I'm not implying that, Susan, but he is someone to be wary of, I mean the man will do anything if it's to his benefit."

"Hugh, what would you have had me do? Pass him by? The wheel had rolled off his truck to center of the highway. It wasn't as though I could ignore him."

"Just be careful. I don't think my gut feeling of the man is wrong. He can fend for himself. I treasure you." Suz reached across to place her hand on his. "He will be wanting you, Susan."

It was hard to shrug off. After he left, she watched Hugh through the kitchen window. Could he be justified in his way of thinking? Not particularly that Kane would make any advance toward her because he had been a gentleman but Hugh was truly troubled. Twice Kane had undermined their business deals…but then he'd helped with the Cotton Ball, donating those columns. Sparse compensation when one considered twice they'd thought they purchased land to find Kane with his easy money had wrecked their plans.

She asked herself, what was Hugh really thinking? But Hugh was transparent, what you saw was what you got. She doubted there was a more honest man anywhere. Still, he had called her Susan and when he did that, Hugh meant business. Affectionate names aside, something strong stirred within his heart.

How many people had asked what Kane Alberson was after, helping with the Cotton Boll Ball? But Hugh's remark was farther from anything she ever could imagine, "he will be wanting you, Susan."

Chapter 18

$\mathcal{H}$e couldn't get her out of his mind. Susan Preston had been crying the day she found him in the middle of the road retrieving the wheel that ran off his truck. Only one thing made a woman cry, in his experience early in life he disappointed one when he refused to marry her. "I am not the father of your child," he denied. "Go find some other fool to lay the blame at his feet." He remembered as if it were yesterday. Tears of disappointment in him ran down Emily's face, tears of fear what her parents would say as she faced them alone and tears for the future not knowing what would happen to the baby she carried. "You know I've not been with another man," she pleaded, "why are you being so heartless?"

Heartless, he supposed was the correct assessment but she could not understand not only his father but his grandfather would have a say in the matter and she did not want that. They would mold the child to their way of thinking and the child would be worse than him. He supposed that was his only decency in the situation, not allowing them to get their hands on another human being. Heartless? Maybe he was, back then, and now but he saved the boy that once born he could not deny, for Thorn resembled him completely and not at all the man who married the girl he made love to, unsure to this day if he had ever loved her, he shook his head wondering that they both lived in the same community and through the years encountered each other. Thorn had no idea as he grew, but now surely he was aware of their likeness. Little mannerisms, handed down through the centuries…how many claimed the boy?

It wasn't Emily he remembered or longed for, nor Gina his second wife. It was Susan Preston captured his thoughts and gave him hours of mysterious wonder. How could it be? He had never so much as laid a hand on her. When Emily married Sam Lansky his grandfather called him into the study. Sitting there in his three piece suit, his hair combed austentiously to one side of his wide forehead, the large square ring sliding around on his thin finger, he pointed that finger toward Kane, "how do you feel about that marriage, Boy?"

Kane had flinched, wanting to say, my name is not Boy and I'll not answer until you use my name, but he'd said instead, "I'm fine with Emily marrying Sam, Sir."

"It should worry you non-stop," the old man replied, his voice sharp with no hint of caring. "Had you married the girl, as I instructed, we'd have someone to carry on the business when I'm gone and don't be patting yourself on the back, left on your own you'll lose it. They'll foreclose within two years of my leaving."

"There's my father."

James Terrill Alberson snorted, "Your father is a glorified bookkeeper and nothing more. He doesn't know how to make deals nor add clientele to the business."

"You should speak of your son with more respect; after all, you did spawn him, didn't you?"

James Terrill's eyes squenched, his expression more pinched, "That remark will cost you."

It had cost him. Even now he would not unlock the memory of that punishment. He picked up the phone and dialed. Sherry answered. "Are you coming home this weekend?"

Sherry's laughter came across the line. "No, sugar, I have woman-work up to my ears all weekend long. This Cotton Industry has more little women needing attention than I could ever make you believe."

"Don't their husbands pay any attention to them?"

"I don't know about their personal life, Hon, but knowledge is key and the board wants them educated to the product. We have an independent bunch of women who really don't give two cents about the Industry trying to make them understand buying cotton products is the key to their husband's success and money in the bank for them. So the industry entices them, a tea with luxurious gifts if they attend."

"You should know, Sherry, talk about independent."

"Well, that's true and if I didn't work for the Cotton Board, I'd not be emphasizing how important it is to tell people to buy cotton when we all know other materials don't wrinkle as bad, unless its rayon."

Kane began to laugh. Leave it to Sherry to be hung up on the most mundane subject when he was at one of those low moments of life but she did have a way of bringing him out of despair. "I get the picture, darlin.' But cotton is comfortable. I'll just go out and bury my doldrums in a barrel of Jack Daniels."

"Oh, you down, Sugar?" Sherry was quiet for a moment. "I've been telling you, you need to find yourself someone to love."

"You and I are the most compatible," Kane replied.

"No, Hon, we'd kill each other. We know too much." Her low throaty laugh let him know she needed to hang up.

"All right, you lost out on a really nice evening. I'd even welcome that raggedy old T shirt you wear."

"Bye, Kane. You be good now, you hear?" The line clicked and Sherry was gone.

The intercom buzzed, J.T.'s voice came over the line, "Kane Alberson, you get in my office, quick."

"Like a school boy," Kane muttered to himself. "Yes, Sir," he said, rising. "I'll be right there." He gave a look around his modern office, black granite and silver wherever possible, black leather chairs and a mirror on the wall, no framed photos of the descendants. No, Sir, he got enough of them in person. He walked down the hall, knocked on J.T's door and went in. "You wanted to see me, Sir."

"News has come to my ears by the grapevine." J.T.'s eyes were snapping. "Sit down." He waited for Kane to settle into the plush velvet chairs that he'd had recovered three times, the fillings replaced to each cushion and the cherry wood shined to a patent. Pictures of the ancestors stared down from the walls and in one corner a bar was complete, adorned by sparkling crystal and silver accessories. Once Kane asked who the ancestors on the wall were but J.T. refused to answer. Kane decided they were fakes and probably if they were J.T.'s relatives they would have been dressed in plain material sporting canvas cotton sacks. That was what he saw in other places of business in the agricultural area.

"It has come to my attention you have been in my shed again. The columns to our former mansion are missing and word has it they are now attached to the community center as the main focus of that building."

"I imagine the good folks would love to personally thank you for your contribution in making the community a better place to live."

"Are you being sarcastic?" J.T. picked up a paper weight and examined it as though it were the grandest piece of glass he had ever seen. "How many times have I told you, ask my permission before entering what is my private domain. You have nothing there, nor do you own even one inch of that property."

Thank God, Kane was thinking until the next words out of J.T.'s mouth caught his attention. "Furthermore, I hear you have been riding the road with that Preston woman. She's married and off limits to you. Do you understand?" J.T. had risen as if his grandson was not paying attention and his stature would make Kane take notice he was speaking directly to him. "We cannot face scandal."

Kane's face turned red. He felt his blood pressure spike as he slammed his body from the chair and met J.T.'s stare. "Don't talk to me like I'm a fifteen year old boy that you have a say over. I came back to run a business and I do it very well. My underhanded way, keeps you from soiling your goody too shoe reputation, when we know you are as decrepit as any man could ever be, but while I take the blame you supply the money…so tell me, grandfather, whose the biggest fool here, me or you? And while we're at it, don't be telling me what to do about a woman. A wheel ran off my truck and it was either ride home with her when she happened to come by or walk. I doubt you would have walked."

"I'm told; at the Cotton Ball you could not take your eyes off her." J.T. barked. "Handle it. Leave her alone."

Kane walked out of his grandfather's office. How many times had they butt heads? He was tired of it. This time he was not going to drown his trouble in Jack Daniel; he was hungry, surely he wouldn't be in trouble filling his belly. He drove through town. Every building bore a contribution from the family holdings. That was what it took in a small community to keep it going. The proprietors were good honest people but comparable to a church, sometimes a contribution was needed. Jones, the town's hamburger joint had needed a new roof, J.T. saw to it. The First Church of the community needed new windows and the elders had not hesitated to come to J.T. How did J.T. compensate? Gathering up land holdings, using Kane to push through the dirty deals, the clean ones he took care of himself.

Kane pulled into the new franchise; His family had a standing invite, come in be seated and let us take your mind off your problems, anyone that's been as good to us as your family, well that's it, we're family. Words rang in his ears and there on the wall was the ribbon cutting of the new place, J.T. and Tom, his father, on one end of the ribbon and himself on the other while the new owner cut the ribbon.

They seated him privately behind a see through screen. He could feel the heat of the fireplace and see those who entered but no one could see him. "Are you alone, Sir?" The waitress took his order. He sat there nursing the iced glass of tea thinking it did not have the strength of whiskey but he was keeping his vow and then a second waitress seated the couple on the other side of the screen; Susan and Hugh Preston.

"How do you feel?" Hugh asked.

She smiled. "Today, I can't tell there's a problem. You and Barkley letting me sleep made a difference."

"I can't stand to see you tired. Whatever it takes to get through this, tell us. Let us help." Hugh reached for her hand, brought it to his lips and kissed her fingertips. Her smile was gentle.

"Thank you. How could one country girl be so lucky to find you?"

Hugh's laughter was low and husky, "I think we know who the lucky one is. Me."

Kane carried their conversation home that night. Their love was balm to an angry hurting soul. His. They spoke of Sophia and Barkley at a ball game in nearby Brighton, of her parents growing older, a few evident health issues and their children were the prize they shared but it was Thorn and Sophia's situation they mentioned that left him puzzled when they said, all we can do is pray. Sophia is coming around. If she and Thorn should marry she will have to quit emphasizing her opinion or she will lose him. Caught up in the meaning behind the words, the previous balm left Kane to be replaced by frustration. How could he have messed up so badly that he had none of the peace that seemed so evident in their lives? Back home he opened the cabinet and searched for a bottle but he had thrown those out in an effort to keep his own personal vow. He crept down the hall to J.T's office. The door was locked and he did not possess a key. Why had Hugh asked Susan how she was feeling? All he needed was a drink. J.T. never locked the office unless he was leaving and he wasn't gone. Their encounter was still fresh on Kane's mind.

He left the house and drove to the neighboring town. He didn't care who knew he needed a drink but he didn't want to encounter the happy couple. Angry with them, J.T. and himself he found a bar and kept the bar tender busy. Twelve o'clock was marked by the loud gong of the clock on the wall. He glanced at Ralph, they were friends now. "I'll have the same, again." Ralph gave him a strange frown, pointed to the clock on the wall. Kane read his lips that seemed to be speaking in slow motion. "Closing? You're closing? The night's young."

"Sorry, Buddy. Got family at home. I need to go home. You think you can make it home? Where do you live?"

"Just around the corner." Kane collected the hat on the next stool, did a two finger salute and tried to walk a straight line to the door.

"Take it easy, Buddy," the barkeep said.

"You bet'cha." He fumbled for keys to the truck, found them but had trouble getting inside. Leaning back, his head on the rest, he let his body ease as his eyelids closed. He had no idea how much time passed until Ralph pecked on the window.

"You okay, Buddy?" Kane nodded. "Then you better move on out, before the police make their rounds." Kane turned the key and headed home. Few people were on the road but once he swerved to miss a small car, whether it was his fault or the other driver's he didn't know. With both windows down, he was able to find his street but when the garage door wouldn't open, he got out of the truck, let himself in through the utility door into the garage and after a time remembered the code numbers to press to the back door to get into the house. Once inside he fell onto his bed and let the drunken stupor take control.

He was awakened by someone pounding on his bedroom door. "Kane, I think you better come out here." Blinking, Kane followed the sound of his father's voice. "I don't even want to think what your grandfather will say. Come look at this mess. Couldn't you even think to turn off the motor of your truck?" Together they stared at Kane's new gray truck that replaced the one that lost a wheel.

"Guess not," he replied, seeing his truck had come through the garage door but for lack of a better explanation the truck moving forward in an idled state had been stopped by the metal plate installed at the bottom of the door due to one of Kane's previous episodes. The truck had missed his grandfather's long nosed Lincoln Town car by a hair. "Lucky me," Kane quipped.

"Somehow I doubt that," his father said, shaking his head. "I thought you were giving up drinking."

"After this, I'll probably have to. I'm sure grandfather will see to that. I won't get paid for a while."

Tom was scratching his head. "You might get by this one if you can find someone to fix it today. Your grandfather left last night with his old buddy. They're headed to Nashville, coming home tomorrow." Tom started inside, then turned back to stare at his son. "Seeing as I woke you, I don't suppose you've heard the news?" Kane didn't catch the meaning. "The news on the radio or television," Tom repeated.

"No, Sir." His father went in, as usual shaking his head, foregoing speech. "Maybe you should."

Kane returned to his room, turned on the radio and flopped back onto the bed. On the hour the news began; "a teenage driver and her younger brother were run off the road last night near Brighton by the driver of a dark Gray pickup truck. It is believed the driver of the truck was drunk. The young lady and her brother were returning home from a basketball game. She was able to call the Police but the driver of the Gray pickup has not been found. Thankfully, neither the driver nor her passenger was hurt. It is a good day today for Sophia and Barkley."

Sophia and Barkley? Brighton? For a moment his encounter with the small car he passed on his way back from Brighton entered his mind… surely not Susan and Hugh's two. But what were the coincidence of two other siblings being named the same? His blood went cold, to think he could have caused the problem that could have been much worse. He stripped bare, stepped into the shower and let cold water run over his body. But the possibilities that he was the driver that ran Susan and Hugh's children off the road left him in a spasm of remorse and fear that he could be responsible for someone hurt, maimed or dying.

An hour later his father found him sitting at the kitchen table, the coffee pot was half empty and it was tradition who ever rose first made a full pot. Tom T. poured his cup and sat opposite Kane. "So it was you?"

"Possibly," Kane replied, studying his father with new eyes. "I don't know how you've stood it all these years under the old man's thumb."

"We're always under some one's thumb, Son." Tom studied the calendar on the wall, his gaze returning to rest on Kane. "Does it really matter who? We have to come to grips with the situation and find our own solitude, J.T. couldn't find it for me or me for you. The question is when we find it, what we do with it."

"Dad, I've wronged you all these years in the way I thought. You're a strong man to put up with both of us. God help me, I plan to do better. On Mother's grave, I'll try."

"You're sure you are all right?" Susan interrogated both, Sophia and Barkley. "I am so thankful nothing happened to either of you or your car, Sophia." She studied her children. "To think, your dad and I were having a pleasant dinner while this was happening."

"Oh, Mom, now that it's over, it wasn't so bad." Barkley pushed the cereal bowl away. "I thought the Policeman might think it was Sophia's fault, but he was nice about it once he checked her license." He turned to Sophia. "You didn't start crying or none of that stuff. I was real proud of you."

"Well, thanks, Barkley." Sophia held up one hand for five. Barkley tapped her hand and they grinned.

"And you couldn't identify the vehicle?" Susan questioned further.

"Well, it looked like that new one of Kane Alberson's," Barkley replied.

"You can let that one rest. Your Dad said Kane's truck was parked outside the restaurant where we ate."

"Mom, where's Dad? I want to talk to him before I leave for school. I know this worried him."

"Sophia Raine," Susan went to her daughter, putting her hands on Sophia's shoulders to stare into her face. "I'm so proud of you. Thinking of dad is about as nice as you could get this morning. It did shake him up. He put his hands to his face and there were tears but do you know what he did?" Sophia was shaking her head. "He said, thank you God that you protected our children. I am so grateful and I love you."

"Dad always talks to God," Sophia said softly. "I'm trying, Mom, but I haven't got the hang of it yet."

"Hurry, Sweetheart or you'll be late. I think Dad's out in the shop. I saw him stop to talk to Bert."

Tossing her keys to Barkley, Sophia pulled on her jacket, "Get us ready, Bub, and I'll go see Dad. It's important." She was out the door and running to the shop, arriving just as Hugh opened the door and she ploughed into him. Giggling, she said, "Dad I needed to see you before I left for school. I'm dropping Barkley off, then I have a first hour study and class the second." Hugh listened, his arms around her. "Dad, thank you for not being mad about last night. It wasn't my fault but I was afraid you'd think so."

Hugh placed a kiss on her forehead. "There was a time I might have questioned, but Sophia I trust the young lady you have become. I pray every day for your safety. God hears our prayers, you know."

"I'm trying to learn that, Dad. Thorn says we're getting married when I finish this last year of college, but I want to be sure we're right for each other. He's too good a person for me to ruin his life."

"Why would you do that, Sophia?" Hugh started walking with her back to the car. "Don't you know if you love him? You spend an awful lot of time together, if you're uncertain."

"I do love him, Dad but you know I get really antsy and sometimes I just want to learn new things."

"Honey, I promise you one thing for certain, marriage teaches you something new every day."

"You like him, don't you Dad? Mom does too. No one would believe he's Kane Alberson's son, would they?"

Taking a deep breath, Hugh replied, "Thorn's a fine young man and your Mom tells me, in regard to Kane Alberson, there's a bit of good and a bit of bad in every person, no matter who they are, even..."

Sophia was giggling as she got in the car to drive, "Oh, Dad, I don't believe there's anything bad in you but Kane Alberson, I'd question if I didn't know Thorn is really his son and Thorn is so good all the way through...you'd wonder that Kane Alberson could have produced a good..."

"It's none of his doing," Barkley interrupted, "Sam Lansky and Miss Emily have raised Thorn and they are really nice people."

"And how is it you know them?" Hugh asked a puzzled expression on his face.

"Why, Thorn's sister and I met at the Beta Convention and her parents were there as chaperones."

Susan had joined them. These were her babies and they'd just been through an accident. Now as the car pulled away and on to the highway, she and Hugh held each other's gaze.

"Does it ever amaze you the information our quiet boy comes up with?" Hugh asked. "I declare, I don't know Thorn's family other than we were class mates' years ago, but our boy..." Hugh stared up at the sky, "Seems like he has a handle on a lot of people...but he's none too fond of Kane Alberson, is he?"

Susan's laughter filled the air. "Neither are you, Mr. Preston." She felt his arm go around her as she leaned her head against his shoulder. "The poor man, if we'd pray for him, instead of review the reason we formed this dislike through the years....hmmm, no telling what God would do with him."

"You pray and I'll try to deal better with the situations he manages to contrive." Kissing her on the lips he turned toward the shop. "I better get to work before Bert fires me."

Chapter 19

$\mathcal{K}$ane drove past the Preston headquarters. A car driven by Sophia had entered the highway ahead of him. Vaguely, he believed he remembered it from last night and he wished it wasn't in his memory. He saw Susan with her head against Hugh's shoulder and then Hugh kissed her and walked away to his shop. A pain of longing for someone pressed through Kane's mind, fast fleeting and noticeable.

Now he stared a moment at the brown bag his father asked he deliver to the church. "It has to go in today, Son," Tom explained. "I told the Pastor I'd see it come in on time. Leave it in the office."

"Must be important," Kane had replied. "Yeah, I'll drop it off for you."

"And Son, while you're there, take time to go in to the altar, ask God to help you with your endeavor to stay sober. That's the only way you're going to do it and no one will be there, just you and Him."

Kane gave a deep sigh, his breath coming out ragged as he was under pressure. Deliver the bag, that was easy enough but he hadn't talked to God in a while, that might not be so easy. He knocked on the office door but no one answered and he recalled there were no cars on the parking lot. Evidently the pastor came early each morning to unlock the door.

Kane walked to the front, the altar consisting of the preacher's pulpit, behind that the many choir seats and in front of it, a simple long bench knee length high, made from cherry wood and attached to the floor. He stood there, staring at the scene painted on the wall behind the baptistery, clouds, nothing but clouds and a light descending as if from heaven with a cross midway. No Jesus, no words, just the cross. He sit on the bench but he couldn't see the cross. Self consciously Kane glanced around making certain no one was present as he slid to his knees but that seemed to slap at piety he neither understood nor owned. He stood and in so doing his eyes caught a glimpse of the cross from a different angle and on the cross was Jesus.

His breath caught. The figure on the cross was not there minutes earlier. He knelt again, rising to see the form of Jesus on the cross, but when he stood the cross was empty. What a trick, he supposed an artist could make anything happen on canvas. But he digressed, as his father's words returned, "go to the alter, Son, it's the only way you're going to stay sober." He stumbled through memory, trying to bring up words, "Father, forgive me. I want to do better but I'm weak."

He shook his head, trying to remember, when did his father become active in the church? How had he failed to notice his father's attendance? Now it came to him, how lonely they were after losing his mother but he hadn't spent a lot of time trying to ease his father's sorrow, no, he was too busy tipping the bottle to drown out his own. And what was his mother request, "Son, take care of your daddy, he's going to feel so alone without me, but you can make a difference." And he hadn't.

Regret stung, causing his shoulders to slump and he wanted to sit on the bench and hold his head in his hands but he could hear traffic picking up on the highway outside the church and the secretary would be arriving. No, he didn't want the grapevine twitter that Kane Alberson was in church this morning. He turned on his heel, leaving the building, closing the door firmly behind as he saw a car pull into the back of the church, a woman getting out with keys in her hand that she wouldn't need. It made him wonder had the pastor opened the door this morning or had God seen him coming and arranged the whole thing?

Once he was safely in his truck, laughing at himself describing the truck a safe haven, he began to drive the roads he'd covered the night before and he saw where a car had left the road and been pulled from the ditch. He drove in to Brighton, slowed as he passed the bar where he'd drank himself into a stupor, but he didn't go in. He wanted to, but something prevented him doing so. Something he'd seen on the wall in the vestibule of the church nagged at his mind. Tom T. Alberson, teacher men and women's combined class in room four. Could it be his father taught a Bible class, or was that before his mother died they had been active in attendance. Members on the church roll? It chafed his spirit not knowing.

He found the carpenter who previously fixed the garage door. Man, I've got others ahead of you. I'll pay you double, so the conversation went and the man left in his van headed for J.T. Alberson's home. Kane rest assured the door would be repaired by the time J.T. returned from Nashville.

He checked with the realtor, no land up for grabs, read the market reports, sold a few tons of cotton seed and was glad when the day ended. He raided the refrigerator, too tired to go out as usual. But he was asleep when J.T. returned, banging his suitcase against the doors, not caring if anyone needed quiet because it was his house. His home. The home he'd built for the love of his life, Rose Andrea, who died of tuberculosis when she was twenty nine years old leaving him to raise seven year old Tommy. James Thomas relieved himself of that process when he hired a Nanny. If she was of the religious bent and wanted to take Tommy to church all was well, it kept the child out of his hair and left him free to work.

Sometimes J.T. was uncertain even Tom T. knew the circumstance of life without his mother and certainly Kane did not. J.T. resisted Tom marrying the Horton girl but in the end he found her quite pleasing. It was her kindness to others, especially him that he noted. The house ran better with Margaret in charge. The help called her Miss Meg and like him, they adored her. He gave his son credit for bringing a good woman into their lives. He mourned her passing along with Tom and Kane. It was as though he lost a child of his own. She always said she saw through his persnipity ways, his thirst for control of everyone and of everything. He wished her son possessed the ability Meg displayed to work with people but no, Kane was more like him; Displeasing and displeased ninety per cent of the time. He was eighty nine, still in charge of day to day envolement in the business and didn't intend to give control to either his son or grandson. The business would flounder before a year passed in their hands.

Kane sat up fast, the blood pounding as hard in his head as his heart until reasoning set in. The noise would be his grandfather hitting the door facings with his roll along suitcase and he wouldn't care. As he always said, if he woke the dead, this was his house and he made it quite clear they were freeloaders taking his good will and turning it into a liability. "We will move," his father had replied, to which J.T. blustered and said they might as well stay, the house needed its rooms filled." A lame excuse that worked. They stayed.

Rubbing his forehead, Kane padded to the bathroom, opening the door to the cabinet above the sink looking for aspirin. The dreams that invaded his sleep left him feeling inept and a foreigner to his own life. The Minister behind the pulpit kept pointing a finger at him. "It is a sin to lust after your neighbor's wife." Was he saying the truth?

Even if Susan Preston was single he doubted she would glance his way. Hugh was a man of principal; the world seemed to like him. The members of the schoolboard met him with open arms. Kane would bet Hugh was a member of his church and knew the reason why. He probably understood why God smiled on one person and frowned on another. Somehow even he questioned the last part of that sentence. God was supposed to be a sovereignty that issued good on all who tried, wasn't he? And Kane found the high road much more to his liking than the low. Until Susan Preston, he had not questioned the hurt he had laid on other men, flirting with their wives to the point of secret rendezvous and once the conquest was won he moved on. Sherry was the only woman smart enough to hold out on him and together they realized what they had was friendship and not to mix that gift, not to ruin a good thing by marriage or any other union.

Sleep was gone. Kane slipped into an old pair of sweats, pulling the shirt over his head feeling the bristle of a day's growth of beard picking at the material. He would walk around the property, and then maybe he'd sleep. But he could not turn off the thoughts. His mind traveled to why Sophia was on the road with Barkley, when she was in college. Maybe he didn't know enough about that either; or Sophia dating Thorn. Thorn would need to be quick on his feet, that one wasn't gentle like her mother maybe that was where Hugh's mother entered the picture. Sharp as a tack, Kathryn Preston could hold a candle to any man when it came to business. If Sophia was like Kathryn, then Thorn would score in one direction. But most men would trade intelligence for the genuine love of a woman. He thought Gina was the one, but her design was on the Alberson business, married or divorced if she was part of the enterprise, Gina knew she had a good living for the rest of her life. Tenacious, she and the old man were tight. Gina would choose J.T. any day over Kane or his father. Tom didn't care but Kane did and divorced her. Let the old man deal with her. If she remarried, Kane had no doubt J.T. would cut her out.

He walked and thought, walked and wished for rest. His mind returning to Susan, her head on her husband's shoulder as he leaned down to kiss her and walked away a satisfied man, secure in her love or he wouldn't leave so easily. Kane leaned against the double fork of an old oak. His father said he climbed the tree as a child. The nanny was lenient, bred from a common family she knew about children playing and accepted they also must learn. "I gave her no problems," Tom related, "my mother was gone and the father I never knew set one room away in his cold stance neither welcoming me nor offering acceptance of any kind. Nanny was all I had and she loved me. It was easy to be good for her."

Tom had given her a royal funeral when she died and his Meg had approved. Sometimes, Kane wondered what went wrong with him; a man with two parents that exuded goodness and he ran the road to destruction, never building a relationship always intent on tearing one down. Tired and dejected he wandered back to the house, the moon the only light until it occasionally hid behind a cloud. "I've got to find myself," he whispered, his words fading in the wind. "Lest I perish."

He was so depressed and down on himself, any previous day he would have head toward the bar where others drown their sorrows and buoyed up each other, though later they went home to further destruct their world. Some who's children needed new shoes, a wife whose clothes amounted to two pair of jeans and few tops, and then there were the Kane's of the world needing nothing material but salvation of the soul and to understand why they continued life lonely and defiant.

The path back revealed a long necked bottle. He picked it up and threw it, listening as it made contact in the dark against something metal. It was almost daybreak but time for a nap if he could sleep. Satisfied, he entered the house and sank onto the bed. How could he love his neighbor's wife? He barely knew her but then again, he was as familiar with her actions as a man was allowed from a distance. Hadn't he been watching her for years? The phone was ringing. Who would call this early? He checked the number. Sherry.

"What's going on in Memphis?" Suddenly he smiled. "You're coming here? Great. Anything in particular you want to do?" He listened, suddenly quiet. "There's a house keeper and I'd say it's in pretty good shape. Why?" He closed his eyes, not quite believing what he was hearing. "Let me get this straight, you had a tea planned for this weekend with our area farm wives at the Brighton Ladies Boutique. No, this is first I've heard about it...and it burned to the ground last night? Hadn't heard that either." She was talking so fast he was having a hard time understanding. "So you called the city clerk and asked about the Community Center but there's no heat and she said the building is cold...yes, yes, I do understand about the rest rooms and all."

Now he was peering into the mirror across from his bed. "Yeah, I moved back permanently when you said you weren't going to stay with me anymore, what was the use of the apartment?" He was growing leery of where the conversation was going. "Sherry, what do you want from me?" Her request stymied him. "Now that I don't know. You call him; I'm on his bad side right now. If he says yes, I'll help in any way I can."

There was an instant click and Sherry was gone.

Some fifteen minutes later J.T. opened the door and walked in. Kane was dressed and expecting him.

"That girl you date, Sherry something," J.T. began, "wants to bring a group of women here; this weekend for a cotton board tea. I didn't know she worked for them. I said yes. She wants you to be available to show them around, seems not many have seen an old time working mansion complete with farmland around it and the beginning family still living in it. They'll be here around eleven thirty. Food will start coming in around ten thirty as she's had it catered. That crew will see to the white table cloths, the crystal and china. She says they'll have everything that's needed, just be sure Kane's around." He turned back, his hand on the door knob. "I've told you, now don't let me down. You understand?"

"Yes, sir," Kane swallowed hard. "How in the world did she talk you into this?"

J.T. smiled, "We swapped favors. She will be my date for the Cotton and Gin Show. I told her she had better be a knock out. Wear something that made the other old coots wonder if I've still got it."

For once, Kane laughed, "You fox." J.T. did a shuffle out the door and Kane wondered what the trip to Nashville was about. On two occasions he'd seen his grandfather pleasant. This was one of them.

Seemed the world was full of surprises. Had it been that long since he and Sherry talked? He wondered would Susan attend the tea since she was one of the leaders in the community farm wife group.

"Why are you staring at the phone?" Sophia was setting the small kitchen table, her dad and Barkley waiting patiently, their attention on Susan now that Sophia was interested. "You look confused."

"No one told me the Boutique in Brighton burned last night. Did any of you know? That's where the Farmer Wives Tea was to be held this weekend. A group of us were carpooling to attend."

"Yeah, I forgot to tell you." Hugh responded. Sophia and Barkley added, "me too."

"Well, I wish I was part of the family you felt you could share with," Susan snipped, her face flushed and looking as though she might cry. "This just messes up everything."

"Can't they find another place to hold the tea? What's so special about a change of location?"

Susan stared at her family. "Oh, they found a place." Everyone was waiting. "At the Alberson Mansion."

"Can I go?" Sophia's voice was all excitement. "I've always wanted to see inside that place. I hear there are dumbwaiters, a basement where in the old days they actually let the undertakers come in and prepare the bodies of those who passed. Can you imagine?" Her excitement turned to pain as she cried, "Ouch. Did you kick me Barkley James Preston?"

"Can't you see Mom's upset." Barkley seemed confused. "Why are you upset, Mom? Going there?"

"It's a long story." She slumped into her chair. "We were to wear semi-formal attire. Mattie James thought it would be fun for all of us to get together and she hired a make-up specialist, a cosmetologist I think she called her to do all our faces and we were just going to have a good time."

"Well, I think it will be even more fun in that period of grandeur, just think Velvet curtains, settees and everything fringe, not to mention the table settings. It will be grand." Sophia's excitement had not dimmed. "Oh, Mom, is there a way I could go?"

"No, Sophia." Hugh's voice held a strange firmness that settled Sophia immediately to quiet mode. "I think your mother's just disappointed no one told her about the fire and then too, she has surgery scheduled for Monday, perhaps without even knowing it her subconscious is trying to keep everything on an even keel." He reached around Barkley and took Susan's hand. "It will be all right, Suz," His eyes held a message that neither Sophia nor Barley understood but found comforting.

Susan seemed to straighten her body and the gentle smile returned to her eyes though they shined with tears. "What would I do without you," she whispered and they all felt better as Hugh asked the blessing.

After the table was cleared the dishes in the washer and Sophia and Barkley disappeared, Hugh took Susan's hand and led her to their room. Reaching beyond the glassed enclosure he turned the tap, until the water was right, raised the sweater she wore over her head, and waited as she unbuttoned his shirt. Once the other garments were removed they stepped into the shower together.

"How do you always know what I need?" she asked, leaning into his body, his arms around her as streams of water warmed them. For a while they stood there, two hearts beating as one.

"I've been there," he finally replied. "And you always know when I'm down to my last straw. It is then you build me up. What more could I ask? You calm the fears, push away the hurt, if I can do that for you, then God has blessed us both."

Tears of thanksgiving welled in her eyes. "If ever I should leave you, not by choice but by circumstance, I have loved you more than I ever dreamed possible. You are my everything. I am content in your love."

"Shh," he whispered. "You are not going to leave me or the kids. You will grow more beautiful in the way you look and in your spirit as you watch over our family. I never doubt who you are and always will be, Suz. I knew the day you said yes I would never doubt you...but," he pulled her closer into the folds of his body…"I don't intend to share you with that rich villain whose house you are going to this weekend, Never-Ever."

Susan giggled, throwing one leg across his body. "I was afraid you wouldn't want me to go." Her eyes widened, "Whoa, did I make a mistake when I rearranged our body positions?"

Hugh grinned, kissing her firm on the lips, "No, I think that's just about right."

She awoke the next morning to a note pinned on her pillow. "Meeting Bert at the coffee shop, a cousin of his is in…the rich one that has some land he wants me to look at." Beneath the pinned note was a second piece of paper, in Hugh's best hand writing, "Engraved on my heart-forever on my mind." Hugh. He had drawn a heart on back. Susan kissed the note and whispered, "I will treasure this forever."

Friday, cool and damp became a reality and as planned a limousine arrived to pick up Susan. Five other wives were ready to welcome her. "We're having diet coke and sprite," Sheila Connely announced, "but the driver said there's hard stuff if we want it." She giggled. "I don't dare if I want to walk into Mattie's house." They were in high spirits discussing the beautician waiting to work magic. "I hope she uses the airbrush makeup because I cannot get the hang of it." LeAnn remarked, "I think it has to do with how to use the stylus, some little trick, I always have too much makeup. What about you Susan?"

"I was listening to the two of you and feeling a bit intimidated, I have never tried it, I'm still an old fashioned girl." It was true; she was a bit uncomfortable with the group. Helping out on the farm she didn't have a lot of leisure time in which to pursue the latest fashion or trends in anything.

"You always look beautiful." Grace chimed in. "I'm stuck in the same mode and I don't think it matters what you use."

"Hey, we're there. Don't forget your garment bags." Voices blend together as they unloaded to Mattie, void of makeup standing on the sidewalk welcoming them in. Out of all the women it was Susan she hugged. "I bet they've regaled you all the way over, right?" Susan grinned. "Come on, girl," Mattie was pulling her inside and down the hall. "You are in here with me. Lily has already finished my hair and ready to do makeup. Her assistant will be preparing the other ladies skin to receive their make over."

She called back, "Girls, make yourself at home. Lila and Laurie will take your names and tell you who comes in to Lily next, until then, enjoy your facial and foot massage and don't forget the pedicure. We are going to look beautiful." Her laughter trilled above their heads and everyone joined in. "Excuse my messy bedroom, it was all right this morning but by the time Lily's crew brought everything in….well…it's obvious they have the accessories necessary to this business."

Letting her apprehension fall, Susan began to warm to the occasion. Mattie's Lily was a whirl of finesse, make up, scrutinizing them one by one and studying their clothes as she gave their hair a tug here and there to allow small tendrils to frame the face…and then it was six, time to slip into the dresses and head down to the Alberson Mansion. They were ready, down to the pedicured toes on their feet.

"I can't believe the evening passed so quickly," Mattie confided. "I was afraid we'd have boring lulls and she whispered, "I did wonder if we would be out of there by the time my sweet ole Fred came home." She peered suddenly intent at Susan. "You gonna be all right, Hon? I worry about you."

"Thank you, Mattie for treating all of us." Susan said. "I think I'm going to make it through very well."

When they were all reloaded into the limousine Mattie leaned back against the seat letting a huge breath of air escape her lips. "You look beautiful, Susan. I hope Hugh gets to see you before the magic is gone." Susan only smiled and for a time they were all quiet until Mattie leaned forward, staring out the window, "Susan," her voice was filled with excitement, "Have you been here before?"

"Only to the back entrance that holds the garage and utility building," Susan replied, remembering dropping Kane off that one time. From the window she saw the grandeur Mattie was exclaiming over. The road had become brick as they entered an elaborate set of iron gates evolving into an exaggerated u-shape drive in front of the house. Lamppost sporting drapes of greenery off-set by drooping wreathes of cotton lined each side of the drive, the candle like glow giving the evening darkness an ethereal feel and lights in the Mansion window belied the fact of wealth turned welcoming, if for this one evening.

"How could they do this so quickly?" Mattie asked, "I understand only yesterday the location was changed."

"Money speaks," Sheila quipped, "Though I cannot speak personally, being a farmer's ex-wife."

And there at the door, standing host with Sherry was Kane Alberson. While Sherry sported a plaster formation on one foot, Kane Alberson stood tall and handsome wearing tan trousers, a navy sport coat and a shirt so white it shined in the darkness just as the brightness of his welcoming smile.

"That man could light up a tunnel," Sheila whispered, the words echoing back to Mattie's shushing as they were all entering to follow Sherry down a wide carpeted hall to a room filled with white clothed tables centered by cotton in the most appealing arrangements the cotton farmer wives had seen.

"Welcome," Sherry began. "What a wonderful evening we have planned for you wonderful women. It was unfortunate our location had to be changed, but who could hope for a better exchange than Alberson Mansion and our gracious host, Kane Alberson." She turned to Kane as he bowed. "On behalf of the Cotton Council of your state and mine we welcome you to an evening of information that we hope will encourage you to buy cotton and to create an interest in your neighbors who do not understand our industry... to also buy cotton. But first, I've heard you exclaiming over the table centerpieces. And they are gorgeous. Beneath the seat of your chair, there's a square piece of paper that will read, either "I'm sorry," or, "You are a winner." That centerpiece will be yours upon leaving tonight by presenting your winner square. Now, reach under your seat on the right hand side and see what your square has to offer."

There were squeals from other tables, while Susan sat mesmerized by the piece of paper in her hand. "I've never won anything, Mattie," she blushed, "Except Hugh, but look at this." Already Mattie was waving wildly. "Susan wins. Susan wins," in a sing song voice their table companions echoed her name.

"All the winners hold up your hand." Sherry was laughing. "All right girls, you are on the honor system, just let them set until you are leaving. Now, we will say the blessing and you will be served a beautiful meal."

In the silence of bowed heads, Sherry read a prayer from Psalms and personally thanked the Creator of Life for each woman attending. It was when she finished soft music began to play as a dividing screen was rolled away from behind where Sherry was standing to reveal to their amazement a five piece ensemble. "Brighton's very own Mini-Orchestra," Sherry sang out, "The Five Merry Men."

Sheila, ever one to voice her opinion, said, "How does she do this? I mean, she has gone all out." With no little gust of admiration, her eyes strayed to Kane Alberson helping Sherry to a nearby table, "And that fellow is not hard to look at, now is he?" She then scrutinized the musicians, "Nor, are they."

"Cool it, Sheila," Mattie warned. "You have only been divorced a short time, you might be vulnerable."

"No, Honey," Sheila countered, "I just know a good lookin' man when I see one, like Kane Alberson."

They had finished the meal, completely sated and happy with Sherry's choice of food when they noticed a slight change in the atmosphere, uncertain what it was until they saw the musicians had left their instruments while recorded music filled the room and the five were separating to each table to stand before a women with their hand extended. Susan watched as one by one the men's invitation to dance was accepted. Eyes downcast she was relieved when Sheila was chosen from their table but when she glanced up Kane stood before her, his eyes quiet serious, though a slight smile played about his mouth as he offered his hand.

"Oh, no," she managed to whisper. "Mattie?" But Mattie was smiling.

"Go ahead, Susan, it is just a dance and then you go home to Hugh." Her eyes were on Kane, now. "Right, Kane?"

"Exactly," Kane agreed. "Sherry sent me over. She fractured her ankle moving that heavy screen today."

At first she was tense and uneasy as she took his hand and stepped out onto the floor. "Relax, Susan," he whispered, "I'm not going to hurt you, nor make a move on you."

Nervous, she tried to laugh. "Not in front of thirty farmer's wives, I hope not." She took a deep breath. "This is kind of far out, isn't it, Kane? And who knew your home had a room this large?"

"It's kind of sad," he confided. "J.T's wife loved to dance. Her name was Rose Andrea and he promised when they built their home it would have a grand room, large enough to dance and have guests but sadly Rose, my grandmother died at the age of twenty nine." He sighed…"as for the dancing, Sherry is a kind of far out gal…the better story here is about J.T and his Rose, the grandmother I never met."

"And your grandfather never remarried." It was a statement, rather than a question.

"No, I'm afraid J.T. and I are not good at second chances. I tried and failed…but hey," he grinned, "she works in the office for grandfather so I guess he is happy with her. Truth is, she wanted in on the business, not me as family and if you're wondering about Sherry, Gina could care less what I do."

"That's sad." She changed the subject. "What is that song…it's on the tip of my memory…but…."

"He sailed at the dawning, all days he's been blue. Red sails in the sunset, he's trusting in you."

For the first time she smiled. "I'm impressed; I didn't take you for a music buff."

"Buff? Maybe not that but my own mother encouraged I take piano, so I would be with her."

The music changed and Kane escorted Susan back before going to another table.

"Now, that wasn't so bad, was it?" Mattie asked, patting her hand.

"No, but it was embarrassing and I felt very inept."

"No one would ever know it. But I tell you, I'm ready for the lecture and go home to my comfortable old Fred who will be sitting half asleep in his recliner waiting for me. What about Hugh?"

"Most definitely waiting. I think my having surgery come Monday is weighing heavy on his mind." She sighed. "You know what would have been perfect?" Mattie shook her head. "Dancing with Hugh."

It was ten o'clock by the time the Limousine stopped in Susan's drive. Hugh met her at the door. "Oh, this is not good, is it?" He saw the dark circles beneath her eyes. "But did you enjoy any of it?"

"It was different. Trust me, once I'm rested I'll tell you just how different." She was grateful he did not question further but helped her undress. "I'm so tired, Hugh, but it will be easier to shower than to try to wipe off this make up. I just want to be me in my old gown next to you. If I never see this dress again, I don't care."

Hugh sat on the stool before her make up bench wondering why she was not only tired but seemed distraught. When she stepped out of the shower he wrapped a towel around her for a moment before helping dry her body. Almost childlike she raised her arms as he slipped the gown over her head and picked her up and carried her to bed. It worried him how tired she had become the last month and how easily she fell asleep, sometimes in the middle of a sentence. Drawing her near he kissed her lips and listened to the easy breathing ruffled now and then by a sound he heard sometimes from Caroline Dawn's little one when his feelings were hurt. "Please, dear God," silently he prayed. "Please."

Kane reviewed the evening Sherry had created. As Susan Preston had said, "it was a bit far out."

"I think the evening was a success," she had chortled, "Don't you?" And for once she stretched her full height to plant a kiss on his lips. "That's gratitude," she said, "for letting us use Alberson Mansion."

"I'm afraid you kissed the wrong man, then. That would be eighty nine year old J.T. Alberson, himself." Tiredly Kane grinned a yawn catching him midway. "I understand you've agreed to attend the Show with him in tow."

"Stop yawning," she replied, placing a hand over her mouth. "It's catching and boy am I tired." He was waiting. "All right, yes, I did make that deal and it will be worthwhile. Standing by one of the larger cotton growers, letting him expound on cotton's future and profitability to this area, I can do it."

"Yeah, one con-artist to another, he will wear his three piece suit and you are supposed to wear something that makes you irresistible to men. Right?"

"Mercy, does he really tell everything?" Glancing around the empty room, completely void of helpers, she winced as a pain ran through her foot, the boot feeling tight and she remembered the doctor saying there would be swelling and that was when he wanted her off her feet. "They will be back to help load up this stuff in the morning. Is it all right if I spend the night?" For some reason this time she asked.

He grinned, "Just in case, I had your room prepared. I'm ready to turn in, myself. How about I wish you a good night's rest and see you in the morning. Eight?"

Sherry was puzzled. "What no warm welcome into your bed?" Thinking a minute she added, "That's not like you. Have you got a new girl, Kane?" A smile waned across her face, "Anyone I know?"

"Sweetheart, you are worn thin. Let me guide you to your room." Already taking her arm into his, he flipped the switch, the room went dark and they were walking down the hall, except she was dragging that fractured booted foot. "Hurts, does it?" She nodded as he opened the door, stooping to peck a brotherly kiss on her cheek. "Goodnight, Sherry."

She was shaking her head. "Whoever she is, you have got it bad."

Placing his clothes on the nearest chair, Kane lay back on the bed thinking maybe Sherry was right. He wanted the privacy of his room to think about Susan's reluctance to dance with him, but most of all to remember the feel of her near, soft, gentle and enduring. What was it about the woman made him want to protect her? From what? She was as strong as any he'd known...but even the strongest need rest and there was the rumor of surgery. He felt a flash of memory; the cross and the image of Jesus that was there and then it wasn't. How did one pray for another? His body still, Kane drift away...to sleep and dream. "Leave me alone," Susan said, "I am Hugh's wife...I belong to him."

Chapter 20

Caroline Dawn called early that morning. "Mom," wispy voiced, her concern evident. "I'm praying, Mom. I wish I could be there but I can't. Dad promised to keep me updated, so I don't know what else to say, Mom, except I love you."

"I know, sweetheart, and it is all going to be okay. I love you, too. Kiss little Ollie for me."

"Mom, can I talk to Dad?" Susan grinned and hand the phone to Hugh. "She needs to hear your voice."

Sophia was leaving for class, "Mom, I'll get supper tonight, once you get home stay on that bed. Grandmother Kathryn said she was coming over for us to cook together. We'll clean the kitchen after, don't worry." She pecked a kiss on Susan's cheek, punched her dad on the shoulder and was gone to return quickly, "Where is Barkley? He better not make me late. I have to keep a rigid schedule every day, and he knows it." Going to the hall she bellowed his name. "Get your butt in here, now."

"I told you, I'm not going." Barkley's words filtered down the way as he stuck his head out of the bedroom door. "I'm going to be there with Dad and if he says no, I'm going anyway if I have to walk."

"Whoa, whoa, whoa," Hugh motioned to Sophia, "Go on, if he's that determined I'll save him a walk." He was laughing as he and Caroline hung up phones. "She says it sounds like the old says. Nothing's changed." Susan stood by the door looking uncertain to what she faced. "All right, Son, if you're going, let's go."

Susan tousled his hair as they went out the door. He was her baby. She smiled. Sophia was the more practical one concerning her relationship with people, what they saw was what they got, sometimes in a blunt striking way, but Caroline would always have that special bond with her dad tiptoeing quietly to reach him, never one to make a big to do over anything, he was her hero, her example of what was right and good. What am I? Susan wondered. She felt she was going off to war, unarmed.

"Mom, you gonna be all right?" Barkley peered across the metal bar they'd raised to transport her into surgery. She hadn't realized he'd grown a few more inches since last they'd measured pant length. He was trying to find her hand in all the sheets. "You are aren't you?"

"Yes, dear." She saw the worry in his eyes. "I will be riding home with you in a short while. Okay?"

"Okay," his grip tightened on her hand; then he stepped back for Hugh to take his place.

They stared at each other while the Nurse secured all the paraphernalia to the bed. "You'll be feeling drowsy any time now, Mrs. Preston." Hugh was stooping over to kiss her as she tried to raise her head but it felt heavy and her arms weren't working either. "I love you," she managed as Hugh said the same.

"Dad, are you sure Mom should go home today?" Barkley fumbled to explain, "I mean, well, if she's having major surgery, shouldn't she stay overnight in case of something going wrong? You know like a blood clot or something…her blood pressure?"

"I know, Son, but that's what they told me, I have nothing to do with it. That's the way it is today."

"But Gramma said they kept her three days when she had surgery."

"That was before everything got out of hand, Barkley and the government stepped in to make things right." They were the only two in the waiting room, Hugh supposed the second operating room was busy and patient's families using the facility that supplied a television to help pass the time.

"I don't know if the government makes things right or not," Barkley muttered.

Catching a glimpse of his son's expression, Hugh said, "I know there's something behind that statement, why don't you just spit it out instead of making me wonder about it?"

Barkley fidgeted a minute and then asked, "I guess you heard Sam Lansky is being accused of chemical misuse when really it wasn't him at all and I think you know exactly who would be to blame."

"Whoa, now Son, that's a powerful statement. I haven't heard this but I've been trying to square everything away all the jobs I could so I can take care of your mother when we get home. Tell me about this and where you got your information."

"Thorn's sister and I stay in touch. Betsy said the government has confiscated her dad's records and he has been forced to get a lawyer. You know who farms the land between the Lansky's and the farm where the crop was ruined?" Hugh was sitting up, listening now. Barkley waited for his father's answer.

"No, I don't know about who is in charge of land in that area. I think Sam lives on about a three hundred acre spread close to the river bottoms but whether he owns or rents, I don't know."

"The Alberson's farm all around their land. She said if the government demands a penalty, which you know means a large fine, then they won't have enough money to finish out the year."

"Son, there are lending…"

"No, Dad, once the government confiscated their records no one wants to loan her dad money, unless they take his whole farm as collateral and he won't agree to that."

Barkley saw the news concerned his father greatly. "It's been bothering me, too, Dad. I like Betsey and from what I've seen of her family they aren't about being big wigs, they just want to take care of their family and have nice things like everyone else."

Hugh laid an arm around Barkley's shoulder and gave him a hug. "That is well said, Son. It's what we all want." He was quiet for a moment and then asked, "Does Sophia know this? Because if she does, I know you two have talked and I'm trying to figure out why neither of you mentioned this to me before."

"I can't tell you Dad."

"Can't or won't?" There was a rustling suspicion growing inside Hugh's chest. "Not knowing is going to be harder on me than you telling me what you've heard. I declare, Barkley, where do you hear all this stuff?"

"Well, Dad, if you went to the coffee shop I think you'd hear it first hand, but you don't and your neighbors that like you sure aren't going to come tell you bad news."

"Bad news?"

"Thorn saw the papers lying on his father's desk; anyway Mr. Lansky's desk and Thorn read them. They just haven't gotten to you yet, Dad. Your name's on those papers, too."

Hugh's heart skipped a beat. Surely something so consequential wouldn't be delayed if a man's name was on the paper. He stared hard at his son. "Barkley, not a word from you or Sophia about this to your Mom. You understand?"

"Yes, Sir." For all his years of maturing, Barkley found his underlip quivering. "Dad, you mad at me?"

"Son, you know I'm not mad at you. It's just startling to hear. We take every precaution to handle the chemicals correctly and to hear this; the neighbors I know next to us would have come to me but not one has suffered damage and now you tell me my names on government issued documents. It's disturbing."

They glanced up at the sound of footsteps coming down the hall as the doctor beckoned. "Mr. Preston, may I speak with you alone?" At those words, Barkley seemed to shrink. The doctor drew Hugh into a corner where there was a table and chairs. In a matter of minutes Hugh returned.

"Mom will be going home as planned but they will monitor her the next few hours before release." Hugh passed a hand across his face. "What the doctor said, amounts to they were able to remove enough around the cancer that they feel the malignancy is gone but there's always the chance a few cells remain. Your mother must heal and then go through radiation treatments as a safeguard."

"Because, otherwise it might get into her blood stream and set up in another place." Hugh was staring at his son. "I know, Dad, I've been reading up on this."

"Barkley, do you plan to be a doctor or a lawyer?"

"Heck no, Dad, I want to be a farmer and work with you."

"Well, it appears we could use one or both of the other." Hugh settled back into the chair and closed his eyes. There was so much he needed to think over while his insides were pounding with uncertainty and he felt a tiredness he didn't recall from the past. When the Government got involved with a fellow, there was no peace and more likely the crumbling of the foundation his life was built upon.

Four Years Later

"Well, how does it feel, Sport. You'll be celebrating your nineteenth birthday." Bert slapped Barkley's shoulder. "I saw you driving that pretty little girl around the other day. How does that feel?"

Barkley tried to smile and think of something to get Bert's mind on another subject. "I declare," he said, "If your legs get any more bowed you won't be able to sit on the tractor seat, you'll have to find you another job, maybe cow punchin."

Not one to be deterred, Bert replied, "Does that mean I'd be a cow boy and I'd have to ride a cow, or you reckon some good ole soul would find me a horse?"

"Get outta here," Barkley gave him a pat on the back before climbing up into the combine.

"Aw, I know you love me," Bert cackled, "Me and Leonie diapered you, young man. We know all your secrets. When you bringing that girl back to visit? Leonie's waiting. She likes your Betsy real well."

"Seriously?"

"Shoot yow," Bert wiped his hands on a grease rag. "Ain't we family?"

Barkley saw the need to reinforce the bond. "Yes, Sir, we are family. None better than you and Aunt Leonie."

"You goin' to see your daddy this weekend?"

"Yes Sir, I don't want Mom driving alone this weekend."

"How about Sophia and Thorn?"

"Well, there was talk, Mom said we might pick up Miss Emily but Thorn has to stay on the farm and Sophia has a speaking arrangement."

"Ain't that just the way it is, life gets busy but your daddy and Mr. Sam too, they'd be down in spirit if y'all didn't make the effort." Bert shook his head. "Near four hundred miles travel one way. Whooie."

Barkley drove out of headquarters, Bert following with the eighteen wheeler. A light rain in the night kept them from starting early and if the moisture wasn't true to last reading he'd have to pull out of the field. But the wind had followed the rain. He passed the cotton field, noting the cotton trying to string from the boll and cotton brought his thoughts full circle to Kane Alberson because Kane's family owned the gin where they must deliver their cotton. There were other gins but mileage was a factor.

He found the arrangement as painful as a soured stomach. He didn't like Kane Alberson, nor his pious old grandfather that rode around in his long nosed Lincoln, his stringy features resembling an old hawk. He just bet even Kane Alberson wondered when the old man would die. They resembled a circling buzzard to Barkley, always on the watch snapping up holdings when an older farmer died or a young one went bankrupt. He was certain they thought the Preston Land would be up for grabs when the Government declared Hugh Preston guilty to crop damage and incorrect use of one of the most hazardous crop chemicals in the history of farming while everyone knew it was the company who made the product should be held responsible. Maybe they'd not had the best attorney, Barkley wasn't sure.

As for funding, the local establishment had refused further association. Susan had drawn herself to full height, stared at the men Hugh had rubbed shoulders with and called friends. "I pray, gentlemen," she said, "You never have to face the turmoil you have caste on us. You know we are good for whatever amount our operation borrows, but in your grandstanding penny pinching way you choose to forsake business and friendship in denying our loan application. Do you think we are so stupid, not to understand you want to foreclose on our operation? In our lifetime, my family may not see justice for your sordid act but you, whether in this life or eternity will rue the day you acted so unkindly. If we have to work our fingers to the bone, we will rise above this and you will see us prosper, God as my witness."

For a time the government held both his father and Betsey's in their respective County Jails, "a mere formality," they were told and after months allowed to return to their farm, hire their own attorney and try to salvage life. Two years later the legal battle drawn to conclusion; each appeared in court and was sentenced to two years in prison. "You are the Scapegoat for all the other farmers," their lawyers said, not a word consoling but devastating as they left family and home and lost all freedoms. In prison they formed a system of support that led to friendship and whether the authorities knew they were from the same area or not, no one else was privy to the information. There was no doubt that information would be used against them.

Barkley had grown up fast. "I'll do home schooling, Mom, but I'm going to help run this farm in Dad's absence. You and Sophia can work with me. I'm smart, Mom. You know my grades prove that. Like Dad said, I read everything. I always have." Reluctant, Susan sought information on home schooling and Barkley excelled. "Do you remember how things are done, Bert?" He asked in the beginning and Bert replied, "Yow, sure, for the most part." And they had made it with the help of Kathryn Preston, who funded the operation and received in return the payments with interest the Association had denied.

"She's not so bad, after all, is she," Sophia Raine teased. He had to concede, he viewed Grandmother Kathryn in a new light but she still seemed cold and standoffish, not like his mother's folks. Where they lacked wealth, their love and encouragement expanded to include even Kathryn Preston. For the first time they were all friends with one accord with a common challenge, everyone must do their best to stay healthy and as Susan coined the phrase, "sane."

Susan's faith had grown. "By the grace of God, Caroline Dawn is still in remission," she reminded, "but she tires easily now that she is pregnant again. Let's all hope Dad is home by the time she delivers the sweet little girl the doctor says she is carrying. And Mom, you and Dad and Kathryn must get your flu shot as they say we will have a bad winter, those old furry worms are wearing heavy coats." And they would all try to laugh.

Laughter was difficult with the love of their life away. He was the one slow to anger, never wanting to do the discipline through their childhood, the voice they counted on in the darkest periods, and he was gone for two years. Barkley had often heard his mother's cries in the middle of the night when she thought he and Sophia were asleep. Standing in the hall, their hearts breaking, Sophia cautioned, "No, Bub, we cannot ease her pain. Gramma says tears wash away the hurt. Let's let her cry." They would return to their rooms and Barkley wondered that Sophia now thought of others. Dad would be proud. He knew Sophia was waiting for Dad's return to walk her down the aisle. Patience had never been Sophia's virtue. And what had he learned? That there was nothing like having good parents. In his more Christian moments he wondered what happened to Kane Alberson and with the flash of Kane's grandfather's image across his mind he thought he knew, but there was the father, word had it Mr. Tom was a man you could count on, faithful in his church, even teaching a class. Too bad he didn't run the operation, instead it was said he was the bookkeeper, not always agreeing with the ways of his father.

Nineteen years old, Barkley realized he had a lot to learn. "Treat people fair, Son." His father's words rang in his ears. But Dad wasn't there. "If you are kind, that kindness will return to you." Barkley thought in spite of the prison stay on his father's record, he still would be considered a man of integrity, one people would be proud to call friend and if they didn't it didn't matter, Hugh Preston was the father he loved. As a son, he knew the truth, there had been no damage, no neighbor next to their daily operation suffered loss, some person unfamiliar with designated land had compiled a record that held up in court. There were times he wondered if a person with authority or wealth had added fuel to the fire, not necessarily to hurt his father but to hopefully gain a land purchase and Hugh Preston paid the price.

Farming was competitive, as Bert defined, "a dog eat dog business. There's men around here will smile to your face while stealin' behind your back." Bert would slap his hands together and finish, "it weren't that way back then." His eye on the header, Barkley was satisfied, the beans were running through the combine, the wind had dried them out and by night fall he would have another patch finished. Spring had been a challenge with the rains but they'd lucked out even planting late the ground warmed up and the seed sprouted and popped through. Then there had been several rains at the right time reduced the irrigation expense.

"It's like if God knew what was needed," Gramma Caplan remarked. She was well aware the tole the absence of her Son in law was causing Susan. "Sometimes, I think if your daddy and I would just die, at least you'd have the money from the life insurance policies. Alive, we're worth nothing to you, dead the money you'd receive would help out."

"Mom," Susan shushed her mother, "just knowing you and dad are with us is a great comfort."

Funny how his mind went from one thought to another while the combine hummed along and Bert waited each round for him to empty the bin into the truck. Betsy's smile flashed through those thoughts and he felt his heart do a skip and a beat. He loved her and he'd almost guess it was comparable to the love his parents knew. Maybe when Dad come home he could buy her an engagement ring. Right now, the whole family concentrated on keeping the budget his mother set up. Oh, Dad," he sighed. "Come home soon."

He and Bert locked up around nine. Maybe he'd call Betsy but they'd be together tomorrow, leaving at five in the morning in order to arrive when the visiting hours began, then they'd leave at three when visitation was over and be home on the back side of seven. It was a tiring day, but it made them happy.

Susan closed the books. She had worked through dinner. Sophia was with Thorn, probably changed to denims and riding the combine. Their courtship was no different than hers and Hughs but no one would have convinced her and Hugh they would be in the predicament they were now facing. She was so relieved Barkley could drive the trip to see Hugh.

Two years had passed since her bout with cancer. Hugh had been with her through the radiation treatment and the next year as she gained ground and returned to her old energetic self. Had she known then Hugh would be convicted of the crime that sent him to prison or prepared to meet the hefty fine served on their farming operation she now sometimes wondered if she would have given up.

It had not been easy facing the community although in her heart she knew Hugh was innocent. She had traveled every dirt road and beaten path to the fields they farmed and she saw no evidence of damaged crops. When she and Hugh studied the Platt book that showed the location of their rented properties they did not find names to match those on the government documents that stated wrong doing but unable to prove Hugh's innocence he was serving time in a Federal Prison. Once he had remarked, "you won't believe the people I've met here, Susan, nor believe the wrong-doing they have suffered. It's an humbling experience." Then his eyes would turn sad as he reached for her hand. "I miss you." The agony in his voice brought tears to her eyes. "When I first arrived here, I thought I would die." With tears running down her cheeks, she nodded. Only those who experience it know, she thought. Prison, military service… yes, they know.

To even touch each other, their hands must be visible or the attendant would come and usher her out. "I didn't know," she said when it happened. "Now, you do." There was no understanding in the voice, only threat. "Lady, this is a Federal prison, we have people of every caliber thinking to do wrong." That, too, was in the beginning. Together, they had learned what was allowed and mostly not allowed.

She arose the next morning from a fitful night's sleep, rest had not come, only anticipation. She and Barkley drove to the Lansky's home. She sat in the back seat with Emily and Betsy sat up front with Barkley.

"How are you this week," she asked Emily and Emily faced her with the same sad eyes Susan often saw trying to smile from her own mirror. "We're here," she whispered, taking Emily's hand. "We have to hang on. Two more months, Emily," She sighed. "And four hundred miles to prepare our happy face."

If arriving was difficult with its personal inspection, identification and disrespectful attitude, leaving was harder. Both men seemed to shrink from their tallness to remind them of little boys being left behind. A sense of normalcy might have been the goal, but truth was the challenge. It was what it was.

"You have to go in to the Gin Company," Hugh reminded. "It's end of year, you need to collect the money." His eyes rest on her, "Next week, Babe, if there's any problem, there's papers for proof."

Returning home she was tired, emotionally spent and spiritually beaten. She realized God had brought them this far, but two more months seemed an eternity. Seeing her Mother's expression, the stoop of her shoulders, Sophia put her arms around Susan. "It will be over soon, Mom. Come on, let me help you get into bed. I know you didn't sleep well last night, I heard you tossing and turning but tonight you will."

"When did you turn into such a good daughter?"

Sophia laughed, "You of all people know it took a while." Trying to ease her mother's mind, she continued, "Thorn and I had quite a day, a picnic on a combine, how do you like that for starters?"

On Monday, remembering Hugh's words she collected the necessary papers she might need when she went to Alberson Gin Company but another day was needed to bolster her strength, today she didn't have it. By eleven on Tuesday she was headed that way, praying aloud, that Kane would not be present. But he was. She parked by the building, avoided walking near the scales and entered the door. Jenny, a girl familiar from church greeted her, but Kane Alberson, a pair of glasses barely perched on the bridge of his nose stepped forward, offering his hand and ushered her into his father's office, closing the door behind them.

"Dad's working from the home office today, Susan, how may I assist you?"

Susan hand over the papers she and Hugh had discussed. "I don't understand the papers. I hope they're self-explanatory. He said your father would help me. I had no idea I would be speaking with you."

"Is that so uncomfortable, Susan?" Kane peered over the wire rimmed glasses. "I haven't seen you at all this year. Do you avoid coming here because of me?"

Susan forced her body to relax, she dare not fidget nor allow Kane Alberson to know the truth. Instead, her gaze rest on him, her eyes a clear blue that held no hint of the animosity she felt. Here was a man who had trifled with the rights of many while her husband was locked away in a prison cell. She did not doubt he knew the prison sentence meant a government program supplied to farmers was withheld from Hugh's operation. Somehow, knowing the Alberson's were the ones who committed the wrong brought no relief, her presence here was yet another punishment.

Fully aware of what it cost for her to come to the office, Kane appeared to be studying the papers. He knew they had signed up within the allotted time; a first payment had not been drawn, probably due to her lack of knowledge and possibly the family's stress in Hugh's absence. There were a number of factors that would have added income to their operation. Had he not known through his father's friendship with Hugh's mother, Kathryn Preston that she was funding her son's farm, he would have personally worried; all the while aware his hands were tied unless he conceived some brilliant plan to help them anonymously. Their pride was as obvious as ever and too, anything he might do would not set well with J.T. Alberson, if anything the man was more driven than ever in his lust to achieve property. His eye was on the Preston's holdings, but Tom T. was adamant in explaining to his father, Kathryn Preston would see it did not happen. Undaunted, J.T. had threatened. "You find a way."

Susan sat, a perfect lady, her hands folded in her lap, her knees straight with the seat of the chair, the skirt discreetly draping mid knee and her breathing even. Kane had noticed the strand of pearls, similar to the ones his mother had worn. He did wonder was her hair professionally streaked or was Susan graying due to the family ordeal, whatever the reason Susan was as attractive as ever and his heart had quickened upon seeing her. It was true absence made the heart grow fonder. He had not forgotten her for a moment.

"I'll make a call, Susan. I'll get back to you within the week but as you leave, if you will stop by Jenny's desk, this year's check for the cotton we ginned for you is on file. We do not like to send them through the mail." She remained silent, acknowledging his words by rising from the chair. "If I may ask, how is Hugh?"

"How would you think he is, Kane?" Her eyes flickered with malcontent. "Have you any idea what a man must feel locked away from society, an innocent man?"

"There are many forms of imprisonment, Susan." A sad smile about his lips did not reach Kane's eyes. "In your happiness I doubt you have considered the wretchedness of others."

"Touché'," she whispered. "I suppose I deserved that."

"No, Susan, I suspect you will never deserve the unkindness of others."

She gave him a strange look and left his presence. He heard her soft voice as she spoke with Jenny.

It would be another year until he saw her again, unless fate intervened. Rumor had it that Hugh would be returning by the first of the year. He could not help but wonder how the man would fit back into society or the routine he had left behind.

Sherry had unintentionally left photos she had taken of the tea J. T. allowed at the mansion. There was one of Susan, sitting at the table with her friend, Mattie and one as they stood her hand in his. He often smiled wryly studying her composure as they danced together, not by her choice. Still, eventually relaxed Sherry had captured the moment. Lest prying eyes ask questions Kane placed the photos at the bottom of a drawer in his room, but as a drugged man he often brought them to light, wondering that Hugh Preston had found her first.

Susan felt the quiver of her body as she fastened the seat belt. Jenny was kind and the meeting with Kane had gone well enough, then why did she always feel there was unfinished business between the two of them? She shook her head as if to ward off an unwanted spell. First, she would deposit the checks at the bank and then go home to finish the end of year tabulations for the bookkeeper. Both Barkley and Sophia were at the Lansky's. Emily had called to ask her over for spaghetti but she declined. "I appreciate it, Emily, but I'm finishing up here and going to bed."

"I know the feeling," Emily replied. "I don't know what to do with the evenings with Sam gone, but the children fill a part of that time for me, without their laughter…" Her voice had ebbed away.

Sleep did not come easily. Kane's words circled her thoughts, "no, Susan, I suspect you will never deserve the unkindness of others." What had he meant? Did she treat him unkindly? No, she countered all interaction with him. Was he responsible for Hugh's incarceration? She had no intention of dwelling on Kane Alberson until the night of the tea at the Alberson Mansion reared up. He had called her name as she in leaving was going down the steps carefully. All the women were busy admiring the light post wreaths when all she could think of was the sanctuary of her own home.

"Susan," he called, coming behind her, the centerpiece from the table in his hands. "Sherry says you forgot this. Here, let me help you into the Limo and hand it over to you." A true gentleman she remembered, taking her hand, waiting for the folds of her dress skirt to clear the door, still holding her hand in his by some quirk of fate as he looked into her eyes.

"You look beautiful, Susan." It was not the words but the longing she saw there. "He will want you, Susan." She gasp and turned; Hugh could have been standing between them. Tiredly, she leaned back against the seat and closed her eyes. "Are you all right, Susan?" She nodded hoping the hand she was waving feebly was motioning Kane away.

The phone rang around ten thirty that evening. "Mom?" Caroline Dawn's voice came across the line. "Mom are you in bed?" Susan heard surprise in her daughter's voice for a moment, and then, "Mom, I think I'm in labor, any way my contractions have begun and they're seven minutes apart.

"Oh, Sweetheart, I'll get my clothes on and come on down." She listened to light rain on the window.

"Mom, Dad will be so disappointed. He wanted to be here. I wanted him here."

"Shh, darling," Susan was already moving around the room, collecting items of clothing and cosmetics she would need. "First, Dad would want you to be well and the baby's delivery normal. Please, don't fret." She padded down the hall to Barkley's room, hoping her children were home as Sophia opened her door. Taking her daughter by the arm, she held the phone where Sophia could hear, as sleepy eyed Barkley sputtered, "What's wrong?" She heard Caroline saying, "I have to hang up, Mom, my water just broke. Hurry. Okay?"

"I'm going to Caroline's, she definitely seems to be in labor and you two will have to carry on here. Sophia you have that final test and Barkley, the men need your guidance on that repair job you have started. This is all we can do. I don't know how many days I'll be there. I'm so thankful you are both home." Her mind was trying to cover all bases. "I don't have much cash."

Barkley was finding his jeans, pulling his wallet from the pocket. "I have," he counted the bills, "Here, this will help." He was awake now. "What do you need me to do? You know it's raining and windy?"

"See if the car has enough gas and Sophia if you will find that large insulated glass and fill it with something that has caffeine." She hugged her children. "I need to get on the road, Caroline sounded all wispy. I think if it's a woman's tenth child there's still a mystery and a fear of something going wrong."

A light rain was falling as she left the drive, her children standing on the steps calling, "be careful."

Within an hour she was passing the lights of Lowe's and Walmart alongside Interstate fifty five at Blytheville. She noticed several eighteen wheelers pulling into rest areas but two continued on, headed the same direction toward Memphis. She could only wonder had the weather issued warnings for where driving had been chaotic at the moment there was an eerie calm to the wind. Suddenly there was a loud crash of lightening and the heaven's opened to a deluge of rain, as if it was coming down in sheets. She pulled between the two trucks, hoping they would lessen the wind's blast on her vehicle which was becoming exceedingly hard to keep to the right of the center line and she prayed for an increase to her line of vision. They had traveled ten miles, she estimated, when the truck in front of her swerved, it's vinyl sided trailer seeming in slow motion as it met the highway and started a haphazard slide on the side of the road. In passing she barely missed it as a guard rail caught the metal pinning and brought it to a grinding halt half across her lane with its content spilling onto the highway.

Even with debris flying all around, she caught a flapping sound that was hard to define, as the steering of her car seemed to lock and the vehicle was clearly shutting down. With the first truck ahead perhaps two car lengths away, she was rolling dangerously near the open bed trailer that appeared to be carrying long metal beams. All she could do was hope by some miracle she wouldn't roll under it. Then, something happened. She threw her arms over her head to protect her face as everything went black.

"Do you know this person?" Susan heard voices trying to distinguish where she was and who they were talking about. The reply was, "yes." Someone was trying to pull her from the car and she was resisting. "Good luck, Buddy," the voice was saying. "I don't think the car is hurt but it probably felt like hell, with those two tires flat. Look at where the metal has run through them. Looks like spokes. She wasn't a bad driver to take it to the side like that but I bet she thought she was going under the trailer. Lord knows that would have been it. You gonna take over this situation? All right, Buddy, we'll handle the others."

"Susan?" She didn't want to open her eyes, much less talk to someone. "Susan, you're on the side of the road somewhere between Blytheville and

Memphis. You've got two front flat tires and I've called a wrecker to come get your car out of the ditch." His voice raised a pitch. Was he pleading? "Come on, Susan, the lightening is dangerous and it's going to start raining again. Come on, get in my truck."

Someone was literally pulling her from behind the wheel of her car. She was half there and half strung across the console and the seat belt was cutting into her ribs. "Hugh?" She felt his hands ease beneath her, tug, pull, strain and breathe harder and then he was carrying her, placing her on the seat of the truck and fastening yet another seat belt. She forced herself to try to open her eyes as she felt her purse dropped down beside her. There was a thump as something landed on the backseat and she knew she had to wake up. She swallowed, tried to glance around but all she saw was jagged lightening. The driver's side door opened, someone rolled down a window, shook a hat and rolled it back up to warmth and the low hum of windshield wipers picked up as rain hit the glass and the truck shook

"We have to get off this road. It's not safe. The wrecker is pulling in to take your car back to the garage. It will be fixed and ready to roll when this wind settles… according to the wrecker guy. I told him to put two new tires on your car and check the others plus make sure it's safe to drive. He thinks it is."

She was so cold she was shaking. Her coat was draped across her and she hadn't even felt it but the cold was clearing her brain. The voice was not Hugh's but it was someone she knew, it was familiar. His hand came to rest on hers. "Are you all right?" She nodded. "Do you know who I am?" She shook her head. "Susan?" She couldn't bear anything else. She began to weep, no sound, only tears running down her cheeks. "Susan." He said her name, softly. Just "Susan." And then, "why are you out on a night like this?" She struggled to think. And it came to her. "Caroline. Caroline Dawn is having her baby."

"Look at me." Suddenly he was demanding. "You have to get a hold on…things. Look at me."

"Kane?" Even in the dark, she knew her eyes were wide, her voice wider with surprise, more than surprise. "Where are we? I thought I was almost to Memphis."

"You know what happened?" The lightening lit up the interior of the truck. "You must think."

She nodded and the whole past hour came out in gasps and stifled sobs and wonder that she was here and he was there. "Why are you here? How did you...come along?"

"I was having a hard time at home, alone," he admitted. "I decided to go to Memphis to find Sherry. She doesn't know I'm coming."

"I'm sorry, I've made you late." She searched for her purse, found it, searched for her phone. "I must call Caroline Dawn." He was silent as she dialed, listened to her talk. "No, Sweetheart, I'm all right. As soon as the weather clears and the tires are on the car, I'll be on my way. You do what you have to. I love you."

"I've never experienced a baby's birth," he said, softly. "It must be a grand thing." They had recovered the miles. He turned into the street that led one direction to where the Wrecker Service was located; a gas station with a repair galley to one side and the other direction a small restaurant with a sign that declared it was open twenty four hours a day. "I think a cup of hot coffee would help us both."

She practically fell out of the truck. He caught one arm and righted her. She laughed, embarrassed, except there were still sobs locked in her throat, it was a strange sound coming from her.

"Did you have dinner?" He was studying the menu behind the waitress. She thought. No, she hadn't. "I take the silence as a no," To the waitress he said, "We'll have two of your bacon and egg meals, toast and hot coffee." She was writing it down. "Do you have a rest room? We need to wash our hands."

"Ladies to the left, men's to the right. I'll have your food in about twenty minutes," she said, without pointing.

Clutching her purse, Susan walked to the right, "that way," he corrected, grinning. "She was facing us."

In the restroom's cracked mirror, Susan saw she looked like a street urchin, rumpled and worn. Combing fingers through her hair she then washed her face, used the sleeve of her shirt to wipe it dry and went out to find Kane sitting with a cup of coffee in his hand and one across the table for her. As if on cue their food was delivered and they ate in silence, compatible for once, thankful to be out of the storm.

Finished, watching the lightening flashing in the distance as it appeared the weather was moving slowly to the North, he finally asked.

"Susan, we live in the same community. We have to run into each other now and then, why do you not like me?"

Startled at his frankness, she took a deep breath. "It isn't that I don't like you, Kane. But we are adults and we both know there's a lot of water under the bridge, a lot of incidents through the years that are not without grievances. You are off limits for me."

"Off limits." She barely heard him. "I'll have to look that up. I find you very likable, Susan. I envy your husband."

She held up a hand. "You've been very kind to me, tonight, Kane, but please, don't go that route."

He felt the rebuff. "If it makes you feel any better, this is no more than when you came to my aid the evening the wheel ran off my truck." He rose quickly. "I'll check on your vehicle."

Susan pulled into the parking lot of the Methodist Hospital as the morning shift came on duty. She raced down the hall, glanced in to the OB waiting room and saw Ceciley, then Charlie and Howie. "Am I too late for the birthing, are they both all right?" Charlie was hugging her fiercely, the expression on her face scaring Susan.

"I think she's just waiting for her Momma to deliver that baby, now," Charlie was saying, as Susan glanced around the room for Alistar and Oliver. Charlie was trying for a smile now. "It's her blood pressure. Susan, why don't you go down the hall and let them know you are here. Just tell the nurse, I suspect they'll gown you up to go in if they think that will settle Caroline's problem."

Susan bent to give Ceciley a hug and was running down the hall when the nurse met her. "Are you Caroline's mother?" Susan nodded. In minutes she was gowned and entering the room where Caroline lay, her face beaded with sweat, her hair matted to her head and clutching Oliver's hand in a death grip.

"Baby. Sweetheart," Susan fought to control her voice. "Hey, Caroline Dawn. Mom's here. Let's get that baby girl out and into the world." Tears were running down her daughter's face, Oliver's and her own and the doctor was saying, "Push." It was mere minutes until a wobbly little cry filled the air and Caroline and Oliver's little baby was laying on her stomach, red, almost purple and mad as a wet hen from having to stay inside longer than she wanted.

Emotional, Susan turned and hugged the doctor and the doctor, relieved and worn around the edges hugged her back. "We've been at this a good twelve hours", he explained," we were getting worried."

"I thought the procedure was…" Susan caught both the doctor and Oliver's eyes on her. "Oh," immediately she felt they were trying to tell her there was another problem, it had to be Caroline's health. Silently her words stifled but her thoughts were not. Not the leukemia, please God, she prayed. The nurse was saying they must clean Caroline Dawn and the baby was being whisked away. Would they please wait outside?

The doctor accompanied Oliver and Susan to the hall. He spoke to Susan. "You were going to say you thought Caroline would have a C-section and that was the earlier plan but then she decided she wanted a normal, or I should say regular birth, which I agreed to if she maintained reasonable levels…" his words dropped off. "During the pre-tests we discovered the leukemia is no longer in remission but we were concerned as to starting treatment with the baby's due date upon us."

"But now you will?" It was as though her blood was rushing ice cold through her veins. Susan found her body shaking while the doctor waited. "It's bad?"

"Severe." He agreed, "And she has to recover from giving birth, if all was well that would be a week or two she would have her energy return, but this has to weaken her. She wanted to nurse the baby but I said no, it would only serve to pull her down and the baby needs full nourishment formula will supply."

Susan turned to Oliver. "Does she know?"

White as a sheet, Oliver was leaning against the wall for support. There were tears in his eyes and his voice broke as he shook his head and replied. "No, she's been so happy, showing Ollie all the new baby things and explaining why the new baby can't wear his clothes." Susan put her arms around him.

"Oliver, we will weather this storm."

She noticed the doctor did not second her word; instead he spoke directly to her. "It is rare a patient's remission halts during pregnancy.

Caroline asked me early on if that happened would I delay treatment because she was afraid it would harm the baby. We were almost home free, then when she went into labor…" He closed his eyes. "Could we take this up tomorrow? It's not that I'm insensitive, but I've been on my feet all day and mostly the last twelve hours with Caroline. I wouldn't change it…it's just that I have more mothers coming in tomorrow to have babies, if at least one doesn't jump the gun, tonight, I'll be lucky." He gave them a tired smile "I hope you understand". He turned to go down the hall. "I'll check on both before I leave this floor." They thanked him and he was gone.

"I'll be staying the day with Caroline, Susan." Oliver's gaze now settled on movement at the end of the hall. "They said I can stay in the room with her because they are going to put the baby there too." He was digging in his pocket to produce keys to the apartment. "Granddad has Ollie and Grandmother Cecily will be going home to help with him."

"After I look in on her and the baby, I will go to the apartment and freshen up."

"She should rest this morning, Susan, if you want to take a nap. I know you are beat from the drive and the weather." He took a deep breath, shaking himself free of the last twelve hours. "We can only hope."

It was when she was getting out of the car at the apartment a moment's spasm of anxiety overwhelmed her. She jerked open the door to the back seats and then hurried to unlock the trunk. Her suitcase was nowhere in sight. She had to think. When it was raining so hard and she was pushed into Kane's truck there was the thump of something falling into the back seat before he crawled into the front seat to drive to the garage?

Her suitcase was in his truck. She had nothing of her own, no clothes, toothbrush or cosmetics and Caroline Dawn was a much smaller replica of her mother. Susan doubted she would find a piece of clothing to fit. She would have to wash the clothes she was wearing.

At this moment, it wasn't the absence of clothes, nor the flat tires that were replaced, nor the fact that her daughter had just passed through an ordeal…it was everything. Once inside, she went straight to the bathroom, turned the tap, and waited for warmth. She had to rise above her aching body and the troubled cloud hanging over her mind. Defeat was not her way, it was her enemy but for now strength was gone. Tears streaming down her face; Hugh, she whispered, please God bring him home…

Later placing clothes in the washer, she heard her phone ringing. Seeing an old brown robe in a pile of folded laundry she claimed it, slipped into the robe, and was wrapping her hair in the towel as she raced back to grab the cell and hear Sophia's voice, "Mom. You didn't call."

"Darling, I was in terrible weather, the tires of the car were ruined and I've been in such a state of..."Suddenly she laughed, standing there in Oliver's robe. "I was in such despair but hearing your voice, I think I'm better..." the laughter filled her soul, "Yes, I am much better. We have a beautiful little girl..."

"Mom, I know, I called Oliver about an hour ago and he said Caroline was not doing well. I've been waiting for your call. Should Barkley and I come now?"

The smile faded from Susan's face. "Let me check again, Sophia, I have only reached the apartment and had time to shower. When I left Oliver said if anything changed he would let me know. Let's hang up and I'll call you back immediately if you should come."

"Mom, we aren't going to lose her, are we?" Sophia was crying. "Mom, Dad couldn't take that."

"No, darling, none of us could."

"But Caroline and Dad have this..."

"Yes, yes, I know. Let me make a call and I'll get back to you. I love you, sweetheart, tell Barkley too."

Her call went through to the nurse's station, "no change, Mrs. Preston, at this time they are all three asleep." Susan's voice caught at the good news. "Yes, ma'am," the nurse replied, "we took the baby in about an hour ago, they have both held her...and for now, all is well. You get some rest, too."

Once more, Susan reassured her children. "No, no, Oliver meant it didn't go well for a few hours last night, the doctor will talk with us this afternoon and then I'll call you. Try not to worry, sweetheart." Good advice, she thought as she closed the cell. Now she had to remember her own words. But first, she needed clothes to wear. While checking on the washer, she heard the door bell ringing. Oh. Oliver had returned but without a key. She hurried back to the door and opened it a crack. There stood Kane Alberson with her suitcase.

"Kane?" Surprised. She just stood there. "How did you find me?"

"Could I come in rather than stand here and explain?"

"Well, yes, I'm sorry." Embarrassed, she started to explain her appearance, thought better of it and ask again, "how did you find the kids apartment?"

Looking a bit uncomfortable, Kane glanced down. "I, uh, thought perhaps you might have something to help me out, in there…" he pointed to the suitcase, "and you did."

Puzzled, Susan tried to make a connection all the while motioning toward a chair. "Since you are here, Kane, if you don't mind sit down and I'll go slip into clothes since now they are here…." She left the words hanging, picked up the suitcase and hurried out of the room…"I'll be right back."

Trying to grasp the presence of Kane in the other room, the fact she now had clothes and she was wearing Oliver's oversized robe with her hair wrapped in a towel, she opened the suitcase and found why he was there. At some time she had taped a card of information to the inner lining of the suitcase, with family addresses, lest any time traveling she encountered a problem. In haste, putting things together before she left she hadn't noticed it was still there….and, too, she was traveling.

Kane heard a click and recognized the fact Susan had locked the door between them. He smiled. Did she really think him the ogre he had perceived last night when she rebuffed his question, or was she only being a lady? He wished the latter but he'd had time to rehash her words, grievances she said and water under the bridge and off limits. All he had offered was friendship. True, he wanted to forget the past mistakes of making her husband and her own life miserable. Not that he was changing….

She returned, offering her hand as she stood, waiting for him to rise. "Thank you for bringing my clothes."

"My pleasure." His expression was grave. "Susan, there has to be a reason I came along last night, could you drop the obvious dislike you have for me and from this point on when we meet," he cleared his throat, the words seeming to drop between them like stones when he was trying, "at least let us speak with civility?" She had withdrawn her hand but he plunged on. "I have acknowledged I find you a strong woman, I admire your ability to go on with your husband away... all I'm offering is a friendship of sorts, perhaps we could treat each other with respect much as acquaintance in business..." He took a deep breath..."Well, hell, Susan, it's no secret I find you interesting, I even harbor thoughts of wishing I'd found you before Hugh."

A glimmer of something different lit her eyes, but Susan's hand went up, warding off further words. "Kane, you are rambling. I get it. If you are as weary as I am," she sighed. "We were up all night, you helped me and I'm eternally grateful, I just haven't had time to process the whole thing. Now, Hugh and I do have a new granddaughter. Caroline Dawn is not doing well and I need to return to the hospital. No doubt, your resilience to a new day is a bit tarnished too, with what you went through helping me last night, the wrecker, the tires and even the cup of coffee," she smiled now. "And finding me here in my son-in-law's old robe...." She grinned. "A woman's vanity seems never to ease up."

"You look beau.." Her hand went up again, stopping him before the sentence was finished as she turned toward the door.

"Thank you, Kane. In the future, when we meet, I will remember your kindness and I will couch my words, undoubtedly, should we meet on one of those business situations, but I will speak respectfully as you ask, and I won't forget you were there in a very serious time of my life. Now," she opened the door. "Thank you again and for now, goodbye. I have to call my husband and tell him about our daughter."

He was on his way out, when he stopped, bent and placed a kiss on her cheek. She closed the door.

That afternoon, the doctor arrived to find Caroline asleep and he motioned them outside the room.

"Being, for all definitions, a country doctor who delivers babies in the Methodist Hospital," he smiled, I'm not just one that delivers babies but I have the privilege of seeing my patients on all issues, sniffles to more extreme disease and with Caroline Dawn we have waded through some murky waters." He sighed, "Now, her leukemia strikes again and we are meeting it head on. She can take the treatment, there's no baby the meds will hurt inside her womb and we are going to go forward, optimistic that we can head this thing off, get her back into remission and let her watch those two youngsters grow up." He searched their faces. "How does that sound?" They both nodded. "I'm going to keep her in the hospital a few days, run more tests while she's here and the time will also give her additional days to gain strength with someone else caring for the baby which we are going to also keep."

"But will my insurance cover the expense?" Oliver worried out loud.

"I'm going to list this in a special way. Today, my secretary is calling your insurance to explain the situation and if I personally speak with them and send them a written page of reason why I'm keeping her in the hospital I believe we can hope for the best but first, give us today to do our magic. Agreed?"

Four hundred miles away, Sam Lansky walked the cold gray hall of the prison, around him the sounds of men's laughter, crude and colorless as the walls as he searched for his friend. It was cold outside and near time for the evening meal, and then he saw him, Hugh away from the groups, his arms stretched high, hands against the stone of the building, his head hung low and he knew without seeing there would be tears running down his friend's cheeks into the solid gray T-shirt that held him together.

"What's wrong?" He asked, knowing when a man was away from his family and he could do nothing was heartbreaking. He listened. "Hang on. Man, hang on. Two months and then you're free."

Chapter 21

$\mathcal{T}$hey were there, his family, Caroline Dawn and Oliver with young Ollie running around and Caroline sitting in the chair near the Christmas tree, little Hope in her arms two months old and growing. She was as pink and perfect as her mother was white and thin. Crossing the room he dropped down beside the chair. Across from them Sophia and his mother were deep in discussing fashion.

"How're you doing?" His voice was little above whisper, but Caroline Dawn smiled and reached for his hand. Some miracle had allowed her Dad to come home on time although there'd been threats and innuendoes his stay might be lengthened. She had fought to live but sometimes she wondered how long she could hang on. Would God in his mercy grant she raise her children?

"Daddy, I'm doing well now that you are here." The wispy tone of her voice did not leave these days. "I was so afraid, Dad, that they'd keep you and I'd not see you for Christmas and my heart was aching."

"Mine, too," he traced a finger along the line of her hand, the blue veins prominent. "Now that I'm here we'll pick up the pieces and you will get well and from there, no telling what life will bring to our door."

"How did you make it, Daddy?" Sometimes she slipped back into calling him as she had all those years when they sit in the porch swing making good things out of situations that could go either way. "I don't think I could last ripped away from my loved ones."

"But we have to Caroline," the timbre of Hugh's voice dipped in huskiness, rose back to normal as he wiped a tear from her cheek with his thumb. "When a man has people as wonderful as all of you waiting for his return; each day he prays to God to help him until he can hold them in his arms again."

"I'm trying, Daddy, but sometimes I'm scared."

"That's normal, babe, but you just stay focused and do the best you can to trust in the Lord."

"I dreamed of you, a lot, Daddy. When I was carrying Hope I would watch Ollie playing and I couldn't wait for you to see how he'd grown."

Hugh laughed as Ollie ran to touch his mother's knee, picking up the little boy that was beginning to look more like Caroline than Oliver. "I believe this boy has long limbs."

"I not got limbs," Ollie cried. "I a little boy with ombs."

"Ombs, huh?" Hugh sit Ollied back on his feet to the floor. "Well, they look like arms to me, maybe they're not limbs."

And so it went. Hugh drank in his family, his eye always glancing away to find Susan. Whether she was near or far in the room, their eyes met and the sweet smile would linger around her lips, the smile he'd known since they were kids when he'd said, "one day I'm going to marry you," and she'd replied, "okay." She had come for him, alone, and as they left the prison grounds he looked back to wonder for two years he'd been thrown into a world he could never have imagined; a place where you became a number, your days were not your own; nothing but the thoughts of your mind belonged to you.

Forced by unseasonal storms they had to spend the night in a hotel a stone's throw from the Interstate; Perhaps it was the best thing, God was orchestrating each step of Hugh's reentry to life as he had known it and he held her, this bride who blessed his life sweet warm and giving he held her.

The following May Hugh walked Sophia Raine down the aisle. This time the church was decorated with white lilies and sprinkles of some mystical white budded flower so tiny they were held in clusters with white satin ribbon to each pew. When Thorn stepped forward with his groomsmen to stand by the Pastor, the smile on his face reminded Hugh of the day he married Susan. Ollie carried the ring on the pillow that was sometimes upright and other times tucked under his arm, for Ollie was a busy little man and Susan had made certain the ring was tied in center of the pillow; a good thing.

Ah, Barkley, my man. Hugh's eyes fell on his son, standing next to Thorn with his gaze fixed on Betsy. It was obvious to Hugh, here was the next to marry and it wouldn't be long until Barkley would bring home his wife to the chaos and happy confusion of their family. They were complete. His heart was full. Today he felt he could weather the storms, but still his gaze returned to Susan, beautiful, serene and happy on this day their daughter would wed. They'd come full circle, leastways once Barkley and Betsy tied the knot. God was good.

After the wedding, the reception and Sophia Raine left with her Thorn, the gifts were loaded in to the back of Sam and Emily's Suburban, friends helped clean the church and tired and spent Hugh placed Susan in the car. Quiet they drove home, holding hands on the console between them.

"Have I told you lately how much I love you?" He asked.

"Only this morning," she replied, "tell me again."

"You know that song Sophia and Thorn danced to? That's our life."

"This kind of love makes me feel ten feet tall… I felt your love when I heard those lines and I glanced up to find your eyes on me."

"I know." He squeezed her hand. "I pray we all have many more years."

"You're thinking of Caroline Dawn. She seemed a bit stronger."

"She's scared but we all go through those times. It's all in God's hands, still we have those emotions."

"How did you make it through," she studied the line of his face visible only by the lights on the dash.

"God's mercy towards me," he replied, "and you," He pulled into the drive, got out and went around to open the door. There beneath a deep blue sky with a few white clouds dipping toward the earth, Hugh smiled as the breeze ruffled her hair and she put her hand in his. He pulled her close. "You, Susan. You are engraved on my heart. Should I die, I would go to heaven with your love engraved on my heart."

Five years passed. Hugh had reestablished himself in the community. There were still struggles between his land and the Alberson holdings. It was said J.T. was ailing. He was in his nineties, still driving his Lincoln town car, the hood appearing longer as other cars seemed smaller with many replaced by suburban's.

Kane Alberson's reputation had not diminished though something had tempered his way but who could forget the past? Word will leak from any business. All those years J.T. Alberson, the power behind the throne, widened his kingdom by using others to build his coffer and Kane was his hench man but true to life, every deed has a day of reckoning. J.T.'s own son was caught in the middle; he helped build the business but now he was older, still too weak to fight his father. The employees talked and it was said, Kane threatened he would no longer do the dirty work…if that's how it was to be he'd leave…and Kane was gone. Now, a landowner by his own purchase, without family money, Kane kept to himself and the community only saw him pass by. They did not know his business.

J.T. wasn't having it. Either Kane returned or he would personally see his grandson behind prison walls.

Barkley scoffed, "why would he reveal what Kane did, when he did a hundred times worse?"

Hugh heard the rumors. "That has nothing to do with us," he told Barkley. "Kane's past is wrapped around him like a shroud. He had a choice, way back then, that's when he should have left. The only way he can change it now is when the old man dies and the business falls into his hands, then if he treats people with respect and doesn't steal their profits, then… he has a fighting chance."

Bert came in on the end of the conversation. "Don't hold your breath, but I heard J.T. is dying. He has two options, deny his heirs and leave the business to Tom who won't step up to the plate or make amends with Kane. Even in death the old man wants control. I'd think by now a man would be thinking about where he's going."

"If you make a deal with the devil," Hugh replied, "can you have a say in where you're going?"

Bert scratched his head, "The next question would be, does God stop dealin' with a man or is there hope to the end?"

"Well that doesn't seem fair," Barkley injected, feeling the moments spasm of remembering all the animosities of the past, "does it? Someone like the old man, or Kane takes advantage of others all his life and then at last minute God forgives his sins and he has the same promise of heaven as a person that's been good all his life?"

"Son, salvation...if that's what we're talking about, salvation is a gift of God. You know that, not a man's works, the scripture says, lest any man would boast." Hugh's eyes rest kindly on his son. "We don't need to judge, then we fall into the same category as the world...it's not our place to judge."

Barkley stubbed his toe against the concrete. "No, but it ain't easy to forget people's meanness, is it?"

"No, no it's not...but I wouldn't wish prison on any man." Hugh felt an inner shudder at the memory.

"I think he deserves it," Barkley was not giving up his opinion, "both of them, Kane and his grandfather."

Three days passed. Bert came to work shaking his head, "We're in a new era now," he said. "J. T. Alberson died in the early mornin' hours, one of the help there what knows Leonie called, now there'll be a grandstand funeral and all the people of the community will turn out whether they liked him or not." Bert poured a cup of coffee, waiting for Hugh to give him a work list for the day. "You'll see a lot of suckin' up to Kane, if he's to be the new oversee, and grindin and nashin of teeth behind the scenes."

"You got a strange way of puttin' it, Bert." Though he was busy, Barkley knew his dad was listening.

"Yup, but that's about it." Bert poured a second cup of coffee and handed it to Hugh.

"You going, Dad?"

"Yes, Son, we show respect, often times even when we think there's none due. Mr. J.T. may have had unscrupulous ways, but still we learn from people."

"I don't get what you'd learn from that old coot," Barkley retorted, his anger toward old injustice surfacing.

"He never let up, Son. His goals may have been tarnished; his treatment of others wrong, but the man did have work ethics. All those years I never heard of a day he wasn't at that office or riding around his holdings in that town car. If you want to grow, you watch your business; no one else will do as well."

"But he was wrong, Dad."

"Yes, I agree but his money was put on about every building in the community and church roofs," Hugh took a sip of coffee, "you get the picture, Son? Even men with unscrupulous ways benefit others."

"It ain't right," Barkley wasn't having it. "If Kane takes over, we're in for it, just a repeat of the old man."

"Son, I know you show respect when you talk to any man whether you like him or not, but there's a lesson here you've got to learn. The Kane's of this world, will always be with us. If fate tempers their way of handling things, so be it, but if not and you have to deal with him, do the best you can, don't bow to their level of pettiness. Be the man God expects you to be."

"He wronged you, Dad. Kane Alberson wronged you and smiled while he was doing it." Barkley stomped away.

The funeral of J.T. Alberson, was as Bert said, carried out with the finest regard. The community had lost its king, the church J.T. put a roof on but never darkened its door, served the people. J.T.'s long nosed Lincoln was spit polished and sitting at the edge of the church yard, a symbol to remind the people what he'd done for them.

Singers were brought in from Memphis, said to have known and loved J.T. People accepted the story and loved to retell it. J.T. and his wife's wedding picture set to one side of the casket. None of their son, nor grandson. The only flowers was a spray on top, white lilies with a touch of red berries, said to be the old man's favorite, while a painting of J.T. and his wife before she died and the mansion was new set on the other side. J.T. request nothing else be added that would take away from the setting. He had chosen the Bible scripture to be used and placed a large sum of money in the pastor's hand to say what he wanted said.

Hugh and Susan attend to find Tom standing at the door as they entered. "Thank you for coming," he said, his countenance was sad, the one who had given him orders was gone. Now he must remember the schedule and follow it; that was all he knew. He glanced toward Hugh's mother. Kathryn had come early to lend support. Sometimes he thought Kathryn the only true friend he had. "Your mother's sitting just there," he said pointing. "I can't tell you what her friendship has meant through the years."

Hugh stopped to kiss his mother's cheek and Susan gave her a hug. "You look so pretty, Kathryn," she said. Kathryn patted her hand. "I'll check on you later, Mother," Hugh whispered.

At the casket, Kane stood guard, shaking hands and listening to old tales, some he'd never heard about J.T. The line was long, people shifting on their feet, waiting. Then it was their time. Hugh extended his hand, "I'm sorry for your loss, Kane." Kane's eyes held with Hugh's for a moment as if discerning whether there was truth in the simple statement and then he reached for Susan's hand.

"Hello, Susan. Thank you for coming. I hope you are well and how is Caroline Dawn and her family?"

"We are all well, Kane." She realized he was holding her hand a bit too long. "I pray you can work through the transition of losing your grandfather, Kane. God bless you."

Kane thanked her and the line moved. There were several in between and then Barkley stood before him, a pretty girl by his side. The girl smiled. Kane's smile was almost benevolent, one of a person who had watched the boy grow wondering how that one would have progressed, not forgetting their dark moments. Barkley's eyes were cool, calculating, no spark of friendship, merely a show of respect he felt his parent's expected. Their hands touched. There were no words necessary.

That girl, Kane was thinking, is sister to my son. He glanced down the line. Sophia and Thorn were not visible. Of course Thorn would not attend, nor Emily or Sam. The fleeting thought of seeing them would have been too much. He was glad they were not there. The line moved again.

They did not go to the grave site. They were not insiders. "Let's go somewhere and have dinner," Hugh suggested. "Seems like a let-down, doesn't it?" He gave a deep sigh. "You deal with people all your life and in the end you just feel sorry for them." They were driving to the next town, silent each with their own thoughts when he reached for her hand. "Do you feel it too?" She nodded. "We are so blessed," he said.

Home, that night, Barkley came to knock on their bedroom door. "Can I come in?"

"Sure." Hugh was lying in the bed. Susan at her dressing table finishing removing her make up.

Barkley seemed energized at the late hour. "Son, you all right?" Hugh asked.

"Yeah, Dad, I am. I talked to Mr. Sam tonight. I asked him if it was all right for me and Betsy to marry."

Susan turned from the dressing table. "What did he say?" A smile was lightening her eyes. "No?"

Barkley grinned. "He said he would be happy to have me in the family."

"Are we in for a long wait?"

"No, we're getting married next month. We've been planning this for awhile."

"Well," Hugh said, "she's a fine girl and we are happy for you, aren't we Momma?"

Susan hugged her son. "Yes, we are."

The wedding was in Sam and Emily's church. A different town, a lot of people Susan and Hugh had never met but the young couple would live near them while Betsy settle into a teaching job in her home town and Barkley would continue to run the farm with his father.

They had returned from the wedding reception, not having to help with the clean-up issues. Caroline Dawn and Oliver were driving their little family back to Memphis. For once, there was color in their daughter's cheeks and she said she was feeling well. Hugh pulled her to his side as she said, "Daddy, I think I'm going to make it." His smile was all she needed. Sophia and Thorn were expecting their first child, she wasn't showing but her face was a bit more full and her smile was bright. "You're good, too, aren't you, Babe?" Hugh asked. And she replied, "You know it Dad, or I'd tell you."

He was a content man. Now as Susan was in their room putting away the day's clothes. Hugh went to the shop to check on a piece of equipment that was painted that week. The sky was cloudy with rain imminent and if it rained the dampness would prevent the tool drying down. As he thought what to do the first drops of rain could be heard on the metal roof.

Hugh passed by the wall where he'd always sought privacy to speak to God during troubled times. He stretched his arms above his head, placing those big hands in the grooves that were so familiar. "I want to thank you, Heavenly Father, for the happiness you've given me, for seeing me through the hard times when I didn't know if we were going to make it, for being there when I went to prison and I had to let go of blaming others for the injustice, thank you for helping me to learn to let go or the poison would kill me." His voice grew husky, "Thank you for Susan and the love we've always known and the children." Tears sprang from his eyes, "The children God, please Lord, let Caroline Dawn stay in remission and raise those babies. And Sophia Raine, Father, she seems to be settled and not as impulsive. She is like Mother, and my mother, Lord, watch over her. If she and Mr. Tom can be friends then I'm all right with that, but your mercy Lord, I thank you for that...and most of all that you've let me be loved all these years. My heart is full. I love you, Lord. I'm just asking you to help me to be the man you want me to be."

No one knew exactly what happened.

When Hugh failed to return, Susan went to find him. She had heard a noise and thought he had started one of the larger tractors to move it inside but although it was raining now the shop was ablaze with fire. Whether Hugh had turned on the gas heat and there was an explosion would have to be determined but it was as though a blast had thrown him across the room.

Evidently Hugh had turned away. Susan found him lying on his stomach, arms outstretched, his face to the concrete. His back had suffered burns that charred the material of his shirt into the flesh. Hugh was dead.

Susan was a widow at the age of fifty one. Many said she and Hugh had already lived a life time but she ignored them; what lay ahead without Hugh, the warmth of his love, his voice in her ear, his arms to comfort and hold her, it was over when she thought a second phase of their life had just begun. Their plans to travel when money and time permit, to love their children and watch the little one's grow...how could she fill the hours, when would her mind settle and she become a person on her own who could make decisions and learn to move in a world that now seemed foreign?

They laid Hugh to rest in the community cemetery, not far from an old oak tree said to welcome those who came to remember the loved one whose body was abiding there. Kathryn's grief was overwhelming at first, the loss of her only child, laid to rest there beside his father, four empty plots waiting for family though no one could know who would fill that place ;she by her husband and Susan next to Hugh...unless...Kathryn's thoughts could not fathom Susan loving another man beside her son.

In the weeks to come Susan went about the business only she could attend to, often her mind going back to her last days with Hugh. The terribleness of the fire, sweeping through the building; it was a wonder all things had not been reduced to ashes, but the flame had its intent and Hugh was the victim and the small towns around had sent fire trucks to reduce the damage. It was her heart that ached, her arms that had no one to hold, her mind still resting on the loss of Hugh's love.

Parking on the street, Susan walked through the cemetery. In the distance someone was setting a head stone. Hugh's was ordered but she was told the process of setting one up took time. The local welding shop had cut a heart with Hugh's name and the date he died on it from metal until the stone she chose arrived. She sit on the ground there by the heart and with one finger traced Hugh's words to her, said so often, Engraved On My Heart. Those words would be on his head stone but for now whoever cut the metal had done a good job. "I miss you," she whispered. "What am I going to do without you?" Tears ran silently down her cheek. She wanted to stretch her body over the grave and feel the warmth of his...but it could not be... as they believed he was not there but in some better place. Overcome, she succumbed. Full length, her face resting on the palm of one hand, she lay there feeling the late spring rise in the soil...and smelled the earth...as memory of Hugh trickling dirt through his fingers came and their walk over new ground when he took her hand and said, let's ask God's blessing.

Month after month she returned, in the heat of August, the cold of January. Hugh's stone was set. The words on the mount no more obvious than the ones engraved on her heart. And then it was February, she found work being done on the road to Hugh's grave. She had changed vehicles, her old car to all purposes died. Barkley said, "Mom, get a suburban, if you're going to haul for the farm, you need the space." However, this one was not without problems. Now she left the vehicle on the side of the road and walked the distance to Hugh's grave. It was when she returned she found she had either locked the key inside or dropped it along the road. She was searching when a truck stopped and a voice called out, "lady, can I help you?" Then a truck door slammed. Someone came around the vehicle and stopped suddenly.

"Hello, Susan."

She studied him quietly before replying. "Hello, Kane."

"Something wrong?"

"I…ah, I've either lost my key or dropped it and I can't get into my vehicle."

"Do you have an extra key at home? Have you called Barkley to bring it?"

"I do but Barkley and Betsy are on a little trip. There's no one to bring it." She felt foolish. "Normally, I do have the phone with me." She sighed, her breath rising in a vapor. "The road condition threw me."

Kane glanced at the cemetery road work. "Then come get in and I'll take you to get it."

"There's another problem, I don't have a key to my house, it's in my purse inside the vehicle."

"Well, you can't stand out here in the cold, come get in and we'll see what we can do." Reluctantly she walked to his truck. "Do you have a door to your house that maybe the lock doesn't fit just right?"

"Maybe." She had to think.

"I have used the old credit card trick a few times through the years. If you haven't thrown the second lock it might work."

"I don't put the second lock on unless it's night time," she said. "I try to think no one bothers in daylight."

He chuckled. "Well, that's one way of thinking about it." After a while he asked, "How have you been?"

"Lost." She replied. "I did receive your card of sympathy. It was worded nicely."

"It took me awhile to find one appropriate. I know how you feel about things."

She was quiet.

"Hugh's gone, Susan. I still find you intriguing, maybe more now than ever."

"Why?"

"Because you are alone. I hate that for you. Being alone isn't easy."

"You don't have to be."

"Neither do you." He glanced her way. "I'm very interested, Susan, for all the right reasons."

"Those reasons being…"

"What I think I feel for you would have gone away a long time ago, if there wasn't something to it."

"I don't think we need this conversation." She turned her head staring out onto the roadside.

"I'm going to say it now, while I have the chance. I know you have a strong faith. Yes, I realize you lost the husband you loved but he's gone, Susan, and I believe God has allowed me to see you through the years and if I've wanted just to speak with you from time to time because I felt you were a person, no holds barred, I would appreciate knowing…then that's what I think. I'm not asking anything of you, other than friendship. See where that takes us."

"I don't think that's possible."

"Give me a chance."

"My children remember the past."

"Build on the future and those memories will dim."

"I can't do this…."

"I've had my say. You think on it." His gloved hands tightened on the wheel. "First things first."

"Meaning."

He grinned. "Find a way to get in your house for the keys. Then I'll take you back."

"Nothing more."

"Agreed." He replied. "It's a beginning." He glanced her way. Stubborn as always and beautiful.

She didn't speak. It's a one-time thing, her mind whispered. One time. He's rich, he's handsome and he thinks he can win me over to prove a point and toss me aside. Never.

For the first time in a long time, Kane Alberson felt different, maybe it was hope, he didn't know. The one thing he knew for sure was he had changed. Suddenly he felt a song in his heart.

The End

www.ingramcontent.com/pod-product-compliance
Lightning Source LLC
Chambersburg PA
CBHW050354190726
48284CB00007BB/2276